Every Tom, Dick & Harry

Also by Elinor Lipman

Ms. Demeanor

Rachel to the Rescue

Good Riddance

On Turpentine Lane

The View from Penthouse B

I Can't Complain: (All Too) Personal Essays

The Family Man

My Latest Grievance

The Pursuit of Alice Thrift

The Dearly Departed

The Ladies' Man

The Inn at Lake Devine

Isabel's Bed

The Way Men Act

Then She Found Me

Into Love and Out Again

Every Tom, Dick & Harry

A NOVEL

Elinor Lipman

HARPER

An Imprint of HarperCollins*Publishers*

HarperCollins books may be purchased for educational, business, or sales promotional use. For information, please email the Special Markets Department at SPsales@harpercollins.com.

FIRST EDITION

Designed by Nancy Singer

Library of Congress Cataloging-in-Publication Data
Names: Lipman, Elinor, author.
Title: Every Tom, Dick & Harry: a novel / Elinor Lipman.
Other titles: Every Tom, Dick and Harry
Description: First edition. | New York, NY: Harper, 2025.
Identifiers: LCCN 2024035528 (print) | LCCN 2024035529 (ebook) | ISBN 9780063322257 (hardcover) | ISBN 9780063433380 (large print) | ISBN 9780063322271 (ebook)
Subjects: LCGFT: Humorous fiction. | Romance fiction. | Novels.
Classification: LCC PS3562.I577 E94 2025 (print) | LCC PS3562.I577 (ebook) | DDC 813/.54—dc23/eng/20240802
LC record available at https://lccn.loc.gov/2024035528
LC ebook record available at https://lccn.loc.gov/2024035529

24 25 26 27 28 LBC 5 4 3 2 1

For Suzanne Gluck

Every
Tom, Dick
& Harry

1

My new business card reads "Estate of Mind," and below, in italics, "We empty your nest." Though I've been working alone since my parents retired, I've retained the "we" for sentimental reasons, and to sound less like the one-woman operation I hope to keep afloat.

I've been estate-sale adjacent since I could add and give change, spending weekends at a table, wrapping and bagging purchases. If buyers tried to negotiate, I'd point to the stated price on the tag or sticker and ask blankly, "Do you *not* want it?"

But the grown-up me has learned to be kinder and more psychiatric. I know when to handhold and when to hard-sell. Some clients can tell a story about every item in their house if I let them, and sometimes I do. If anyone is convinced that the unsigned portrait over the fireplace is an Old Master, I don't argue. I let the small local auction house with which I have a relationship (I recommend them; they recommend me) be the bad guy. As ever, they agree that the work in question is either NSV (no sale value) or TFO (the frame only). Yes, I can get $100 for a decent still life by an unknown artist, but it's small comfort to the surviving children, who grew up expecting that their inherited treasures would be auctioned off for millions.

*

I wish I could say that no two houses are alike, but Harrow, Massachusetts, has several subdivisions where only the paint colors differentiate one property from another. Inside, there are few surprises. I know what the big-city, apartment-dwelling beneficiaries *won't* want: the gas grill, the Weber grill, the porch furniture, the fireplace tools, the lawn mowers, the rakes, the snow shovels, the hedge clippers, the left-handed golf clubs and warped tennis rackets, the recalled playpen, the crib bumpers, the furry toilet seat covers and crocheted tissue-box holders; the DVDs, the cassette tapes, the VHS tapes, the college textbooks, the shag rugs, the sewing machine, the electric typewriters, the souvenirs bought at airport gift shops, the aluminum saucepans, the grape-jelly juice glasses, the empty mayonnaise jars.

I'm proud of our excellent Yelp reviews complimenting our bedside manner and my parents' talent for curing a lifetime of buyer's regret. One written salute to their "Midas Touch" is now reproduced on my invoices. Still, it's not my calling; the accolades don't stop me from thinking, *Just one more summer . . . just one more sale.*

My parents are torn; they want their old business—formerly Finders, Keepers, renamed by me to a more zeitgeisty Estate of Mind—to thrive and to outlive their retirement, yet they want me to be fulfilled, and to put at least one of my degrees to good use.

My most recent one, attended online, in narrative nonfiction, makes them nervous. They ask, "If you're supposed to 'write what you know,' wouldn't that lead to a tell-all in very bad taste?"

I'm not going to do that. How could I forget my father, widowed young, smiling, shaking his head in something like wonder, asking as we loaded a cracked mirror or a wheelbarrow into a stranger's car, "Did you ever think your dad would be having as much fun again in this lifetime?"

2

As to "my parents," clarification is needed.

Nineteen months after his first wife, my mother, Annie, died, my father married Beth Williamsen. I'd known and liked her well enough, the way a child likes anyone who waves and smiles from her porch and doesn't mind the neighborhood kids cutting through her yard.

Looking back, though not grasping it at the time, I sensed that she wasn't the only woman who'd set her sights on my heartbroken young father. Even to me at seven, he seemed deaf and blind to the blandishments of the women in pursuit, except for the competent and pretty Mrs. Williamsen, who mowed her own lawn and hung her own Christmas lights.

She was divorced. Mr. Williamsen, I would eventually find out, had been a ladies' man, and an indiscreet one. They had no children. She got the house.

Not long after my mother died, Mrs. Williamsen knocked on the back door while managing a cake on a cake plate. "For Emma," she told my father. I was present, eating or drawing at the kitchen table.

"Emma," my father prompted, "see what Mrs. Williamsen brought you. A beautiful cake! Can you say thank you?"

Saying thanks from the table was deemed inadequate. "Over

here," he prompted. I obeyed. At the door, my father stood behind me, both hands on my shoulders.

"I hope you like chocolate cake," Mrs. Williamsen called, now at the bottom of the stairs, in polite retreat.

I nodded. My father said, "She's quiet with strangers, but I know she's touched."

The tragedy of my mother's death from breast cancer was handled as well as such things were dealt with twenty-five years ago. We checked out books about sick, dying, and dead parents from the library. The school psychologist sat me down with paper and crayons a few weeks in a row, and even at seven I suspected that the colors and pictures I drew were supposed to say something about my feelings. Appropriately sad or *too* sad? I didn't want to make my father feel any worse. I put green leaves on trees, a big, beaming sun, a stick-figure daddy and a stick-figure little girl with a giant bow in her hair, and a dog not yet owned, in case this would be translated as aspirational. After four visits, I didn't have to go back.

My father had devoted friends among his fellow teachers at Harrow High School. Even more protective were his three older sisters, my doting aunts, all living in neighboring counties, eager to mother me. As Beth was introduced in small social increments, the aunts were split on the coupling, two against, and one philosophical. He was so attractive, their heartbroken baby brother. The two sisters who were anti-Beth thought she was insensitive to the etiquette of mourning. "She didn't wait a minute" was the naysayers' motto. The philosophical one said, "He knows her better than we do, which is not at all. Let's give him some credit."

Eight months after my mother's death, my father brought Beth to Thanksgiving dinner, always at Aunt Unity's, the eldest. When all three sisters were gathered in the kitchen, basting, chopping, advising, and I was pretending to be deeply engaged in cutting rounds of dough with a biscuit cutter, Beth took the opportunity to make the speech she'd prepared in advance. She knew John-Paul was still grieving. He'd never get over Annie's death. She herself understood heartbreak. She'd never do anything to disrespect Annie or—her voice dropping—"your Emma."

Their Emma! The magic words. I was the youngest grandchild and only girl. Aunt Pamela was childless. Aunt Unity had big boys, old enough to drive and to be nice to a little cousin who worshipped them. Aunt Celeste had married a divorced man with a son who'd aged out of the every-other-weekend custody agreement.

My father and Beth were married at Harrow City Hall. At eight and a half, I wasn't old enough to be an official witness, but I was there, in a new pinafored dress I adored, my hair in French braids, Beth's handiwork. My three aunts and their husbands attended because we were not a family that would boycott the wedding of a beloved brother, no matter the doubts. Until that day, I'd been calling Beth "Mrs. Williamsen." She asked if I'd like to call her Mom. My dad said, "Or maybe just 'Beth'?" Beth said quickly, "Of course."

The aunts came around. Beth remembered every birthday, not just with cards but with notes. She stepped up to host Thanksgiving the year Aunt Unity's contractor missed the deadline for her kitchen renovation; contributed to every bike-ride and walkathon for Aunt Celeste's favorite causes. When the aunts collectively offered to send me to boarding school at thirteen, my dad said no thanks, and that was final. And how would it look—a public school teacher sending his daughter to private school? He'd miss me too much. They both would—their only child!

Beth agreed wholeheartedly. Send the girl who'd lost her mother away for her all-important high school years, when "Finders, Keepers" told our story in two words: *Finding, then keeping*? As for the claim "We empty your nest," no way; no takers here. Emma's not going anywhere.

3

Finders, Keepers's first client was Beth herself, after she'd sold her house and moved into ours. While shopping around for the best estate sale company, she'd interviewed Goldie of Goldie's Oldies, which would become our main competitor. Did they advertise? she asked. What about flyers? Signage? Liability insurance? Did they have a mailing list (which at the time meant the actual mailing of postcards)? It didn't take long before Beth was asking herself, *How hard could such a business be?*

That inaugural sale set the style that Finders, Keepers would be known for. Beth dressed up and greeted customers as if she were hosting a holiday open house. She made attractive groupings of unwanted knickknacks. She studied which rooms customers visited in what order, what sold and what was destined for Goodwill. Customers were invited to open closets and bureau drawers. They wanted the oddest things! A man who hadn't even gone to the same high school as her ex bought his yearbook! It got her thinking . . . if John-Paul and Emma could help on weekends, she'd do the advance work, the photographing, arranging, pricing.

After conducting a half dozen sales, she quit her job at a Springfield furniture store. The experience she'd gained there as both bookkeeper and saleswoman served her new venture so well that it seemed foretold.

They managed with the help of my aunts when I had games

on Saturdays through junior high and high school. Unity had the best eye, occasionally spotting something auction-worthy that Beth had underpriced. Pamela was the best mathematician, calculating sales tax in her head. Celeste viewed her time at the checkout table as a lark. "I can hardly keep a straight face when I'm wrapping up some hideous thing! Sometimes I want to say, 'You're kidding! You're paying ten dollars for *this*?' "

Finders, Keepers didn't make anyone rich, neither the home-owners nor us. Still, Beth and my dad persevered. His teacher's salary got us by, plus the 40 percent commissions that the semi-monthly sales brought in. Though I was accepted at BU and BC, I went to UMass on in-state tuition and majored in art history, not with an eye to appraising future properties but because it seemed the polar opposite of commerce.

Summers I was back at the checkout table, already feeling as if I knew every person, every house, every cellar and attic in Harrow. After graduation I was of less and less help. I worked part-time at various retail jobs at Shoppers' World, convenient to Framingham State where I was studying for my first impractical master's degree, English. For years I dated my on-and-off college boyfriend, who finally joined Teach for America without asking me to consider the same.

Beth and my dad announced with some ceremony at my thirty-second birthday dinner that they were looking at a town house in Buzzards Bay.

"Winters are milder on the Cape," said my dad. "And I might get a little dinghy."

I asked what "looking at a town house" meant. As a rental property? Can't be for summers, could it—Finders, Keepers' high season? Surely not a full-time move, as in . . . retirement?

"That's where you come in," Beth said, raising her champagne flute. "The logical heir to the throne."

They were asking, at this shockingly early juncture: How would I like to take over? Finders, Keepers was mine if I wanted it.

I didn't want it. I'd helped out because I had to. I wouldn't be good at wooing or charming clients. I wasn't vivacious Beth or genial John-Paul. Who retires the second they turn sixty-five? They were busy and healthy. Buzzards Bay? A dinghy? They were Harrowites to the core, or so I thought. "You'd walk away from Finders? Isn't it your baby, your nest egg?" I asked.

"No," said Beth. "It was your college fund. It may seem out of the blue, but we've always loved the Cape."

"And my back is telling me no more hoisting sofas onto people's trucks," said my dad.

"And no more Sunday nights leaving the property"—air quotes—" 'broom-clean.' I hope I never have to hear that expression again."

I said, "What about me, though? *I'd* be going for broom clean. *I'd* be hoisting sofas onto truck beds for people who should've brought along their beefy sons."

"Sweetheart, at thirty-two you'd be the CEO of one of Harrow's most beloved homegrown businesses. You'd be ready right out of the gate, no training needed," said Beth. "And you won't have a gap on your résumé between school, J.Crew, Nordstrom Rack . . . and whatever's next."

"You'd keep 'family' in 'family business,'" said my dad. "No small matter."

Our celebration was taking place at the town's white-tablecloth restaurant, Beardsley's, named after the British illustrator, judging by the black-and-white prints on every wall. It was the restaurant of choice for special occasions, and for my apparent doubleheader: Happy Birthday and Happy Keys to the Castle. As early as over salads, Dad and Beth exchanged a look that I recognized as *Should* I *tell her, or should you?*

It was my dad who delivered the bombshell. "We think this may provide an incentive and a cushion: You'll stop paying rent on your apartment and move home. No, wait; listen: home but without the stigma. You couldn't be a boomeranging adult child if we're no longer under the same roof, right?"

With Beth nodding her encouragement, he continued. "With the mortgage paid off, it would be rent-free, and if you couldn't swing the taxes, the utilities, the fuel, the upkeep . . . we have a solution."

I was shaking my head, thinking their solution was throwing more cash at my unprofitable lifestyle. I said, "If you mean helping out once again, there's only so much—"

But my dad was saying, "With three bedrooms, and as far as we've gleaned, no boyfriend/partner/companion on the horizon— why not a boarder! Not a roommate in the traditional sense; not someone to socialize and share meals with, but someone who merely rents a room. You'd take the master bedroom, and he'd get your old room."

"And would keep to himself," added Beth.

"Himself?" I repeated.

Of course they had someone in mind, practically lined up: Frank Crowley, my old algebra teacher and one of my dad's colleagues whom I'd known my whole life, recently widowed— *but*, they assured me, coping remarkably well.

"Recently widowed" told only half the tale. His wife had died instantly and famously on the golf course about a year ago, struck by lightning, front-page news for days.

"He would *not* be a gloomy presence," Beth continued. "He just wants a room of his own."

"But a roommate *your* age? I've never called him anything but Mr. Crowley."

"On a trial basis," Beth said, then let slip, "He's very keen on the idea."

My dad said quietly, "He was there for me. Most of my colleagues didn't know what to do or say when your mother died, but Frank had lunch with me every single day for months after I returned to work. You'd be doing him a favor, and me, too."

I must've looked slightly less disinclined because Beth coaxed, "How about breakfast with him at the Over Easy? You'll talk; you'll see if it feels right."

"If I decided to move back home, I'd ask a friend. Or at least look for a roommate on Craigslist."

But ex-bookkeeper Beth reached into her briefcase-size handbag and brought forth a sheaf of bills. Even just the levies from Harrow's property and school taxes were scary. She said, "We're figuring if a boarder brought in even a hundred dollars per week, it would make a nice dip in the red ink."

"Or I'd keep my apartment and you'd sell the house."

Ignoring that, Beth testified, "When I kicked Brad out, I had a series of roommates, one nightmare after the other. You can't ask someone, 'Are you a slob? Do you never wash a dish? Do you drink too much? Do you have the creepiest boyfriends? Do you throw things down the toilet that result in a three-hundred-dollar visit by a plumber?' And not easy to evict, either."

"How do you know Mr. Crowley wouldn't be a nightmare?"

"Frank Crowley is the least likely nightmare that ever walked on God's green earth," said my dad, his voice choking.

How could I say no to a breakfast with the man who moved my father to near-tears?

Beth added, "He wants to keep to himself, to read, to tinker, to watch football and baseball. He once told your father that Ginger made him watch Red Sox games with the sound off. I don't mean with the volume turned down. I mean off! And he has a snow blower."

They raised their glasses to toast my generosity of spirit, even if so far withheld. I said okay. The least I could do was have breakfast with the guy who'd been there for my dad, who'd been through so much himself, widowed by a strike of lightning. "But just Mr. Crowley and me at the Over Easy, okay?"

I didn't need them putting their thumbs on the scale.

I was honest with him. I told him I didn't understand why he'd want to be a boarder in someone else's house rather than live in his own.

The waitress had just arrived tableside, pen poised. Frank closed his menu and said "Just coffee and a cruller for me. Emma?"

"The Mexican scramble, extra jalapenos, and cocoa," I said, which for some reason made him smile.

As soon as we were alone, he explained. "The house was in Ginger's name. She left it to her two daughters."

I might've muttered "What a bitch" in any other company, but Frank was looking more embarrassed than sad. He said, "They've given me a grace period. I can stay until I find something else."

I asked if his wife's nonbequest had come as a surprise.

"No. We had a prenup." And with an apologetic smile, "I was husband number three."

I hadn't known Ginger. I did remember her wearing a fur coat to whatever math department family get-together I'd attended, evoking eyerolls from Beth. I was tempted to ask if he'd loved Ginger, meaning *Are you devastated?*, but said only, "I should've sent a note. I'm sorry."

"Your dad was the first person I called after her death was confirmed."

"I know it was sudden."

He shrugged. "It's sudden for us all, isn't it? One second you're alive, and the next second you're dead."

Very true, forensically speaking, but with a detachment that reinforced Beth's claim that he was coping remarkably well. Across from me, he looked exactly like the high school coach he used to be, his gray hair a few millimeters longer than a buzz cut. Had I known Ginger's daughters? Were they close to my age? Had they gone to Harrow High?

"Younger," he said. "She sent them away to boarding school."

Our food arrived, giving me time to frame my biggest worry. I buttered a half piece of toast in slow motion and finally said, "With this arrangement, I'd be living with my former algebra teacher. It might look funny."

"You have to be completely comfortable with this. But at the risk of being hard-sell, please know I'd keep to myself. A room with a TV and a desk sounds just right. Oh, I *would* need a modest use of the kitchen, maybe one shelf in the refrigerator, but I'd know my place."

His place . . . a stellar colleague and bosom buddy of my father's who'd put on a tie for this meeting, talking about "his place"! I asked, "You're sure this is what you want, a monk's life?"

He closed his eyes. "Exactly."

I was still torn, annoyed with my parents for dreaming up this potentially awkward home life, but already fond of this unassuming man in a crew cut and cardigan. He volunteered that he'd looked at a few places, studios, but all out of town. "I can afford a place of my own. That might still happen." He smiled. "I could find out that I don't want a monastic life."

I was out of arguments, and empathy was winning out over fear of domestic discomfort. "What if we gave it a shot. A one-month trial?"

"Makes sense."

"Did my dad mention a figure?"

"He did. But I didn't take him seriously. It was almost a joke."

What to charge someone who's merely sleeping and watching TV in one room and using a single shelf in the fridge and the lesser bathroom with its fiberglass shower? Should I go higher than my parents' bargain-basement $100? I did, but barely. "How's a hundred twenty-five per week?"

"Five hundred a month? More than fair."

"Deal," I said.

4

I knew almost immediately that landladyhood was working. On day one, Frank corrected the time on my coffee maker and programmed it to brew four cups at 6:30 every morning. He took the trash and recyling bins to the curb the first Wednesday he was in residence, noticed what needed tightening or oiling, and performed tasks unknown to me such as emptying the crumbs collected at the bottom of the toaster.

One evening he came downstairs, found me watching *The Bachelorette* in the den, and said the Sox were losing by ten runs in the eighth inning, too painful to watch. Did I have a minute? There was something important he wanted to discuss with me.

I paused my show, surprising myself by feeling worried. Was our arrangement not working out?

No, it was this: He was asking my permission to get something that had been unattainable when Ginger was alive. Could he get a dog?

"Unattainable why?" I asked. "Was she allergic?"

"No," he said sadly. "She didn't like dogs. She was afraid they'd shed and tie us down."

I told him I'd always wanted a dog too.

He said he'd go to the pound; maybe there would be an older dog whose owner had died? Fully trained.

One day later, enter a squat little girl, part pit bull, part basset hound, brindled in brown and gold. She was orphaned, of indeterminate age—maybe two, maybe three years old, guessed the vet—and instantly in love with Frank and, to a slightly less ecstatic degree, me. She'd been named Sad Eyes at the shelter, which Frank softened to a relatable long-I "Ivy." We placed one dog bed—a fleece-lined cave that looked like a pita pocket—in the kitchen, and another halfway between our two bedrooms. She stopped crying as soon as she was permitted sleepovers in Frank's room.

Frank made Ivy soup from beef shin bones to moisten her mail-order premium kibble. As for his own meals, he made oatmeal every other morning, enough for me, alternating with English muffins. He had lunch at the Over Easy, and seemed content to make himself a cheese-and-tomato sandwich, a burger, an omelet, or a frozen turkey dinner at night. Not that I was any cook, but his choices made me sad. He ate early, leaving the kitchen to me at a later, more fashionable hour. The meal that changed our routine happened the night we were both twisting limbs off separate but identical roast chickens from the Big Y.

"What's wrong with this picture?" I asked, pointing at the two carcasses side by side in their plastic boats.

"Maybe one would do, you mean?"

"I never finish mine," I said. "Do you? After two meals in a row, I lose interest."

That was one accommodation we made: a shared roast chicken, then soup with the carcasses, bones carefully drained for Ivy's safety.

Frank took on more chores around the house, slowly, as if too many would be stepping over some line. Vacuuming? Did I mind? Did I have any new bags, or should he pop over to the house on Greenough—Ginger's—to get a package? I announced that I was cutting his rent by $25 a week. How clean and orderly the house had become since he moved in! He didn't agree or disagree, but when the first check came in, it was for the full, agreed-upon $500. I asked, waving the check, "Did you forget?"

It was my own fault. I had a bad habit of yelping when I opened bills—electric, gas, the whoppers from the town for real estate and school taxes. Heading out the door with Ivy, both of them smiling, or so it seemed, he said, "I don't know what you're talking about."

Unsolicited, Frank packed me a sandwich for the opening day of an unpromising sale.

"Why so glum?" he asked.

"For starters, it smells funny . . . urine-y. There were litter boxes everywhere. Air freshener didn't help."

"Did you open windows?"

"I tried."

"What if *I* tried?"

He quickly assembled a second sandwich, put Ivy in her crate with her favorite stuffed buddy, came with me, and unstuck and opened windows. "Why don't I stay?" he asked.

I told him I'd be hiring a teen, once I got around to that, to do what I used to do.

"As in . . . bag the purchases, take the money, give change?"

"And add up the sticker prices."

"An ideal job for a retired mathematician with time on his hands, don't you think?"

Suspecting that Ginger had chipped away at his self-worth, I asked, "It wouldn't be like the retired teachers who I see ringing up my purchases at the Dollar Store?"

"Degrading? Embarrassing? I don't know where you get these ideas."

*

Next up: an estate sale at a house that had been built in the late 1700s. On a walk-through before the doors opened, Frank suggested some price adjustments. He knew his stuff. Ginger had loved antiquing but hadn't driven since a parking-lot collision had caused her airbag to deploy. How many times had he spent whole weekends at the Brimfield Fair? Too many times. The accumulation . . . he wouldn't know where to begin.

Those antique garden tools? Rusted? So what? Rust could be beautiful. You can't buy those anymore. The weathervane I hadn't lifted my eyes to notice? Surely two hundred years old. Let the buyer figure out how to get it down. And most helpful and profitable, the mysterious wooden thing that Frank recognized as a cheese coaster, explaining that all cheese used to come in wheels, and this is where they rested. I tore up the $5 sticker and with his urging priced it at $99, with a note explaining what this rare and valuable antique was.

Yet again we had a friendly, disingenuous squabble about compensation—me for, him against. His argument: He enjoyed seeing what people bought—it was an education, really—and the socializing. So many parents of ex-students! A pleasure! He was so happy to help.

No, he couldn't accept an hourly wage. Too complicated for me, filing W-2s and such. But he agreed to one concession: He'd let me pay for the pizza and Chinese food deliveries, but no more than once a week.

That was it, his big ask. Of course I said yes, but it made me wonder once again: How beaten down by Ginger had he been, that this new spartan life was an improvement? Thirty-plus years his junior, I was feeling more and more maternal about my old algebra teacher, as if I were the shelter, and Frank the rescued Ivy.

I needed to make a gesture. I knew a present would embarrass him unless it could masquerade as something for the house. I looked around the kitchen. The Mr. Coffee had arrived with Beth when she and Dad married. And the soup he made for Ivy simmered for hours, requiring his attention. After research online, I ordered the Rolls-Royce of stovetop pressure cookers, and a coffee maker that boasted hot and cold foam technology. It needed whole beans, so I signed us up for a subscription to a coffee roaster in Seattle, starting with two pounds of a big seller with low acidity and heady notes of vanilla.

5

I came downstairs one morning to find Frank Swiffering the linoleum kitchen floor. "Hope you don't mind," he said. "Swabbing the decks was always my job."

I wanted to say, *Wasn't your job being head of the math department at Harrow High School?* Trying to sound lighthearted, I asked instead, "And what were Ginger's jobs?"

"Golf. And so-called collecting," followed by a barely audible, "I knew what I was getting into."

Instantly intrigued, I sat down and invited him to join me. He did; he said he was going to get the dust mop, the carpet sweeper, and all the cleaning products from Greenough Street. "I'm entitled to that much," he added.

It was another reminder of Ginger's unjust bequeathing. How to learn more, while sounding like a neutral party? I tried, "Your late wife . . . there's so much I don't know about her."

His worried expression said *Not that again.* I forged ahead just the same, asking how and where they'd met.

"We were on some foolish Founders Day committee together. For reasons I never understood, she set her cap for me. I think it was because I was age-appropriate, single, straight. I was flattered." After a pause, apologetically, "She was a very pretty woman."

"And?"

"Hair colored to match her name . . . and a big yellow dress."

I didn't want to interrupt his narrative by asking what he meant by "big," so I just nodded my encouragement.

"There was coffee and cookies after the meeting."

Was I seeing a preemptive reddening of his face? It made me skip a few polite questions and ask a blunt, "Who came on to whom?"

"Ginger struck up a conversation with me."

"About . . . ?"

"I don't remember. Probably about the tricentennial. And then . . ."

I could tell he was gauging what was appropriate, what might be crossing a line. I said, "Frank! I'm thirty-two years old. I'm not a kid. Did she ask you out for a drink?"

"No. She offered me a ride home because I'd walked. The community center was less than a mile from my house."

"Okay . . . you got in her car. Then what? Did one of you make a move?"

Eyes averted, he said, "A rather big move."

I waited. "Did she kiss you? Or try to?"

"Eventually."

"That sounds sweet enough. Why are you turning purple?"

I could see him trying to counter that, to put a swagger into an unconvincing smile. "I'm taking a wild guess that she offered . . . to do you a big favor?"

He looked surprised. How had I guessed Ginger's exact overture? "I was flabbergasted! Stunned. I'm still stunned now at how willing I was to . . . consent."

"A pretty woman, someone upstanding enough to be on the Founders Day committee?"

"It was like something that happens in a movie. 'So nice to meet you. Are you here alone? Do you need a ride home?' What followed without any warning was behavior that was as bold and as, as—forgive me—libidinous as I'd ever experienced."

I whispered, "Did you go back to your place? Or hers?"

He shook his head. "We went somewhere private that she knew. Along the river. I'd never been there."

I didn't admit that I knew exactly where they'd gone—where every Harrow teen took their girlfriend or boyfriend.

"I still can't believe it was me—the parking and the . . . partaking. Me, of all people!"

"Stop it! Obviously she was attracted to you. She spotted you across a crowded room and probably thought, *I'd like to get to know that guy.*"

"Perhaps . . . I quit the committee after that night. I felt as if I had a big red A on my chest, even if neither of us was married."

"But you must've kept going out on more . . . dates. Obviously you enjoyed her attentions."

"Enjoyed? I was in a daze. I was like a teenage boy who was seduced by the high school prom queen and couldn't get over his good luck!"

"Okay. But why so *Scarlet Letter* about it? You kept seeing her."

"Kept seeing her? I married her! God help me!"

What does one say to that? Sorry/not sorry? "Previous girl-friends?" I asked.

"A few. It had been a while."

He meant, of course, it had been a while since he'd had sex when Ginger undoubtedly took her hand off the steering wheel and reached for him. "Who proposed marriage, and when?" I asked.

"When? Six months? Despite what you're hearing about her being a modern woman, she wanted that ring on her finger."

"How'd you feel about becoming a stepfather?"

"I welcomed it. I thought it was a bonus. I'd always wanted

kids. Ginger's daughters were just eight and five. But they were shipped off for whole summers and then to boarding school, against their wishes; against my better judgment, too, but it wasn't my decision."

I retreated to one of my favorite Ginger grievances. "Do you think she left them the house as a way of saying 'Sorry I sent you away'?"

"No. They got the house because her lawyer was protecting it from husband number two. She'd had an ironclad prenup, the same one I signed."

"Can you apply one husband's prenup to the next guy?"

"Same terms, but a new draft, with my name on it. I was still seeing through rose-colored glasses."

I asked if he thought the daughters would move back to Harrow.

"Doubt it. They're both in Manhattan."

"So they'll sell it?" I asked, as Beth would want me to.

"They *can't* sell it," Frank said. "If they don't want it, it redounds to Stefan."

"Stefan? Who's Stefan?"

"Her first husband, the girls' father." And then with an uncharacteristic curl of his lip, he spelled S-T-E-F-A-N, adding, "The great love of her life."

I winced. "She told you that?"

"She didn't have to."

"Did you know him?" I asked.

"He made himself known, believe me. And I can guess your next question: Why'd she divorce the love of her life?"

"Because he did the divorcing?"

"No! Because she took up with husband number two while still married to Stefan."

"And number two lasted how long?"

"Two years. He was young, a handsome specimen, and a liar."

"But she didn't get back together with Stefan?"

"He was done with marriage. He'd had his kids. I suspect he had other women. He was punishing her, so she punished *him* by marrying me on the rebound."

What a job that floozy had done on Frank's self-esteem! He sighed and sent a longing glance over to the idle Swiffer. It was my cue to give the topic a rest—at least for the time it took me to scramble an egg and talk about the weather forecast. Back at the table with egg and toast, twisting the peppermill, I said, "It helps to talk about it, don't you think?"

"I never talk about this. Especially with an ex-student."

"You have to get over that."

After a long pause and much brushing of invisible crumbs off his placemat, he said, "I was away at school all day. . . . He had a very recognizable car, a red Audi—"

"Who did?"

"Stefan! Even that name . . ." He shuddered. "Chuck Mendez, our next-door neighbor. His wife was home during the day and saw the car in the driveway for an hour most days. Sometimes more, sometimes less. A helluva thing for Chuck to have to tell me, but he said *he'd* want to know."

I'd had Mr. Mendez for Spanish and sophomore homeroom. I also knew Mrs. Mendez, a Finders, Keepers devotee who never missed a piece of Wedgwood.

"Didn't I already know her history? What a coward I was! I'd come home from school, and she'd be in a dressing gown! Not a word from me! No recrimination. No scene!"

I gave his nearest hand a quick pat. "But then she got struck by lightning," I pointed out. "Kind of biblical."

"I've thought of that," he said. "Neither her caddy nor the friend she was playing with were hit. A direct strike. Just Ginger."

I noticed he'd been twisting his wedding ring with various degrees of agitation from the moment I began my interrogation.

I pointed at it. "Some widowed husbands might've taken it off by now."

He looked down, gave the ring a meaningless tug. "I can't get it over my knuckle."

"But you'd take it off if you could?"

After a long pause he said, "I suppose. What's the point?"

Unsaid: For some, the point would be remembrance and love, if the marriage had been happy. I gave the table a take-action slap, went to the sink, and motioned for him to join me.

"Left hand," I ordered.

He offered it, turning away, bracing himself as if I had a needle poised to scrape out a sliver. First I tried liquid soap, then bar soap, then canola oil. Once the oil was on, one decent pull was all it took before the ring slid over the knuckle, went flying into the soapy water and down the drain.

"Oh shit!" I yelled. "I should've put the stopper in. Oh fuck!"

"What?"

"It's gone. Down the drain. Shit! I'll call a plumber. What an idiot!"

He reached in and swished the soapy water around, excavating, finding nothing, saying nothing. He wiped his hand on a dish towel, held up his naked left hand, and laughed.

6

My dad and Beth sent postcards from Buzzards Bay, from Race Point, from Martha's Vineyard and Nantucket, from cranberry bogs and whale watches. Retired life was great! They were walking two miles a day and eating more fish. What a luxury to attend estate sales as mere customers!

Win-win, they often said, meaning their enjoying life and me keeping Finders, Keepers alive. They wanted to hear everything. Was I managing, breaking even, covering utility bills? Occasionally and more delicately, they asked if I was writing.

I said not yet, but I'd be using the third bedroom as my study.

"Dating?" asked Beth. "I heard there's a site where women make the first move. You'd be good at that."

I said I'd look into it. I walked to the front door, opened it soundlessly, rang the doorbell. "Pizza's here!" I said. "Talk soon!"

As the months went by, I reported in less and less detail about Finders, Keepers 2.0, skipping over some new wrinkles I'd introduced but confessing that it was now officially "Estate of Mind." An easy, neutral topic was Frank as value-added times two, residentially and professionally. They loved hearing about his discoveries—the cheese coaster, the weathervane, a sled that had to be a hundred years old.

"Rusted runners, I bet," my dad said. "How much?"

"Sixty-five. Hardly rusted. It was a beauty."

"See?" said Beth. "I can hear it in your voice: the treasure hunt! You're getting bitten by the bug."

The bug that was biting me wasn't job satisfaction but the novelty of answering only to myself. I'd begun tagging items with prices in dollars, pounds, and Euros, thinking it might add some international intrigue to the more valuable items. Frank did the calculations and conversions.

Also new to Finders, Keepers 2.0: the more careful inventory of clothes. Beth had believed that owners and/or beneficiaries wouldn't bother washing or dry-cleaning anything left behind. She might make a sign saying "Items of clothing, $5" without noticing the vintage Gucci dress under a Dior trench coat, due to her low expectations, fashion-wise, in a town the size of Harrow.

Had she not seen the bridesmaids' and prom dresses? A silk kimono, a vintage tuxedo, men's cashmere and herringbone overcoats, a loden coat with toggle buttons, and once a stole of indeterminate fur that brought $100. I spotted hand-knit sweaters with such small moth holes that no one would notice; a wedding gown, an academic gown, a christening gown; scarves, pillbox hats, fedoras, and cowboy boots. At one sale, just to amuse myself, I answered the door in a green satin cocktail dress I wouldn't have worn in real life, a price tag hanging from the armpit. Same for wearing a menagerie of rhinestone animal and bird pins, the more the better, to catch someone's eye.

Though unopened canned goods used to go to the food bank, I turned them into arrangements, adding a cookbook, a spatula, a potholder. Occasionally when a customer left a bottle of wine behind—surely undrinkable, probably a gift from a teetotaler who didn't know good from bad—I'd add that to the grouping.

I introduced gift-wrapped surprise packages for only a dollar, usually books or a shoebox filled with duds like clip-on earrings, pens, spools of thread, a deck of cards. No one complained, since I always added a coupon entitling the holder to one dollar off their next Estate of Mind sale. I had to make the best of it, didn't I?

Midweek, following a middling sale on Fairgrove, the doorbell startled me awake. Who'd be visiting at 8:30 a.m.? Hearing muted but companiable-sounding exchanges, I knew that Frank was up and tending to it. A friend of his, I figured. No need to rush downstairs, other than curiosity and the smell of the cinnamon that Frank always added to our oatmeal.

I dressed, brushed teeth and hair, went downstairs, and found a uniformed policeman seated at the kitchen table. Unsmiling, he half rose, nodded formally, sat down. As one of Harrow's three police officers, Luke Winooski was known by all; everyone, including me, had gone to school with a Winooski sibling or cousin. But this wasn't the Luke I'd graduated with. Once a chubby redhead who played drums in the HHS orchestra and marching band, he'd returned from the police academy and a decade on the Worcester force fit and nearly unrecognizable.

"What's up?" I asked, with an involuntary check of his left hand.

"It isn't social, I'm afraid," Frank explained. "Chief Winooski is here on police business."

Was it about Frank? Surely not anything that would make me wonder how clueless I'd been to open my door to a criminal. "Does he need a lawyer?" I asked.

Luke smiled, a fleeting relief—except that he was now saying, "No, but *you* might."

Surely he was joking. I smiled.

"Emma," said Frank. "We weren't supposed to be selling alcohol at the Moriartys'."

"What alcohol?"

"The Spumante," said Frank.

Luke added, "And reportedly a bottle of peach wine."

"That's what brought you here? A bottle of peach wine?"

"You need a license to sell alcohol," he said.

Taking issue with "sell," I explained how we practically gave it away. "We designed groupings, maybe with wineglasses, a corkscrew, an apron. Once in a while, if I found an unopened bottle—"

"Did someone *buy* this grouping?" Luke asked.

I looked at comptroller Frank, who nodded.

"You need a license to sell beer and alcohol," Luke repeated. "We got a complaint."

I asked if it was a local, state, or federal crime.

"It's a town ordinance," he said. "Not my call."

Frank said, "We won't do it again, Chief. We'll consider this a warning." He was signaling something to me, nodding toward the table. I interpreted this as *Don't just stand there, join us*. I asked Luke if he'd like some oatmeal, which he declined.

"Mind if I finish it?" I asked Frank, wooden spoon poised over the pot.

"All yours," he said.

Maple syrup, milk, spoon, napkin. I took my time, then sat down again. "Frank cooks it with a stick of cinnamon," I announced. "He's always up first."

"Oatmeal on Tuesdays and Thursdays," Frank added. "Otherwise toast, or I scramble an egg."

After a few moments Luke asked, new color behind his freckles, "How long have you two been living together?"

Frank raised his hand in the manner of *Full stop/let me answer that*. "I'm a boarder here. Emma's father and I were colleagues and friends. Of course you know Ginger died." And to me: "Ginger's caddy called nine-one-one. An ambulance came, and so did Luke."

"I missed that," I said. "I was living in Framingham at the time."

"You and Luke were in the same class at HHS," said Frank. "Surely you knew that."

I said, "Of course."

"And he moved back to replace Chief Mankopf. Lucky for all of us."

"Lucky?" I repeated.

Frank glanced at Luke. "I'll leave it at 'bent cop.' Is that unfair?"

"We'll leave it at 'he had a heart attack,'" said Luke. Then, to me, "You need to get your van inspected. Your sticker expired at the end of last month."

I said I'd take care of that today. Thanks for noticing. Then, hoping to sound enthusiastic about the municipality that employed him, I said, "It's nice being back. As you obviously know, I took over the family business."

"She's introduced a lot of new features," said Frank.

Finally, a laugh from Luke. "So I've heard."

Were we off the hook? I said, "We didn't know we were breaking the law. I just spotted a bottle of crappy wine and said, 'Here, take this, too.'"

Luke said, "Ignorance of the law doesn't excuse a crime."

I put out my hands, wrists together. "Then arrest me."

"Maybe next time."

"I think Chief Winooski is pulling your leg," Frank said.

"No more selling alcohol, even if it's for two bucks." Luke took a final sip of his coffee, thanked Frank, nodded to me, and stood.

I looked up. "Didn't I used to be taller than you?"

"You missed my growth spurt."

"Thank you for coming by," said Frank. "Don't be a stranger."

"I grab lunch at the Over Easy every day unless I'm in court or rounding up criminals." Luke took a business card from his wallet and put it on the table.

Frank said, "I'll walk you out."

I watched them through the window, talking next to the police car, continuing when Luke was in the driver's seat, window rolled down. When Frank returned, I said, "That was a nice long tête-a-tête."

"He had me for homeroom," said Frank.

"Were you talking about old times?"

"Not exactly. I asked him to send my condolences to his mother. His father died last year. I meant to go to the wake."

"Or you could send your condolences yourself."

"It might be seen as . . . never mind. Luke said he'd tell her."

I filed this away. Maybe the next time Mrs. Winooski's name came up, I'd deliver a subtle version of "Go for it." He needed an ally and a cheerleader. I could push and pull for him in a way I might not do for myself.

I was adding my bowl and mug to the dishwasher and contemplating the dirty saucepan when Frank shooed me away. "Go do what you usually do after breakfast. Cleaning up was always my job."

What wasn't his job? Something else to add to my grudge against Ginger and their marital inequities. It motivated me to pluck out of thin air, "I remember Mrs. Winooski being pretty."

After a long pause, he said, "I know what you're getting at . . . but it's not even a year since Ginger died."

"Of course. Sorry."

I figured that the sigh that followed was about my helter-skelter loading of the dishwasher until he asked, "What kind of recently widowed man asks a woman out for a cup of coffee?"

A rhetorical question, for sure, but still I said, "A cup of coffee is not a night on the town."

More silent cogitation, and then: "I can't just call her out of the blue."

"Why not?"

"I only know her as a parent. Expressing condolences a full year after her husband died? How transparent is that?"

Admitting transparency, I thought, was a good indicator of his wishful thinking.

Pocketing Luke's business card, I wished Frank a nice day and went upstairs. I checked my email, gave Luke twenty more minutes to reach the station, sat on my unmade bed, then called what turned out to be his own line. He answered with a brusque "Winooski."

"Emma here, Emma Lewis. Thanks for the house call and for giving me the benefit of the doubt."

"Did I?"

"I'm sure you did." Then, a line I'd worked on in advance: "From now on, Estate of Mind is on the wagon."

No response. Hadn't that been a little charming?

Okay, then; why pussyfoot around with a busy and distracted police officer? "Here's why I'm calling: I was thinking it would be nice if Frank and your mother got together, maybe for a cup of coffee."

Silence.

"He sent his regards, right?" I continued.

"His condolences."

"That's a start. Someone's got to get the ball rolling. Do you know if she's already seeing someone?"

"Jeez, Emma."

Men as matchmakers? The worst. I said, "What's the big deal? Just pass along his regards. It could be enough."

"I think you're mistaking me for a girlfriend."

I ignored that. "Tell her you were at my house on official business, and Frank Crowley happened to be there. And—I hadn't even thought of this until now—how you and Frank share a bond. You were there when his wife was struck by lightning—"

"Except I wasn't. I was called to the scene. And he wasn't there, either."

"Trust me," I said. "You'd be doing her a favor."

"Look . . . I can send his condolences. But the other stuff—way outside my comfort zone."

"You're a cop. You have a dangerous job. You must go outside your comfort zone ten times a day."

"Debatable," he said. "Why can't Mr. Crowley call *her*?"

"Because he thinks he should be in mourning for a whole year, that it's too soon for him to ask someone out—which this wouldn't be anyway. When did your dad die?"

"June fourteenth. Flag day."

"I'm sorry," I said. "I should've said that when I found you in my kitchen. You might want to throw in that he's widowed, too."

"She knows. Everyone knows. It was on the front page of the *Echo*. Mrs. Crowley was the first person ever struck by lightning at Eaglecrest, let alone killed."

"How about this: You say Emma Lewis, his landlady, is putting me up to this. She thinks it would be nice for him to meet someone in the same boat. By the way: He's in good shape emotionally. His wife was a tyrant."

"I am *not* setting up my mother. I'll pass along Mr. Crowley's condolences, but that's it. And only to end the harassment."

"Good man," I said.

7

Three days after I spoke with Luke, a card arrived for Frank from Mrs. Winooski. I played innocent as I delivered the envelope, casually placing it between junk mail and a bank statement. Frank was in the den with the morning's *Echo*, Ivy snoring at his feet. I was already feeling successful, given the quick turnaround, and because the envelope's return-address sticker testified to Mrs. Winooski's support of the Humane Society.

Like Ivy hustling a treat out of sight, he excused himself, card in hand, and headed for the front porch. I gave him a full five minutes before I joined him, casually, as if on my way out. He was on the glider, Ivy lolling belly-up, a front paw on Frank's leg, hoping to engage him.

"I'm checking out the Duggan place," I told him. "Do you know them?"

"Um . . . not sure."

"A daughter, Hannah, is the one who reached out to me," I tried again. "She had my father for something."

He nodded, as unmoved as I'd ever seen him at the mention of my dad and a course offering.

Small talk was getting me nowhere. I pointed to the card. "From Luke's mother?"

"For better or for worse . . . a sympathy card." He held it up.

Below white flowers, maybe lilies, was the phrase, "There are no words to take away the sadness when you lose someone you love."

I slid my shoulder bag to the floor. "I see what you mean. Kind of . . . off message?"

"It's the timing. She must think Ginger died recently."

Without quoting Luke, lest Frank know of my meddling, I said, "Trust me. She knows when Ginger died. Everyone does. And I think the etiquette of sympathy cards is the same as for wedding gifts: You get a year to send them." I stepped over Ivy and sat down. "She sure didn't waste any time getting back to you. I don't understand why you're not beaming."

He handed me the card. Inside, under more bereavement reassurance, she'd written, "My son mentioned seeing you at your friend's house."

Was it the ambiguity of the word *friend* that was troubling him? I read aloud, triumphantly, "'Sincerely, Constance Winooski, mother of Michael, Alex, Peter, and Luke.' And for god's sake, her phone number! She's asking you out!"

That produced a weak smile. After what looked like further pondering, he said, "I'm trying to remember which of her boys I had for which subjects."

I groaned. "That isn't the point. That is so . . . literal. She won't remember which kid had you for what. She wants you to call her!"

Though he nodded, I could tell he was unconvinced.

"Are you having second thoughts?" I asked. "You better not be, because if this arrived today, she ran right out to buy the card as soon as Luke sent your condolences."

"I know," he said.

"But . . ."

"Don't be impatient with me . . . I'm remembering her as an attractive woman."

"And you're an attractive man!" I yelped, adding a white

lie—that several of my friends had crushes on him back in high school.

"Students! I never would've acted on such a thing," Frank protested.

"I know! That wasn't my point. My point is that Mrs. Winooski wouldn't be sending you her phone number if she didn't want you to use it."

"I intend to use it."

"When? *Mañana?* Please don't tell me that you're worried about breaking some rule of posthumous dating."

"Shouldn't I be?"

Impatient with his oversolicitude, I asked, "Would your late wife have agonized over an invitation from a fellow widower?"

At long last, he smiled. "A *fellow* widower? A man? Ginger St. Pierre Giordano Crowley? Not for one second."

Luckily, we were due for a shared dinner, or at least that's what I announced, calling upstairs at six o'clock, "Pizza? Or the Indian place on Church Street? They deliver now."

He came right down, looking close to jovial. I coached him through the menu, and ordered what I considered beginner Indian.

Table set, food delivered and unpacked, beer poured, I started with the Duggan house appraisal. "Parents dead. None of the three kids wants any of the furniture. Dutch colonial, midcentury, window treatments, sets of dishes for every holiday. There's a barn, which I'd have you scope out. They're leaving most of the furniture. It's not interesting, but it's in good condition."

I expected the usual questions about potential valuables and street parking, but instead I heard, "Aren't you going to ask me if I followed up with Connie?"

"It's *all* I wanted to ask you about."

"First, I want to thank you for giving me the pep talk. I needed that."

"You're welcome. *And?*"

"I left a message, and she called me back. She'd been at her book group, which meets once a month."

"Okay, she called you back. Then what?"

"We talked mostly about her sons. Three of the four are married, including her gay son, and she has two granddaughters. I didn't have to make conversation, which suited me fine."

"Please tell me you arranged to meet."

"We did. We *are*. Tomorrow."

"At the Over Easy?"

"No . . . not at the Over Easy."

I said that made sense, especially if her son hangs out there. Where were they meeting?

"Her house. It was her idea. Neither one of us needs to start tongues wagging. Plus she said I could bring Ivy. She doesn't have a dog now, but she had a rescue."

I didn't want to restart my harangue about his chronic worry over widower etiquette, so I asked if any of her sons lived at home.

"Do you mean Luke? No. He lives at the station."

"At the police station? That can't be right."

"It's an apartment. Separate. I'm guessing rent-free for the chief."

I moved away from the topic of Luke to a neutral, multi-son question. "Did she tell you where the other three live?"

Frank smiled. "Do I have to repeat every word that passed between his mother and me?"

I said, "I like your attitude. And I like where this is going."

"I'm nervous, but in a good way. And I have time to work on some conversation starters."

"Easy!" I said. "Tell her about Estate of Mind, how you put

your calculator of a brain to good use, and especially about your good eye. Give her examples of some treasures you spotted. The weathervane, the first-edition *Valley of the Dolls*! Everyone loves homegrown *Antiques Roadshow* stories."

"That wouldn't be bragging?" he asked. "It wouldn't come across as immodest?"

"Not from you," I said.

8

For someone whose face was a mirror to very little, Frank returned from his coffee date looking wonderstruck.

"Nice time?" I asked.

He held up a brown lunch bag. "Blueberry scones. She insisted."

"Nice house?" I asked.

"I didn't go beyond the kitchen—which was sunny; pretty blue-and-white Delft tiles on the backsplash. Then we sat in the backyard, at the picnic table. She grows her tomato plants from seed, indoors on a windowsill all winter."

"Amazing."

"She only bothers with tomatoes. And of course herbs." He was unclipping Ivy's leash and complimenting her on her stellar behavior while visiting Mrs. Winooski.

I asked if he'd cleared everything up.

Squinting, he said, "Remind me."

I waved a hand around the kitchen. "This. Your living situation. And that you weren't widowed, like, two days ago."

"No need. There hadn't been any misunderstandings. I told her how you were willing to take in a boarder when I was looking for a new situation, and whose daughter you are."

"Did she ask why you weren't staying in your own house?"

"She did. I told her the truth: that it never *was* my house. The whole town knows I wasn't Ginger's first or favorite husband."

Yikes. Was Frank sounding more Ginger-cynical than before? Maybe having a few hours with a pleasant, supportive woman was giving him some perspective. Blunt me asked, "Did you tell her that Ginger cheated on you with her first husband?"

"I didn't have to."

"She knew?"

"Everyone knew." He shrugged. "Maria Mendez is in her book group."

"Who brought this up?" I asked.

"One thing led to another. I found myself opening up. We had quite a few good laughs."

"Laughs about your—no offense—terrible marriage?"

"I wanted to appear . . . what's the right term? 'In a good place'? Not angry or bitter toward a woman who died tragically."

"Excellent instinct. A lot of first dates—and I'm not saying this was a date—begin with a pissed-off guy railing about his old girlfriend. For me, that's a dealbreaker."

He'd moved to the sink, where he was refilling Ivy's water bowl. After shutting off the faucet, he didn't turn around, but seemed to be staring straight ahead at nothing more than a shelf of juice glasses.

"You okay over there?" I asked.

He turned around. "You don't often talk about dates. Or dating."

True; a road we hadn't gone down except in his lane, given my aggressive matchmaking of the past four days. Maybe the turning point was Constance Winooski; maybe she'd asked questions about me he couldn't answer. *Is your landlady married, engaged, seeing anyone? Gay? Straight? Something else?*

I said we hadn't touched on my dating because there wasn't much to tell. I gave him the condensed version of my love life: the on-again/off-again college boyfriend who signed up with Teach for America at thirty. Went to Louisiana. End of story. I smiled as if I too were in a good place. "Does that do it?"

Apparently not. "I suppose you'd like to have children someday," he said.

I sensed it was Emma homework he'd been assigned. "I know what you're saying: Time can run out. . . . Was it something Mrs. W. brought up when she heard I was over thirty?"

"Actually not. I feel . . . well, I would've liked to have had a child. Ginger still could have, just about . . . age-wise, if you know what I mean. She allowed us to try, but it didn't happen."

She allowed us . . . Another checkmark for me in the overbearing-Ginger column. "You were how old when you two got married?" I asked.

"I'd still have been in my forties when/*if* we'd had a child. Not too old. My own father was forty-three when I was born, and there was a sister after me."

Though I'd only glimpsed Ginger once, and that was across a buffet table, I silently convicted her of lying. She probably didn't want his child, and never stopped using birth control. Had his conversation with Connie, mother of four, brought back that old ache?

"Did she talk more about her boys?" I asked.

"Somewhat."

"Personal stuff?"

"Quite."

I waited. I could tell he felt he owed me more. "Is she not crazy about one of the daughters-in-law?" I guessed. "Or the son-in-law?"

"No, no, not at all." Then, a whisper: "Just that one of the couples is doing IVF, told in confidence to Connie. They know it doesn't always work." Without prompting, almost apologetically, he added, "You might want to know that Luke has a girlfriend."

Mind-reading aside, how had Frank gleaned that I'd want to know such a thing? I said as breezily as I could, "A serious girlfriend?"

"That I didn't ask. She lives in Worcester, where he worked before Harrow."

Of course he would have a girlfriend. And Worcester wasn't far enough to make it a doomed, long-distance relationship. "Big promotion to chief," I said, "even if they were small shoes to fill."

"We talked about that—Manny Mankopf, the corrupt former chief. Luke was brought here to be clean as a whistle. He speaks to school groups! Connie said, 'Don't try to pick up his check at the Over Easy. He's incorruptible.'"

"Proud mom, huh?"

"Very. And Peter, the third son? His husband is a professor at UMass. More bragging rights." He gave his forehead a smack. "How did I forget to tell you this? When I brought up my pitching in with Estate of Mind—you were right about her enjoying my self-style *Antiques Roadshow* anecdotes—she sent along this tip: Lois Mankopf is selling her house on Quail Ridge Road, a beauty, and we should give her a call."

"Manny's widow?"

"Not widowed. Ex-wife. He didn't die. He just left town in disgrace."

A very promising address, Quail Ridge Road. I'd had a friend whose parents were both doctors who lived in an outlandishly cantilevered house there, and another friend who had an infinity pool in her backyard.

"Please thank Mrs. Winooski for the tip next time you see her," I said. "Which is when?"

After all the talk about adultery and infertility, it was this topic that made him blush. "Saturday."

"In other words . . . tomorrow. Doing what?"

"Her second oldest does lighting for the theater at Holy Cross. We're going to a performance he told her about, not sure exactly what, but we're taking our chances."

I turned to the ever-attentive Ivy. "And you? How did you like Mrs. Winooski?" As soon as she heard my voice traveling in her direction, she whipped her tail back and forth. I went closer, kneeled, stroked her head, and sweet-talked, "Are you doing anything Saturday night? If not, we could take a W-A-L-K around the reservoir before dark"—producing even more strenuous wagging that shook her butt.

"She's so smart," bragged Frank.

"Mrs. Mankopf's first name again?" I asked.

"Lois. She's something of a character,' Connie says. It's a big property. Endless bedrooms." He pulled his phone out of his back pocket and consulted it. "Ten-ten Quail Ridge Road. She gave me a phone number, too."

I told him to email whatever he had. Later, I checked the listing on Zillow. Asking price $2.1 million, nearly unheard of in Harrow, Massachusetts. Former five-star bed-and-breakfast.

This could be good, I thought. *This could be big.*

9

At 9:30 a.m. the following Monday I called the number Connie Winooski had supplied. The local 413 area code didn't tell the story, because I reached and woke up an angry Californian who demanded to know who was calling at this ungodly hour. I supplied as many recognizable proper nouns as I could rattle off: Harrow, Emma Lewis, John-Paul and Beth Lewis, Estate of Mind, previously Finders, Keepers, Constance Winooski, who'd given me this number.

"Why did Connie give you my number?"

Connie, not Constance, I noted as I rushed to explain, "Your house on Quail Ridge is for sale, and I'm—"

"You don't call the owner about that! You call the agent—"

Which was when a male voice yelled, "Hang up!"

"Shut up!" she snapped back.

I gave it one more pitch. "I'm not a potential buyer. I'm the owner of the highest-rated estate sale company in the county, and I was hoping—"

"Not now. I can't think straight until I've had a cup of coffee. Call me at a decent hour."

"Which is when?"

"Who the hell are you talking to?" the man grumbled.

"Hold on," she said to me. "I'm getting a robe on . . . let me get away from this schmuck."

I waited. I heard the flush of a toilet, then bare feet slapping linoleum, then Sinatra, then coffee beans rattling in a grinder. *Quail Ridge Road*, I reminded myself.

Finally I heard, "Okay . . . estate sales. Doesn't that mean the owner has to be dead?"

Straight from my website's FAQ page, I explained that "estate" did often imply posthumous, but just as often homeowners were downsizing, divorcing, or, like her, simply relocating. "Did you ever get an insurance appraisal that listed everything on the property?" I asked.

"Who the hell knows? I left enough for staging. With any luck, whoever buys the house will want what's there."

I delivered one of our canned pitches: "Which is exactly where Estate of Mind comes in. You can have us sell what you don't want, rather than hoping the next owner shares your taste."

Above a second whirring grind of the coffee maker, she yelled, "So what does your outfit take?"

I knew exactly what she meant. "Forty percent, which I assure you—"

"Ridiculous," she said, and without another word, the line went dead.

Monday mornings were usually a postmortem on the past weekend's sale, but it had been a free and fallow few weeks. Over coffee I told Frank the disappointing news: 1010 Quail Ridge Road was a no-go. Mrs. Mankopf hung up when she heard about my 40 percent commission. Just the same, please thank Connie for the referral.

"Do you ever come down on your percentage?" he asked.

"For some people, maybe, but I'm not inclined to do this woman any favors."

"Bear with me: thirty-five percent of a big haul is surely going to be better than forty percent of nothing special or nothing at all. A house on Quail Ridge? It could bring triple, quadruple the number of customers that you usually get on a weekend."

I told him I was factoring in the difficult-client piece of the pie.

"How difficult? Didn't you wake her up?"

"And him, too."

"Him? Connie didn't mention that Lois had a new husband."

I smiled. "I've heard you don't have to be married to have sex with someone."

"Irony noted," Frank said, eyebrows raised above his coffee mug.

I asked if Connie was friends with Mrs. Mankopf.

"I didn't get that impression. I think it was a simple matter of noticing the For Sale sign. And when I told her about how I help you on weekends—she wishes she'd known about the Wentworth sale and the cross-stitched pillowcases—she said, 'The Mankopf house could be a gold mine.'"

What if it *was* a gold mine? I felt instantly annoyed with myself for my lack of ambition and backbone. Mankopf's hanging up could've been a negotiating tactic. Was she expecting a counteroffer?

I borrowed Ivy. As soon as we got to the end of Montpelier, she pulled me toward the small park two blocks away. I used the walk to quiz myself. What was the corporate goal here—liking the owner or making a living? I could handle difficult clients, both local and long-distance ones. I practiced visualizing. Get the gig. Bring in five figures instead of four. Promise to place ads in the *Echo*, pitch a feature to the business editor along the lines of *The new CEO of this long-standing family business, the thirty-two-year-old daughter of the founders, is breaking some rules* . . . no, *breaking new ground* . . . no, *breaking company sales records*. Then again, would I want to go public with specific numbers? Probably not, but—

Ivy stopped to poop. I looked around. What if I just kicked her shit into the gutter? Would anyone know it was Ivy's? A car or two passed by. One driver, a neighbor, waved. Wouldn't it be a coincidence if Chief Winooski drove by at the exact moment I was breaking the town's feces disposal law?

He didn't. Besides, there were bags for this exact purpose in a pod attached to the leash. Besides, he had a girlfriend. Scooping up the trail of boli distracted me from my flights of journalistic fancy and an imagined scofflaw summons. I checked my phone. It was still too early to call back the hard-bargaining Ms. Mankopf. I reminded myself that I wasn't the only show in town. I might've done such a good job convincing her of her need for an estate sale that she was already comparison shopping.

After ten minutes in the park where Ivy was greeted by name by a number of admirers, all humans I didn't know, we headed home—Ivy to a peanut-butter treat and her fleece-lined pita pocket bed, me to a Post-it that Frank had left on the refrigerator: "Food shopping. Text if you need anything."

If negotiations succeeded, I'd ask him to pick up something celebratory. Filet mignon? Lobsters? Champagne? No, too early and too optimistic. I hit redial.

This time the man answered. "What?" he snarled.

"Ms. Mankopf, please."

"I'm dealing with this."

"Dealing with . . . ?"

"The house. It's a no."

I asked if he had joint tenancy, because if he didn't, I should be speaking to the owner of 1010 Quail Ridge Road.

Silence, and finally, "She's in the tub."

"Please tell her it's Emma Lewis, calling back to revisit my commission."

The return call came from a landline. "Okay, we're listening," said Lois. "Billy's on, too."

"First of all," I said, "I'm experienced, insured, bonded, and discreet. We're a family business—"

"What's the best you can do?" she cut in. "Because there's no way I'm agreeing to forty percent."

I was prepared. "Given the property, I'd be willing to come down a few percentage points—"

"To . . ."

"Thirty-seven and a half percent."

"That's *it*?" muttered Billy.

"Thirty percent," said Lois.

I said, "You wouldn't *want* an outfit that takes only thirty percent."

"You called *her*," said Billy. "Mrs. Mansfield didn't reach out to you."

"Mrs. Mansfield?" I repeated. "Am I not speaking with Lois *Mankopf*?"

"My professional name is Mansfield," she said.

Lots of people have professional names, pseudonyms, pen names. Nothing odd about that. No red flag. I was determined to nail this down. If I lost this job over a few percentage points, it could get back to my parents, the way things inevitably did due to my confessional tendencies. I said, "For you alone, and please keep it confidential: thirty-five percent."

"Thirty-five percent of what kind of money are we talking about?" Billy asked. "I mean, is it worth our trouble?"

"It's no trouble for you. I'd handle everything."

"Have you even seen the place?" Billy asked.

I said I knew the house. I'd driven by, walked the grounds, and I'd be making an appointment with the real estate agent for a viewing, with a clipboard, once we came to an understanding.

Billy asked, "Lo, if you can get the asking price for the house, is it worth the couple of grand you might get for whatever crap you left behind?"

Lois said, "You can hang up—Billy. Not you, Emily."

Should I correct her at this delicate juncture? I didn't. After a confirming click, she said, "Nervy, huh? Especially from someone I met, like, six weeks ago."

I said, "I'll email you the contract. If you have any questions—"

"I have *major* questions already."

"Happy to answer them now."

"No. He's still here. I'll call you after he leaves. I need to talk to my daughter. She'll know exactly what we'll need you to do."

Nothing unusual about that, either. I was used to dealing with adult children and future beneficiaries. We said our goodbyes and set a time for me to call back.

A mother-daughter interview? I wasn't worried. When did I ever get anything but run-of-the-mill questions I could answer in my sleep?

10

A request—or was it a test?—put forth by daughter Vanessa in the promised, determinative phone call: "We'd need you to burn the contents of the file cabinet in the beau parlor."

Beau parlor? Burn? I'd dealt with plenty of file cabinets, one of the reasons I owned a dolly, but I'd never been asked to set fire to anyone's possessions. "I assume you've gone through this paperwork, and know there's nothing valuable left behind?"

When my question met with silence, I continued. "I mean things like birth certificates, insurance policies, wills. I've found savings bonds that the clients had never cashed."

Vanessa asked, "Is incinerating things such a big deal?"

Hoping this would be all the disincentive required, I said, "I don't have a fireplace or a wood stove, and considering the town's outdoor burn bans, I'm afraid it *is* a big deal."

"The master bedroom has a working fireplace," said her mother, on speaker.

Though I could surely find a way to burn any unwanted papers, the task had a dodgy ring to it. Or was it Lois herself who was giving me a lawbreaking vibe? What if it was evidence? What if her ex used his home file cabinet for confidential Harrow police files? What if destroying their files meant I was perverting the course of justice?

"I can always rent a dumpster," I tried.

"We're not talking about *throwing* things away," Lois said. "We need them to disappear."

My next suggestion: I could bag everything and bring it to the dump myself. Unsaid: or straight to Luke Winooski, if what needed disappearing looked suspicious.

Lois herself snapped, "Forget the dump! People meet there! They think it's a flea market and a kaffeeklatch. Just because something's bagged doesn't mean it's off-limits. No way."

Next I tried, "I could shred everything," still wondering, *Tax dodgers? Blackmailers? Or a stash of love letters from a married officeholder?*

"Is it your own shredder?" asked Vanessa. "Because you can't just hand personal things to some drooling guy behind the counter at Staples."

I knew if I kept debating the disposal of unwanted things, my company's raison d'être, they'd hang up and call Goldie's Oldies.

"It's not just papers," said Lois. "I'm talking about photos. And some sensitive records—all of which we'd rather our nosy neighbors weren't pawing through—not at the dump and not at the estate sale."

"Sellable photos?" I asked.

There was whispering between mother and daughter. Eventually Vanessa asked, "Would you be offended by full frontal nudity?"

I wanted this job, and I wanted to sound cool. I said, "Of course not!" Then, whispering, "Are we talking about porn?"

"Porn! Hardly! We're talking art!" Lois said.

Art? Why did art need to disappear? "Are the subjects . . . over the age of consent?"

"You mean are they naked children? Absolutely not. Every woman is over twenty-one!"

"And gorgeous," said Lois, "with at least an associate's degree, and, needless to say, all from good families who don't need to know how their daughters moonlighted."

I, who'd lived in Harrow my whole life, whose father and boarder had taught everyone's children, asked, "From *local* families?"

"From everywhere!" bragged Lois. "From Florida, from New York, from Canada. One of my most popular girls was from Czechoslovakia."

"Slovakia," Vanessa corrected. "I called two of the references on your website. Both swear by your discretion."

Of course they did—the three numbers listed belonged, respectively, to Aunts Unity, Celeste, and Pamela.

I thought it was my job as vendor to point out that tasteful, artistic photographs of nudes would sell, framed or unframed. Back issues of *Playboy* jumped off the shelves.

Lois said, "You don't understand—they were my bill of fare. We didn't parade the girls in front of the customers like a Nevada cathouse. I showed my clients the beautiful photographs, and they picked their favorite—at least for that particular visit."

Why be delicate at this point? I went straight to "You're saying people came to your house for sex?"

After a few beats, Vanessa said, "Mom ran an escort service, so if you're asking if business was conducted, the answer is yes."

"And every single customer was top tier! Millionaires, doctors, ministers, CEOs, CFOs," said Lois. "Lola Mansfield was a brand. Lola Mansfield is synonymous with 'the best, the cream of the crop.'"

Lois was suddenly Lola? And Mansfield, as in Jayne? If I hadn't approached them first, I'd assume I was being pranked. I asked Vanessa if she lived in California, too, or was just visiting.

"Visiting. I live in Boston. Why?"

"Couldn't you just lock up the file cabinet? It's as easy as taping a sign on it that says 'Not for sale. Do not open.'"

Lois said, "Yes! Forget we asked." And to her daughter, "Tell her what we were famous for? What did we make our reputation on?"

"Discretion," said Vanessa.

Out of my hands then. Good.

"Is she still on?" Vanessa asked her mother.

I might've volunteered to hang up so they could talk freely, but I was too enthralled to withdraw. "Please know that everything we've discussed is off the record," I said.

"Don't go overboard," said Lois. "Use whatever will help bring in the most customers. I'm proud of my worker bees! I loved every single one. Beauty and brains, and it went both ways. Men of the highest caliber. It was the best job ever."

At my phoniest and most flattering, I answered, "Wow. How many of us can say that? It's . . . inspiring."

"I didn't have a college degree. I didn't have anything to put on a résumé besides 'Housewife, mother, hostess.' These were the happiest years of my life."

Happiest? As in happiest hooker? Why not ask at this point? "Were you one of these . . . worker bees?"

"As a demimondaine? Ha! Thank you! But no."

What did that leave? "Were you the madame?"

And then, as if it were the most logical and obvious job one could perform at a brothel, Lola Mansfield said proudly, "I was the housemother."

11

Soon after hanging up with Lois and her daughter, I sent my parents the most benign of texts: Do U know Lois Mankopf, Quail Ridge Rd?

When neither answered all day, I followed up with AKA Lola Mansfield? And when that produced nothing, I went straight to The woman who had a brothel? which autocorrected to "brother."

Whose brother? Beth finally wrote.

BROTHEL! As in whorehouse! As in "the oldest profession"!

No answer for at least an hour, then Did hear but I think it's just scuttlebutt.

Though I hit Beth's number, my dad answered. "Hi, hon. What's up?" ignoring my bombshell . . . unless it hadn't been a bombshell at all.

I said, "No reaction to a brothel operating on Quail Ridge Road?"

I heard an apologetic chuckle. "You know your dad. I'm not good at talking about personal things."

"This isn't personal," I said. "This is public! Beth seems to know about it."

"You mother is susceptible to gossip," he said. "Not her best quality."

"It's not gossip. I just got off the phone with Mrs. Mankopf—"

"About a future sale? She called you?"

"No, I called *her* when I heard the house was on the market."

"Good work!"

"But—"

"Quail Ridge Road," he said reverently. "That's all you'd need to say in an ad. How many rooms?"

"I haven't been there." And after a pause: "Have *you*?"

Thank goodness he laughed. *"Been there?* Even the union couldn't save my job over a lapse of judgment like that. No thanks! Hold on. I'm putting us both on speaker."

I heard a quiet "Just hit speaker. No, I'll do it," from Beth, and then, "She fixed people up. This was before internet dating. No meals served, just parties with chitchat and punch. She liked to say she was a matchmaker."

"And that was taken at face value? No one asked what took place at her parties? The police didn't raid them?"

"It's always been a broad-minded community," said Beth. "Plus she had friends in high places."

"Such as?"

"The chief of police, who happened to be her husband, for starters."

"Not Winooski," said my dad, then straight to, "When do you think you'll hear about the sale?"

"I haven't decided whether I can take this on."

"Why wouldn't you?" he asked.

"Because it would be bigger than anything I've handled myself." Unsaid: like invoices that could land some of my friends' dads in divorce court if Vanessa doesn't dump them.

"The parties were a short-term thing," said Beth. "By the time the rumors were flying, she'd turned it into a bed-and-breakfast."

"Do you think the Mankopf house really was a B and B, and not just a cover?" I asked.

"It *was* a B and B—the Quail's Nest. Your uncle Paul stayed there whenever he visited us," said Beth.

I managed to ask, "*Visited* Harrow, but didn't stay with us?"

"We always offered," said my dad.

Uncle Paul, the longtime bachelor uncle. "Not a matinee idol," my stepmother used to say about her sweet, shy ginger-haired brother. I asked if he was the kind of man who'd pay for sex.

I heard a muffled "Where does she get these ideas?"

"When were these visits to Harrow?" I asked.

More silence until my father at last said, "He was still single. It all worked out. He and Paulina are very happy. Did you know she got her citizenship last year? We were invited to the ceremony."

My Aunt Paulina? Was their history suddenly making sense? She was exceptionally pretty, and at least twenty years younger than my step-uncle. I'd been to their wedding, and as a teen, had been starstruck by the bevy of glamorous bridesmaids, who, I'd been told, were models.

"Were Uncle Paul and Paulina introduced by Mrs. Mankopf during one of his stays?" I asked.

"Does it really matter?" Beth said.

What else didn't I know? I said I had to get off. I had misgivings, and some legal questions I should get answered before deciding.

"Don't be a prude! Quail Ridge Road is as good a Harrow address as you'll ever get," Beth scolded. "It has a past! People pay more for things from a house with an interesting, let alone notorious, history."

I asked what they would've done if a potential client had asked them to burn the contents of a file cabinet. Not shred, not mail back to them—burn!

"We did find ourselves in a similar situation," said my father. "It was the home office of a doctor who'd died, leaving patients' records behind. I boxed them up and gave them to the other dermatologist in town, presumably for patient follow-up."

"I doubt there were photos of naked women in the files."

After a pause, Beth said, "He was a skin doctor. He documented the before and the after—rashes and such for his records. You can't take any chance that Lois's photos might expose women who've turned their lives around."

"We'll come up and help with the sale," said my dad.

They had not once, since retiring, come up from Buzzards Bay to lend a hand to any sale. "Don't pack your bags yet," I said.

"Would it help if *I* called Lois?" asked my dad.

"Which begs the question," I said, "of why you're on a first-name basis with the madame of Quail Ridge Road."

"She was on the school board. She voted in favor of every cost-of-living increase the union asked for."

"And your father and I are not the morality police," said Beth.

I felt the need to say that I wasn't either, just lukewarm because I sensed that Mrs. Mankopf and her daughter would be difficult. Very.

"But it would be a humdinger of a sale," said my dad.

Beth continued, "You could hint at its past in the ads—not spelling out 'brothel' or 'prostitutes ate off these dishes,' but something like 'A house of many pleasures,' which could sound like you're describing the contents, and not the services rendered . . ."

Even without seeing their faces, I knew my dad was smiling proudly. "My wife has always had a way with copy," he said.

After thirty seconds of googling, I confirmed that engaging in sexual conduct for a fee is a crime prohibited by Massachusetts General Laws Chapter 272, Section 53A. Was "housemother" a polite word for madame? As a businesswoman in good standing, I had questions I needed to run by someone in authority.

Such as Chief Luke Winooski.

I still had his card. I called him and left a businesslike voice-mail, just my name and a request for him to call me back.

He didn't. That was life, messages unheard, unread, unre-turned. As the chief of police, he'd know that if it had been an emergency, I'd have called 911.

Every time I ran into classmate and reunion co-chair Annette LaChance at the dog park, she tried to enlist me for her commit-tee. When I confessed to Frank about my repeated turndowns, he told me I should accept. Was I not in business? Would their class mailing list not be a valuable tool? My mercantile instincts, he scolded, weren't good. These classmates were just the right age to have retiring parents with houses that needed clearing.

"I guess you're right," I said.

"Where do they meet? And when?"

I consulted the last email from the chairpersons. "At the library, Mondays, at seven."

"You love the library," he said. "Win-win."

I confessed why I'd turned them down: none of the other members were friends of mine, then or now. And one member was Luke Winooski, which would be uncomfortable.

Frank said, "I don't understand."

"I've called him twice since he came by the house. Joining the committee would look like . . . outreach."

"How is it outreach if they asked *you*?"

"True, but—"

"I've never heard such nonsense," he said.

I went dressed for success, the summer version, in a linen tank and a long flouncy skirt. The committee was made up of the four class officers, our starting quarterback, and our head cheerleader, plus Luke and me. Due to my late acceptance, I hadn't expected this to be the first meeting. We went around the table introducing ourselves. The chairpersons, who'd been dating since junior year, were married, with their second baby on the way. Class president Joe Keohane had taken over the family funeral home. Class treasurer Buddy Schneider drew our applause when she announced she was a trans woman and now Brooke. Ex-jock and class VP Keith Duffy ran the pro shop at Eaglecrest. Class secretary/ex-cheerleader Melissa Rodrigues, now Melissa Orenstein, was a sales rep for a pharmaceuticals company and had married an internist. Me? Still Emma Lewis. I'd taken over my parents' estate sale company, now doing business as Estate of Mind.

First item on the agenda: the date of the reunion. Easy; it was always the Saturday after Thanksgiving. The theme was a given, too: "Be Seen at Fifteen!"

Luke arrived in uniform, too late for introductions. He had no choice but to take the empty seat next to mine. "Aren't they smart," he said in greeting.

"About what?"

"Recruiting Entrepreneur Emma Lewis for the committee."

I shrugged. "More like 'took-over-the-family-business Emma.' "

He was, I soon observed, the class notable. Three words into his apology for being late, our chairpersons said almost in unison that they totally understood. Keeping Harrow safe, practically single-handedly. So glad he could make it at all.

When the meeting wrapped up, over decaf, I told him that I'd gotten my van inspected. I'd had a broken taillight, fixed on the spot. So, thank you for noticing.

"Good thing," he said, smiling, "because I could pull you over for that."

Was that merely a fact? Something he'd say to any driver? I'd never know because QB Keith was narrating the experience of being pulled over on the Pike for going seventy but not getting a ticket because, miraculously, the state cop had played for Amherst-Pelham Regional High School, beating Harrow 31 to 7 in the turkey classic of 1990.

Luke gave Keith his full attention, which made sense—the cop talk, plus the Mass Pike setting, surely his route to Worcester, where the girlfriend lived. Even if his "I could pull you over for that" led me for five seconds to wonder if I should ask him out for a drink, the moment had passed.

And seriously, if you have a girlfriend, keep your slightly charming comments to yourself.

12

I owed Frank an update. Over a breakfast of muffins baked by Connie Winooski, I told him that Mrs. Mankopf had an offer on the house, and she and I had come to terms.

"Good work. Is it on the calendar?"

"Not yet," I said, "but as soon as she knows when the closing is."

I studied his face, looking for clues that he, like everyone I'd confided in, knew the true business of 1010 Quail Ridge Road.

"Besides the sale date, what's left to iron out?" he asked.

"Not much." Then, setting myself up for the big reveal: "Dad and Beth think I'm hesitating because I'm a prude."

"Prude? Why 'prude'? . . . It can't be because Mrs. Mankopf had a male friend in her bed when you called?"

I'd almost forgotten about rude Billy and his hard bargaining. I went straight to the unsugarcoated truth. "All those bedrooms? They were used by prostitutes."

He looked more baffled than shocked. "Do you mean they rented rooms from Lois?"

"No. We're talking about a whorehouse."

He'd risen to put the butter and milk back in the fridge, but dropped heavily back in his chair. "In Harrow? Jesus Christ. Was Lois Mankopf a prostitute, too?"

I leaned over the table and whispered, "How do you like 'housemother'—allegedly her job title."

Which is when Frank Crowley muttered two words I didn't know were in his vocabulary: "Fucking unbelievable."

"I know!"

"In Harrow," he repeated. "On that beautiful street. . . . Are you sure this is a job for Estate of Mind?"

I said I'd sent them the contract. Then, quoting my parents, "Estate of Mind can't be the morality police."

I studied his face, looking for clues that he, like everyone I'd confided in, already knew what business was conducted at 1010 Quail Ridge Road. Hadn't neighbors noticed the revolving door of out-of-state millionaires and billionaires? Did Connie Winooski know? To bring her into the frame, I complimented the moistness of her corn muffins.

Frank beamed. "Sour cream."

Then, casually, I wondered aloud if Connie knew Mrs. Mankopf.

"I doubt it. The only time the house was mentioned was as a tip for you."

He was breaking eggs into a bowl and asked if I wanted scrambled. I said, "Sure."

He broke two more eggs, added another splash of milk, poured the eggs into the hot pan, stirred them once or twice, then let them cook. "Plates, please."

When we were sitting down, he took a deep breath and asked, "You know how many girls I've taught over the years?"

Good, a change of topic. "Thousands?"

"I couldn't even name a number. A lot stayed in town. Some were girls who might've needed jobs after dropping out."

I said, "I think I know where this is going."

"Silly, isn't it, where the mind takes you? I mean, you hear about pedophiles skulking around school property. Why not pro-curers and pimps?"

"You'll be happy to know this, then: Mrs. Mankopf bragged about her working girls being college graduates from far-off places."

" 'Happy' wouldn't be the word I'd use in this situation."

"*Ex*-situation. It's out of business. Not to worry."

There was more nonverbal eating until he asked, "May I tell Connie about this?"

"Absolutely. And ask her if she knew what was really going on over there." I pointed at his phone.

"I think I'll wait till Saturday," he said. "Tell her in private."

"Why wait? She might say, 'You're just telling me about this *now*? When did you find out?' " I reached across the table, picked up his phone, handed it to him.

After staring at it, possibly rehearsing euphemisms, it only took one tap under favorites. He whispered to me, "When she's gardening, she usually leaves her phone—" Then a cheery "Hello! It's Frank . . . good, good, me too."

He did more listening, more happy nodding, then, "Looking forward to Saturday. And I was thinking, it's my turn." He smiled, as if proud of the transition. "Emma wanted me to thank you for the lead on the Mankopf house. . . . Not yet, not officially . . . still some dotting of i's and crossing of t's left."

He listened to what must have been a fairly long narrative. I could hear her voice but not the exact words. Was his expression growing gloomier? Then to me: "Connie's asking if you'd want her to put in a good word with Lois?"

"Ask her how she knows Lois," I whispered.

He didn't. Just quite solemnly to Connie, "You'll tell me more about that on Saturday. . . . Six? Six thirty? . . . Good. Till then. Pull into the driveway." He hung up the phone, said nothing. Drank some more coffee.

"Something wrong?" I asked.

"No. Nothing at all."

"Saturday's all set?"

Expressionless, he said, "Yes. She's bringing a pie."

"Why are you looking less than thrilled?"

Absent-mindedly overpeppering his cold eggs, he said, "Something can run through my head and keep playing in a loop. It doesn't mean the worrying about my students is logical." And then, as if he were saying something unworthy of him, "Some of them . . . very pretty girls. Popular girls."

Romantic counselor that I'd become, I said, "Confide in Connie. She'll find it sweet that you worry about ex-students being sex-trafficked right here in Harrow."

"But I don't want her to think I'm neurotic. George was a worrier. She thinks his heart attack came about from too much worrying."

Relieving him of the pepper mill, I asked if the heart attack had been fatal.

"His second one was. He didn't want the bypass surgery despite what the angiogram showed."

I said, "I'm not sure if worrying can bring on a heart attack." And then, "Your heart is fine, right?"

He said proudly, "My primary care doc said I had the heart of a thirty-year-old. Did you know Danny Kellogg? I see him in Worcester at the medical center. He was our starting catcher his junior and senior years. Then Holy Cross and Dartmouth Medical School."

He sounded better, allowing me to ask, "You know what else helps? What's scientifically proven to reduce anxiety and extend a lifespan?" I didn't wait for his answer. I called, "Ivy! Come!" There was a bark of acknowledgment from upstairs, and in seconds she was bounding down the stairs, then skidding ecstatically to a stop at the kitchen door.

"Come here, you silly mutt," said Frank, with his first smile of the morning.

*

A few hours later Frank emailed me, apologizing for being dismissive, for withholding. He wrote, "Connie said that she baked for the B and B, a standing weekly order. That was under the radar, otherwise she'd have to get a permit for a cottage industry and get inspected by the board of health."

My immediate thought, which I didn't write back, was: *Of course she knew.*

Annoyed by my own foot-dragging, I called Mrs. Mankopf at noon. Vanessa answered. After pleasantries, I asked if her mother had signed the contract, which could be scanned and emailed—

"Not quite. She added a few lines, to be discussed in person."

Was she summoning me? "In person where?"

"Harrow," she said.

I asked where.

"Where? At the house we've been discussing in rather too many phone calls."

I said an automatic "Sorry!" then asked if she had moved into the house or was just camping out while it was on the market.

"Camping? Why camping?"

"I got the impression that your mother had left just enough for staging."

"I wish! It's still packed to the gills."

Packed to the gills wasn't bad news; just the opposite. "So I trust you're not sleeping on an air mattress or eating off paper plates."

"Hardly! No shortage of beds! And I could open a kitchen store."

I said a walk-through would be great. I'd be taking notes, taking pictures—

"For what purpose?" she asked.

"For the email I send to my regulars. Emails, plural. I always add photos of tempting pieces as teasers."

"Just emails? Not ads?"

"Definitely ads in the *Echo*, and on Craigslist. And of course I put notices up all over town."

After a long pause, she asked, "Do you think that 'estate sale' says to people 'the family needs money'?"

"Not. At. All. It's the American way of . . . leaving. People move and downsize. Downsizing means deacquisitioning. What else are you going to do, besides have an estate sale?" I brought up the contract again. Did she know what her mother had added to the boilerplate two pages?

"I don't. But hold on. She's here." I heard footsteps, then a knock on a door, then Vanessa explaining that the estate sale woman was asking about add-ons to the contract.

"No parking," said the distant voice of Lois.

"No parking?" I repeated. "Seriously?"

Vanessa said, "Mom means no parking on the lawn. She's seen how latecomers pull up onto the grass rather than parking blocks away because they think they're going to come away with a tread-mill or a Barcalounger."

I said, "No problem. What else?"

"Mom? What else?"

"Music," I heard.

Vanessa said, "She'd like chamber music. Maybe a trio."

"Live?" I asked.

"Absolutely live. She thinks that would elevate the sale. You could hire the same ensemble that played at her soirees."

I said, "It's not something we've ever done," in lieu of *Are you fucking kidding me?*

"Mom? Anything else?" Vanessa asked.

"Remind her that the file cabinet in the beau parlor should stay locked, with a sign on it that says 'Not for sale.' "

What happened to Vanessa taking care of that? I asked, "You'll deal with whatever compromising stuff is in there ahead of the sale, correct?"

Suddenly bordering-on-*Goodfellas* cryptic, Vanessa said, "You don't know what's in that file cabinet, okay? They're business records, period. We're holding on to those files until we find a use for them."

I wasn't going to contradict her. If I needed to be retroactively ignorant, I would. I didn't want to lose this job. Fingers crossed that I wouldn't have to testify at a future trial for the blackmailing of wealthy johns.

Vanessa went straight to "How about Monday morning, ten o'clock, for that walk-through? Do you remember the address?"

"Ten-ten Quail Ridge Road?" I made it sound like a question, and not as if it had been seared into my brain.

13

The doorbell at 1010 Quail Ridge Road played "Some Enchanted Evening," bringing Vanessa to the door, annoyed, wrapped in a towel. She had to be six feet tall, or maybe the terrycloth turban was adding inches. I judged her to be forty-fiveish. Even without makeup, she was tightly unlined and striking. "Why does everyone have to show up on time?" she grumbled.

I said I could wait on the porch while she dressed.

"No. Come in and look around. That's what you do, right? Literally take stock?"

I stepped onto a long red-and-black Persian runner. It was a good start; runners sold, easy to roll up and fit in any car. An enormous house spread out before me, larger than any floor plan I'd imagined. Murals had been painted on the entryway walls: on one side a cocktail party, men in tails and women in gowns; on the other, either a fox hunt or a cookout. The house smelled like whatever powder or perfume had been applied minutes ago by Vanessa.

The first room she led me to could've been a gentlemen's club in London. Its walls were dark green, its wing chairs a tartan plaid. Chess pieces were set up on one table and backgammon on another. There was a stone fireplace, with screens and burnished tools that would go fast, pewter tankards on the mantel, and above, an oil painting of a storm-tossed ship. Next to every chair, a standing brass ashtray. Would I be selling all of this? Did Lois want *nothing*?

I turned the dimmer up and took pictures; too much stuff to catalog on this first tour. Everything was beyond traditional and stuffy, but not a problem. Harrowites loved stuffy.

Through heavy sliding pocket doors was a decidedly feminine room. Its walls were a pale peach; the artwork plentiful, all naked Venuses except for one Lady Godiva. A long black velvet banquette was accessorized with pastel throw pillows. Noted: a bar, with champagne flutes, martini glasses, highball glasses, shot glasses, several cocktail shakers, and two filigreed decanters.

In an alcove that looked like a curtained dressing room was a file cabinet, enameled red. On reflex, after a quick glance over my shoulder, I pulled at the top-drawer handle. Locked, of course.

Still no Vanessa. I took more pictures, too much in awe to take notes.

Next, the kitchen, which reminded me of every Apple store I'd ever been in, with its long rectangular blond-wood table and chrome-legged stools. The open shelves displayed boardinghouse crockery: thick white plates, bowls, and mugs. A gleaming professional espresso machine sat next to two four-slot toasters, two waffle irons, a blender, and an electric kettle. Good. They'd fly out the door.

Then something on the wall caught my eye: a set of brass bells à la *Downton Abbey*. I quickly googled "Bells Victorian Edwardian servants maids" and up came a set. Its asking price: $1,198! Were Lois's bells merely decorative, or did they bring an escort downstairs to meet her date?

Hearing "Where are you?" I yelled back, "Kitchen!" Vanessa strode in, wearing a floor-length dashiki. In just these few minutes her streaked blond hair had been dried to straight, chin-length perfection and she'd applied eyeliner, eye shadow, and blush. Her lips were outlined in red, a pale pink lipstick within. "Okay to open the drawers?" I asked.

"Isn't that your job?"

I found silverware, utensils, wooden cutting boards, brand-new potholders.

Vanessa pointed to the double window. "The porch," she said. "In nice weather, guests took their breakfasts out there."

"Breakfasts" was just the segue I needed. "Continental, probably," I prompted. "Coffee and muffins—stuff like that?"

"Coffee, tea, cereal, bananas, muffins, scones, make your own toast."

Did I need to be coy with this no-nonsense daughter? "Was it Connie Winooski who baked for you?"

"You know her?"

"She's a friend of a friend."

"Mom was happy to give her the business. She had a ton of kids."

I didn't say "Just four boys," or that I'd had sampled those muffins. No need; Vanessa had no interest in follow-up. Instead I pointed to the bells. "Were they a kind of intercom, so a visitor would choose a woman—"

"*Choose?* How about 'fall in love with'? Men are pathetic, aren't they? Their dick gets hard and their brain turns to mush."

Was confirmation required? I said, "I know what you mean," then repeated, "So the chosen woman would come downstairs to meet—"

"No!"

That seemed overly adamant, given the business at hand, already acknowledged. I asked why not.

"Obviously, with the B-and-Bers sitting by the fireplace, we couldn't have the girls come down, practically naked, and lead their dates upstairs. 'Out of sight, out of mind' was the operating principle. Every one of our ads used 'discreet' or 'discretion.' "

"So you had both kinds of customers at the same time?"

"It wasn't hard. Different floors, different beds. Different hours. Different people."

"Different rates, I bet."

She shot me the same pitying look bestowed by my more experienced summer-camp bunkmates. "Once in a while a man arrived as a B and B customer, and if I picked up some vibe—maybe he flirted with me, maybe he asked if there was a scene, a bar in town—I'd tell him about our other services. Those guys would get a special introductory crossover rate."

"It sounds as if you were"—how to put it?—"involved."

"Summers. I made bookings, checked people in and out, changed the beds, and"—finally, a wry note—"pretended I didn't recognize anyone's father." She tapped her watch and said we should move on; she had an appointment at eleven with a criminal lawyer.

"Criminal? Why criminal?"

"Just making sure that Lola's Ladies won't get in trouble."

"For prostitution?"

"No! They were *escorts*. Escort services are totally legal, even in this puritan state, as long as you're not engaging in sex or soliciting it."

Was she serious? Was that dissembling just for my benefit? I was tempted to ask "Then what trouble are you seeing a criminal lawyer about?" but decided it was better not to know, in case I was ever subpoenaed. I asked instead if the words *Lola's Ladies*, or even the initials, appeared anywhere—maybe monogrammed towels or pillowcases? Business cards or signage?

"Because you think it would be value-added? Would your customers know what the L.L. stood for?"

Yes, they *would* know, because I'd tell them. "Here's what I'm thinking in terms of marketing: We'd be honest about the house's past. I think it would triple or even quadruple the number of visitors."

She'd made herself a double espresso without offering me one. Leaning against a counter, she mused between sips, "About once a year, Mom considered going straight."

"But . . . ?"

"But it would be killing the goose that laid the golden egg. She had such great word-of-mouth."

"Amazing," I said.

"What is?"

"The juggling. Who was booking for which thing. Were there secret passwords or codes?"

"It didn't take a genius to know who wanted what. If someone called and asked about air-conditioning or handicap access or checkout time, that was the giveaway. Then there were the guys: 'Greg from Greenwich sent me,' or 'Doug from Darien gave me this number.' Only an idiot would ask outright, 'Are you a brothel?' If some cheapskate asked for the rates, she'd get pissed off and say 'No vacancy.' She didn't want every Tom, Dick, and Harry."

"How'd you know it wasn't someone from a vice squad calling?"

"Harrow doesn't have a vice squad." She smiled. "Besides, we had that covered."

I didn't admit to knowing that her father was disgraced chief of police Manny Mankopf, lest it made my vice-squad question disingenuous. I asked if we could continue the tour.

She opened a back door and motioned for me to follow. "We called this the stairway to heaven," she said.

No wonder. Its white walls were covered with kisses in various shades of pink and red. "My dad painted them," said Vanessa. "He's an artist. Did you see the murals?"

I had. We didn't stop at the second floor but kept going. Attic, I guessed. That was fine; attics had potential.

Except this was a warren of small rooms, each with a double bed that practically took up the whole space; the same red satin quilt, a flimsy white rattan night table, a lamp, a carpet sample on the floor by the visitor side. The skimpiest college dorm or monk's room would be more inviting.

Hadn't Lois/Lola bragged that her clients were millionaires and billionaires? "Kind of bare bones," I said.

Vanessa shrugged. "The men didn't care. We called these rooms the love nests. Get it?"

"Like a play on Quail's Nest?"

"Exactly. We matched each room's wall color to its name: robin's egg, cardinal, peacock, goldfinch."

"Clever."

Without asking, but with a neutral-enough expression I hoped was professional rather than nosy, I opened the storage drawer beneath the first bed, a good place to store linens, hopefully monogrammed ones. Instead: a medley of sex toys.

NSV was my first thought. Or *was* there sale value here? I could designate one room "adults only," or the whole house could be rated R. I was now doing business as Estate of Mind, wasn't I, not the Finders, Keepers of old? My ads could say for the first time ever, "Mature audiences only."

"You're looking a little shell-shocked," Vanessa said.

I said, no, of course not. I was just thinking about the branding.

"The toys weren't for everyone, just on hand in case. A lot of guys came here wanting what they saw on TV and didn't get at home. We had a menu."

"A literal printed menu?"

"No, a spoken one. My mother could say anything without blinking."

I asked if the sex workers actually lived in these attic rooms. Was there even a closet? A shower? Wi-Fi?

She asked why I needed to know. Though it was my own naked curiosity, I said my customers would ask.

"Full baths are downstairs. As for Wi-Fi, hardly any bars up here meant no interruptions, no wives calling." She pointed to an accordion-pleated door. "That's a half-bath. All the love nests have one."

I followed Vanessa downstairs to the second floor, a whole other world: in every room four-poster canopied beds, braided rugs, vintage writing desks, a satin-upholstered chaise longue.

I took picture after picture, then asked Vanessa where she slept when she was home.

"Any vacant room, and always on top of the bedclothes, so I wouldn't have to change the sheets."

What a life. Could a daughter really be so accepting, so accommodating? "Were you all right with all of this?"

"Why wouldn't I be? I wasn't a kid anymore. It paid my tuition . . . and I got an MG convertible for my eighteenth birthday."

I told myself to stop asking questions unrelated to the future sale. Vanessa had an appointment in twenty minutes, and I knew I was sounding increasingly judgmental. I said, "Once the contract's signed, I'll be back to organize, price, and tag. I'll need at least a week for just that. My parents will be helping. I think late August at the earliest."

She said I could stay if I needed more time to look around. The cellar maybe? The garage? Had I seen the statue in the rose garden? I had; a naked woman, sprayed pink, blatant signage that would be too heavy and too hideous to sell. "Yes, for sure . . . but one more question before you leave, about someone who stayed—"

"Nope. Don't ask me about your dad or your friend's dad or your favorite teacher. We don't kiss and tell."

"No, not that. I know for sure that he met his wife here."

Vanessa said, "I know who you're talking about. We were all invited to the wedding. Sweet girl, a real blonde. Innocent-looking. Men loved that. Another friend of a friend?"

"He's my stepmother's brother . . . I was at that wedding, too."

"Mom loved having the bragging rights to two people who met at the Quail's Nest and got married."

I told her that they were still together. She was an American citizen now.

"Have you ever seen a happier groom? He couldn't believe his good luck . . . and her luck, too," that last with a cynical twist of her mouth that I interpreted as *the green-card form of meant-to-be*.

I thought it was safe to ask at this point, as casually as I could, "Do you know if Paul was one of those men who booked a normal B and B visit, then became a crossover customer?"

We were walking down the stairway to heaven. She stopped and caressed one of the painted kisses. "Do you really care whether your lonely uncle checked in for a night's sleep or for female company? Picture him on these very stairs, walking up to meet the beautiful Paulina for the first time, his heart pounding. We always heard that he knew the first time he took his pants off that he'd marry her. Please tell me you're not judging him. *Or* her. *Or* my mother."

"No, no way," I protested. "I'm in favor of . . . everyone and everything." For emphasis, I too caressed the painted wall. I had to. Only a fool would lose the biggest job of her career by insulting an aunt, an uncle, and the madame who introduced them.

14

Engaging in sexual conduct for a fee was only a misdemeanor in Massachusetts, but shouldn't I find out if mentioning that in a press release could still get Lola's Ladies alumnae in trouble?

Maybe the chief of police would know the answer. It wasn't a question I wanted to ask him at a reunion committee meeting; "escort" and "sexual conduct" would have a personal ring to it that I didn't want our classmates to hear. But as I was approaching the Over Easy, I spotted a cruiser that could be his in the diner's parking lot.

I went inside. Luke was indeed there, but it wasn't the right time to engage him in conversation; he was seated at the counter, where every stool was occupied. I backed out without a hello and leaned casually against my van, which I'd parked next to his cruiser. How long would someone on duty—whose plate was empty except for a few fries—linger?

When he finally appeared, I looked up from the takeout menu I was pretending to study and said hello, as if surprised at the uncanny coincidence of us overlapping at the town's most popular lunch spot at the lunch hour. "I'd wait to decide until you get inside," he said. "The daily specials are on the blackboard."

"Not today. It's too crowded." I waved the menu half-heartedly. "I'll keep this in the glove compartment, though."

We both nodded, once, twice. Then nothing. I was surprised

by my sudden onset of shyness. Luckily he asked, "How's the auction business?"

"Estate sales," I corrected, and shrugged. "Mezza mezza . . . but while I have you, there's a possible legal and moral conflict I'm facing."

With a flicker of a smile, he said, "I'll do my best."

"I'm in negotiations with the owner of a big house on Quail Ridge Road."

"Whoa, nice. Congratulations."

"I haven't decided whether I should get involved." I looked around and saw no one, but still lowered my voice to a whisper. "Stuff went on there."

"What stuff?"

I raised my eyebrows. "Entertaining male guests."

"Meaning?"

"Meaning, *women* entertaining male guests."

He smiled. "Entertaining is not against the law, even in Harrow."

"I'm talking about sex for money."

"According to . . . ?"

"The owner."

"Are we talking about the Mankopfs?"

"Yes! Exactly. About her"—air quotes—" 'bed-and-breakfast.' "

He slid his cap back a few inches and forward again. "You didn't hear this from me, but . . . she got herself into some hot water with the planning commission."

Finally we were getting somewhere. Or so I thought until he confided, "She was running that operation without a license."

I said, "You can *license* that kind of business?"

"Everything has to go through the planning commission."

"Are we having parallel conversations? Because I'm not talking about innkeeping. I'm talking about prostitution."

"Luckily not on my watch. It was before I took the job."

"But what about your predecessor?"

"My predecessor . . ." He closed his eyes and shook his head. "Never mind."

"Your predecessor had to know exactly what was going on. Have you ever seen the place? He painted kisses on his ex's walls! I'm thinking he was getting hush money or a kickback."

I could tell Luke was weighing his response carefully. Finally he said, "I think it's public knowledge that Manny's heart attack saved him from being fired." He pointed his key fob at his door, unlocking it.

"Wait! I haven't asked the main question yet."

"If it's about someone breaking a law before I was hired—"

"No. Nothing like that." I had to think fast; it had to be crime-related and Mankopf-specific. So I asked if there was a statute of limitations on prostitution.

He smiled. "Are you considering making a citizen's arrest?"

"No! What I meant is . . . let's say I dropped hints in my promotional materials about the house's past. Would I be crossing a line into libel?"

Was that too contrived? Maybe. Because his answer was "For what? Selling lawn chairs that hookers might've sat in?"

I ignored the professional put-down. "If you must know, there are records that could be proof of something—"

"Vinyl? Or do you mean business records?"

"Business records. Files. Photographs of the women."

"That she wants you to sell?"

"No, just the opposite! She asked me to burn them. I refused. I don't burn people's confidential files! I offered to ship every-thing back, which is as far as I'm willing to go, in case this stuff is needed in court someday."

He sighed. "Do you really think an estate sale could get an ex-madame in trouble? Or you?"

"That's what I need to know. I'm new at this. I can't risk . . .

whatever I'd be risking." Which seemed a very good juncture to ask if I could buy him a drink.

He looked confused. It was 1:10 in the afternoon, and he was obviously on duty.

"Not now," I said quickly. "I meant after work. Some time."

And what was his answer? "Prostitution is only a misdemeanor, at least in the Commonwealth. And this is ex-prostitution, right?"

"Okay, bye. Never mind." I headed toward my own driver's-side door. What was the big deal—a drink? Shouldn't a police chief have more conversational dexterity and better manners?

"No, wait," he called. "Sorry. I was answering your question about a statute of limitations. I do want to hear more about . . . whatever."

"That's okay," I said. I had my pride. "Sorry I took up so much of your time. I hope you don't think I was asking you out for a *drink* drink."

Which was when he said, "How's Friday night? Beardsley's?"

Beardsley's . . . with tablecloths and amuse-bouches and valet parking.

"How's seven?" he asked.

I nodded, still surprised at my own unpremeditated invitation, and his saying yes.

"I'll pick you up," he said.

I must've shot a worried glance at the cruiser, with its laptop and high-tech gadgets between the front seats.

"I have my own car. No sirens, no radar gun, no cherry light."

No girlfriend? I reached over and pinched an inch of khaki on his sleeve. "And I assume . . . out of uniform?"

"Don't be fresh," he said.

15

I told Frank I had a date on Friday. With a man.

"Wonderful!"

I laughed. "Regardless of which bum it's with?"

"I trust . . . not a bum. Anyone I know?"

"I'll tell you, but it can't leave this room, okay? Nothing to my parents, and definitely not to Mrs. Winooski. Let her find out on her own."

"Why would she find out if I'm sworn to secrecy?"

"Isn't *not* telling Mrs. Winooski a big enough clue?"

First there was the visible reckoning, then a happy intake of breath. "Are you going out with Chief Winooski?"

"To Beardsley's. Friday night."

"How nice," he said. "And you can trust me—not a word." A musing silence followed that struck me as advice withheld.

I asked if this personal stuff was making him uncomfortable.

"No, no, not at all. Forgive me. It's just that I was wondering . . . if you've given any thought to what you'll wear."

I looked down at my mistakenly bleached, splotchy T-shirt and my ripped jeans, which he might not realize came that way. "I'm not going like this, I promise."

He still looked worried. "Here's why I'm asking: That one time when you greeted customers in a dress you were hoping to sell . . .

it was very becoming. And I believe it was grabbed up by the first woman who walked through the door."

Not necessarily true, but how sweet. "I should've bought it myself. The green cocktail dress at the Wentworth sale? I think I priced that at twenty-five dollars, designer label and all."

My note of buyer's regret seemed to be just the prompt he needed. "If you wanted to treat yourself to a new dress, but didn't feel you could afford it right now . . . I could help."

So generous on several counts: the financing; the worrying about how I might dress for Beardsley's, and where the right outfit could lead. I said, "I have dresses I got with my employee discount at Nordstrom Rack."

Since he looked no less assured, I brought down two on hangers.

"The black one," he said.

I'd told Frank there was no need for him to answer the door or even greet Luke, which would look unnecessarily paternal. He agreed with such alacrity that I wondered if whatever designs he had on Connie could be detected by a son.

Ivy came running and barking seconds ahead of the doorbell, but she calmed down as soon as Luke patted and sweet-talked her. Not since high school had I seen him in regular clothes, in this case gray slacks, a blue Oxford dress shirt, a navy blazer.

"You're looking very smart, Miss Lewis," he said, one eyebrow arched in such a way that made the formal address sound like a tease.

Our drive to the restaurant went past the Macmillan campus, onto Main Street, through downtown Harrow, where I noticed Luke appraising the pedestrians and the malingerers.

"See anything suspicious?"

"Sorry. Occupational hazard. Just the usual Friday-night scene."

When we passed the police station, I pointed and asked, "Is it true you live there?"

"Above the store, as they say? True."

"Is it, like—an apartment?"

"As opposed to?"

"A room?"

"It's an actual apartment: three rooms. Not beautiful, but you can't beat the commute."

I waited a few beats before saying, "Can I ask you a personal question?"

He pretended to brace himself with both hands on the steering wheel, then said, "I'm ready."

"Does the apartment *come* with the job?"

"Whew. Just that? If you mean do I pay rent, I don't."

"That's great. Is it furnished?"

"Just about."

"Are you missing anything?"

He shot me a quick, puzzled look.

I swiveled my wrist in the air. "Oh, maybe a beanbag chair, a soup tureen, knickknacks, yoga mats, sheets, towels, tablecloths, cookbooks, board games, gas grills?"

"I get it," he said. "When's the next sale?"

"No date yet. Just the location."

"The former whorehouse, by any chance?"

"Exactly."

When we reached the rotary, Luke gallantly signaled other drivers to merge ahead of us. After a few traffic lights heading east on Route 9 East, I said, "Now it's your turn to ask me a personal question."

I expected it would be in the same residential vein as the one I'd asked him: Did I pay rent at my parents' house? Did Frank?

But the question he asked was, "Are you seeing anyone?"

I dared to say, eyes straight ahead, "Only you."

We were escorted to the table by a woman with an abundance of wildly curly ink-black hair, and in a dress that showed a lot of bosom. "Chief," she said in greeting.

She led us to a prize window table. Once seated, napkins unrolled, I said, "Everybody knows you."

"The hostess? She dated one of my brothers. Alex, I think. He's safely off the market now."

"That's not a very guy thing to say."

"Profiling," he said. "Part of the job."

We ordered martinis, gin for me and vodka for him. "So much for a designated driver," I murmured.

I expected him to answer scientifically, along the lines of body weight being a factor in metabolizing alcohol, but instead he quipped, "We're fine . . . zero chance of getting pulled over."

When the drinks were served, with the olives on beaded bamboo sticks, we toasted with nothing more personal than "Cheers." Small talk followed: Black cloth napkins were a thoughtful touch . . . Was Ivy my dog or Frank's? . . . One brother had children, both girls . . . the upcoming mayoral election, and the challenger who'd run for every office in town.

After a few minutes of studying the calligraphic menu, I said as casually as I could, "That question you asked me in the car, if I was seeing anyone—"

"I'm not," he said—too brusquely, I thought.

"There isn't a girlfriend in Worcester?"

"Not anymore."

"Not anymore . . . like, recently?"

"We broke up when I moved here."

Do I confess that his mom told Frank the opposite, and Frank told me? I didn't have to, because Luke was saying none too happily, "I'm guessing my mother was the source of this?"

"Via Frank."

He took a sip from his martini glass and put it down. "She thinks she has to tell people that."

"Because . . . ?"

"Because her other three sons were married before they were thirty . . . and not that she doesn't love Peter and his husband, but she drops 'girlfriend' if someone asks about me."

I whispered, "So people won't think she has two gay sons?"

"Something like that." Then, off-topic—if the topic was him/me/us—"I feel, after Manny Mankopf's sleazy eleven years in this job, I can't be seen running around."

Was that a loyalty pledge or an escape clause? I rattled on too obligingly, "After Manny, that's totally understandable. You have a very high-profile job . . . plus you live above the station, which could be awkward."

He smiled. "How so?"

I had no idea. I kept going anyway. "Let's say you arrested a woman, and were leading her inside . . . not that I know the layout of the station, or if there's a separate entrance to your apartment, but—"

He imitated a plane taking off with his hand and an accompanying whoosh. "Exactly, straight upstairs to bed, *especially* if the perp is attractive and handcuffed."

Luckily, I felt his foot giving one of mine a nudge. "Sorry! I was babbling like an idiot. Of course you don't take criminals up to your apartment."

"No! Don't stop; I enjoy hearing about my imaginary life. Are there paparazzi, too? Are they following my every move?"

"If Harrow had paparazzi, you'd be the first person they'd be chasing," hoping to imply *tall, handsome, man-about-town*.

It was an unambiguous compliment, wasn't it, delivered with a fond smile? Yet he shook his head. "I think you're forgetting."

"Forgetting what?"

"Me in high school . . ." Then, grimly, "Mr. Popularity."

I could've said "Nonsense." Or "I don't know what you're talking about." But instead I said, "I don't care."

We shared the cavatelli special, the Beardsley's signature rack of lamb, and a white chocolate bread pudding. We agreed: no need to rush back, so that was two yesses to decaf espresso, doubles. And he being the chief, and me having been there for my last birthday, the manager sent over glasses of a liqueur made from wild cherries, expounding on its properties and provenance, causing Luke and me to exchange smiles over our glasses.

He waved away my offer to split the bill, unmoved by my argument that I'd invited him, hadn't I? I should've stopped with "Thank you so much. What a treat," but I went on to say, "I hope you know I'd be fine with pizza and a movie."

"Me, too," he said, but nothing more.

Had I made him self-conscious with such a broad hint about a future date? I felt the same wash of worry that his *can't be seen running around* had evoked.

We didn't talk much on the way home. Downtown Harrow was busy, with long lines outside Noodle Dynasty and the ice cream parlor famous for its kitchen-sink sundaes. I said, "Note to self: leaflet outside these joints on Friday nights," hoping it might inspire him to say, "Not *every* Friday night, I hope."

He was a guy. A cop. Was I expecting . . . words? I'd already planned to say something romantically tinged at my front door—nothing major, or nothing at all if his body language was saying merely *see ya around*. My street was dark. Didn't anyone keep their porch lights on, my house included? The moon was no help, just a thin crescent. Luke guided me up the front steps with a grip on my closest forearm, but more crossing guard than date. Thankfully, at the door, his hand slid down to take mine. We faced each other and smiled. I was about to say, "I had a wonderful—" but was preempted by a whispered "Emma . . ."

Later I wondered: When and where does a self-proclaimed unpopular guy learn to kiss like that?

16

I came down to the kitchen on Saturday later than usual, trying to look morning-after nonchalant. Frank asked, "Nice time?"

"Yes, very nice. Beardsley's never lets me down. Remind me to learn how to make popovers."

"And the company?"

"The company was . . . excellent. By the way, Connie is wrong, or maybe spinning it, but Luke broke up with his Worcester girlfriend when he moved here."

"I'm glad. And I got the sense that Connie was no fan."

I poured myself coffee and sat down at my usual place. "I think we have to strategize . . ."

"About . . . ?"

"'How we're going to handle the Winooski coincidence."

When he looked puzzled, I said, "You. Me. Connie. Luke. Don't you think it's a potentially sticky situation? Given that you live here, wouldn't she ask about me? 'Is Emma a good landlady? A good housemate? Does she have a boyfriend or a girlfriend?' "

"How's this: If she asks about you, I'll be as vague as would be credible for two people who live under the same roof." He offered me a half piece of toast from his plate.

"No thanks. I'm still full from last night." Then: "Let's

role-play. I'll be Connie. I say, 'Your landlady, Emma. What's new with her? Is she dating anyone?' "

Smiling, he said, "Funny you should ask. She had dinner last night with your one unmarried son, and guessing from the look on her face this morning, she's smitten." With that, he walked his coffee cup to the sink, humming.

"I can see this is going nowhere."

"She could be having the same conversation with Luke this morning. *They* could be strategizing."

"I have an idea: No matter what she asks about me, you say, 'You'll be the first to know,' which changes the subject back to the two of you."

He shut off the water and turned back to face me. "Run that by me again."

"Saying she'll be the first to know is the same as saying you'll be seeing her again. That's a big worry for women: *Will he call? Will I see him again?*"

"Except that she's no shrinking violet."

"Girls didn't used to ask boys out," I said. "They sat by their phones."

"I could've used your wisdom in my bachelor days, in the dark ages. I may not have stayed single as long as I did."

"You did fine. Didn't Ginger pick you out across a crowded room?"

"When I was forty-four!"

"You probably had a lot of relationships under your belt by then, and were ready to settle down."

He shook his head.

"Girlfriends, I'm sure."

A shrug.

"Crushes?"

After a pause: "I can't answer that."

That was odd. I asked why not.

"It was a crush I deeply regret."

What causes someone to deeply regret a crush? "Because you found out she was a rotten person? Or because her boyfriend beat you up?"

"Just the opposite, on both counts."

I knew I was pushing it, but a hunch was taking shape. "Then regret for what?"

"For admitting my feelings when I had no business to."

By what rules? I wondered. "When was this?"

He knew exactly. "The December before your parents married."

"My mother or Beth?"

"Your mother."

Which is when I knew. I whispered, "What happened?"

Frank sat down again. "I'm not sure this is the kind of thing a daughter wants to know."

Was I going to hear something that would upend my mother's sainthood? Had Francis Crowley *slept* with my mother? Was that why he was looking so repentant? All of those guesses must've been written across my face, because he rushed to say, "I wrote a letter and gave it to her when we were alone in the teachers' room."

"A love letter?" I whispered.

"It might as well have been. It said I had feelings for her, and I had to let her know in case they were . . . reciprocated. I gave it to her, then left before she opened it."

"Did she answer?"

He nodded, his eyes closed. "She wrote back, left a note in my cubicle. Two lines. She said that she was very fond of me as a friend but didn't return my feelings. And she didn't want this to hurt my friendship with John Paul." A pause. "Your mother was a very kind person. What the hell was I thinking! I knew they were a couple! I've never forgiven myself for that stupid confession. Some friend!" After much forlorn shaking of his head, inhaling and exhaling, he continued. "Did you know I was his best man? He only had sisters, so I was the logical choice." And finally, a rueful smile. "I think she was hoping I'd take up with one of the bridesmaids."

"But why haven't you recovered from this? She married my dad. You stayed friends. You married Ginger. All you did was tell a woman that you had feelings for her—in a letter, like a gentleman from another century." I gave his nearest hand a victory tap. "And tonight you're having dinner with the lovely Mrs. Winooski, who *is* going to return your feelings."

No reaction, no recovery, only gloom on a morning that should be anything but melancholy. I needed a better explanation as to why he was still carrying around an ancient embarrassment. I said, "There's regret and there's regret. . . . You tried. I mean, what if you'd never told my mother how you felt? To this day you could be wondering *what if.*"

He said with a weak smile, "You're kind to say that. I was young and naive. And I probably wasn't the first man who professed his love for her. She used to bring brownies and oatmeal cookies to school. Who knows where she baked them when she was still student-teaching, still living in a dorm? Did you know she pitched for the HSS faculty softball team?"

I did, but I feigned surprise at such a marvelous missing piece of biography. "Whatever anyone tells me about my mother is wonderful to hear."

"If I think of other things, other than what's on my own guilty conscience, I'll tell you."

"That guilty conscience has to go into a lockbox. How many years ago did you make a very sweet gesture? Thirty-five? You didn't put a move on her. Some men might've kissed her in the teachers' room. Groped her. Stalked her." Even as I was making my case, it seemed a bad fit for Frank, who hadn't even made the first move on the slutty, handsy Ginger.

"I'll think of more things to tell you about the young Annie. She's still here in lots of ways."

Of course she was—on the mantel, healthy, young, happy, radiant. Engagement, wedding, with baby me. First day of kindergarten. Beth wanted the photos to stay on display, not as a shrine to her husband's deeply mourned first wife but for me. Frank saw them; he dusted religiously, not only with the new Swiffer but the feather duster from his marital home.

He stood up again. "Mind if I get on with my meal prepping? We're done with role-playing, I trust."

"Yes. Tonight will be great. And I'll be out of here by six. You'll text me when she's gone. But absolutely no hurry." I didn't make a sleepover joke; didn't even add a wink, having been emotionally intrusive enough for one day.

"You won't be sitting on a park bench, I trust," he said.

"No. Sushi with Marcia Kirshner, and then a movie."

"Kirshner," he repeated, squinting in a student-recall effort.

"AP calculus," I supplied.

"Your year?"

"Our valedictorian! Now assistant professor of engineering science at Macmillan."

"Wait . . . and something else . . ."

I was already nodding. "Husband Gideon was arrested on fraud charges, big-time. Cryptocoins. Front-page news."

"Of course, of course! Terrible!"

"She's okay. Maybe the most resilient nongrudge holder I've ever met."

"Did Luke do the arresting?"

No. The FBI. Why?"

"I meant, are you going to tell her you and he are . . . what to call it? Seeing each other? Isn't that what girlfriends talk about?"

"No. It's too soon."

But was it? Those kisses. I'd hardly slept.

17

Had I worried that a mere dinner between Frank and Mrs. Winooski had awkwardness potential? How about the fact that her car was still in my driveway when I returned home at 10:25 p.m.?

Marcia and I had lingered till closing time at Noodle Dynasty and then, to waste further time, had a drink at Bell in Hand. I'd filled her in when issuing the invitation: Frank had a friend over for dinner, and I wanted to give them plenty of time for wining and dining without interruption.

"Man? Woman?" had been her first question.

"Woman. Constance Winooski."

"Mother of our police chief? That Winooski? Is she nice?"

I said I'd never met her, but Frank certainly thought so.

Now at 10:29, home, parked on the street so as not to block Connie's leavetaking, I considered my options: head straight up to my room without a hello or, like a cool parent, dip into the dining room, living room, or kitchen for a quick how-do-you-do. Frank would introduce me, ask how the movie was, and a friendly (from all accounts) Connie would ask what I'd seen, and I'd say, "the new Indiana Jones, with [I'd make the point] my friend Marcia."

But where were they? The dining room table had been cleared. The dishwasher was humming. The casserole dish that had housed scalloped potatoes was soaking in the sink. The berry pie was on the counter, covered with aluminum foil. Wineglasses? Not present. Ivy was thrilled to see me, jumping up, her paws on my shoulders. "Ivy, down," I said, but without conviction. If Frank and Connie were home, had they not heard my car and Ivy's excited bark?

I asked Ivy rhetorically if she'd been out, which sent her slip-sliding to the back door. "We're not going for a walk," I warned. "You'll just do your business." I opened the door and watched her bound down the stairs and straight to the square of Astroturf that Frank had laid for that purpose.

I reconsidered: Why not take her for a walk on this perfect night, cooler now than the late-afternoon heat, and give Frank and Connie more time to say their goodbyes without an audience? I bagged the poop, left it for later disposal, said "Ivy, stay!" and went inside for her leash, a flashlight, and my phone,

Should I text Frank? And say what? *I'm home.* Just that? Then why send at all?

I didn't hurry Ivy's pace; didn't tug her away from every pole and hydrant. At the end of Montpelier, I turned back to avoid the incessantly barking beagle on Allerton. I checked the time. I'd only given Frank and Connie an extra thirteen minutes, but I had decisions to make. Do I lock up? Turn off the lights?

Inside, from the bottom of the stairs, I heard voices, Frank's faint, and Connie laughing. It was only 10:47. She could still leave. Was this such a surprising development, I asked myself—two mature adults who'd come of age in the 1960s and '70s? For all I knew, their conversations over the past few weeks could've been increasingly flirtatious, with this night as the mutually agreed-upon consummation. I did quiz and debrief him after every get-together with Connie, but actual sex might be too sacred a bridge to cross with me over oatmeal or pizza.

I sat down on the bottom step, Ivy at my feet, and texted Marcia, who had experience with a near-identical situation.

Though she didn't live at home, her divorced mother chronically dated and overshared. Connie still here, I wrote.

She answered immediately, And?

They're up in his room.

It didn't even earn an OMG. She wrote, So?

I went out to the porch and called her. "Frank, the perfect gentleman? This would be a huge move."

"How do you know? And maybe it was *her* move? He's an attractive man."

Was he? Coach Crowley, with his GI crew cut, his khakis and windbreakers and dabs of toilet paper on shaving cuts every other morning?

"Remind me," she asked. "Widowed, divorced, single?"

"Widowed not that long ago." I felt the need to add, "But she was an awful person and a worse wife. She never stopped sleeping with her ex-husband."

"Wow. But he stayed with her?"

"I'm pretty sure they'd have divorced, but then she got struck by lightning."

"I remember! Struck and killed. At Eaglecrest."

"*Everyone* remembers."

"And how did these two lovebirds meet?"

Without naming Luke as the middleman, I said, "Frank sent condolences over the death of her husband, and she wrote back."

"So what's the problem? Why aren't you rooting for them?"

Against previous testimony, I said, "I am! I encouraged him to call her."

"Then you need to stop sounding like his warden."

"I know! What's wrong with me? They could just be watching TV up there."

"Again: spoken like a true killjoy."

Besides being rightly characterized as warden, judge, and

jury, I was feeling like a bad, withholding friend. I hadn't said a word all evening about Luke and me, treading carefully, not wanting to sound lovestruck in the face of Marcia's separation from and recent humiliation by Gideon.

After hanging up, I ate a piece of Connie's pie, which turned out to be mixed berry, and delicious. Then another piece. I checked my email and texts. I hearted a new photo of my dad, aproned and grilling kebabs. I moved to the study and watched cable news. The vice president was at an economic summit in Geneva, and there were record high temperatures in India. At midnight I locked up and collected Ivy, along with her kitchen bed and beloved ratty stuffed rabbit. I had to: She was used to sleeping in Frank's room, and cried if left alone overnight.

Upstairs, I heard murmuring from down the hall. I didn't undress in case there'd be a knock on my door—Frank explaining that Connie was staying over/not going home/would leave before breakfast/staying for breakfast.

It had been twenty-four hours since I'd heard from Luke. Was it too late or too girlfriendy to text him at this hour—naturally without a single syllable about his mother being here? Then again, he might already know. Some widowed mothers treated their sons like confidantes, like substitute husbands.

I scolded myself. Why did I have to factor Mrs. Winooski into my romantic strategizing? Ivy was peeking out and studying me between the fleecy layers of her pita bed. I said, "Stay. Good girl. I'll be right back. Shhhh," I tiptoed across the hall to brush, floss, and pee. Back in my room I changed into T-shirt and boxers, got into bed, turned off my bedside lamp, turned it back on, and texted Luke, "More thanks for last night. Sweet dreams. Emma."

He wrote back in minutes, "You too."

It wasn't poetry, but it was plenty. I shut off my light, smiling. The overlap—me, Luke, Frank, Connie—was feeling less sticky,

merely coincidental. Harrow was a small town. Lives overlapped.
Frank and my dad and my mother all taught at Harrow High. Lois
Mankopf had been on the school committee. Hadn't my widowed
father ended up with someone who lived down the block?

Connie's adult sons would want her to have a life. And who'd
be a better suitor than beyond-reproach department head emeri-
tus Frank Crowley? What was the big deal? He wasn't my father;
if he married Connie, Luke wouldn't be my stepbrother.

Nothing to worry about, nothing to judge. And was I personally opposed to fast-tracking sex with a willing Winooski? Hardly.

18

I'd have slept later if it hadn't been for Ivy's muzzle in my face, effectively asking what I'd done with Frank. I opened my bedroom door, and off she ran, barking ecstatically all the way downstairs. It was 8:05. I looked out the window. Either Connie was gone, or she'd moved her car far enough away so my neighbors wouldn't jump to the correct conclusion.

Just in case she was there, and this was Mrs. Winooski's first view of me, I reworked my messy ponytail and put on cutoffs, a crisp sleeveless white shirt, and silver hoops.

Frank was alone. Despite the summer heat, he'd made my favorite Irish oatmeal. "Should I steam milk?" he asked, pointing at the coffee maker.

"I can do it," I said. "You sit."

From the counter, I asked him the same question he'd asked me the day before, "Nice time?"

"If I may . . . ," he began. Then: "I owe you an explanation."

"No, you don't."

"Last night . . . it wasn't planned! I mean, I *did* plan every course, and had two movies picked out. But then . . ."

I jabbed a thumb ceilingward: *The sleepover part?*

Frank said, "I had no idea . . ."

"Why no idea? You invited her for a private, romantic dinner, didn't you?"

"For dinner, yes—"

"Frank! You're two attractive, healthy heterosexuals. Things happen."

"And they did . . ."

I joined him at the table. "Are you trying to tell me it wasn't consensual?"

"Oh goodness! I hope you know me better than that."

"I didn't mean"— with eyebrows arched—"you."

He sighed. "It started with margaritas on the porch. I grilled the steaks outside. I'd put the salad together beforehand, and the potatoes were browning nicely in the oven. I dressed the salad while the steaks rested."

If this was what it took to get the play-by-play, I could listen patiently enough. He continued. "We ate in the dining room on the good china—thank you for suggesting that—and as soon as we finished . . . she moved her chair closer."

"Okay . . ."

"She became very affectionate. . . . It was nice, once I got my head around it."

"Meaning . . . ?"

"It was early. We hadn't had dessert yet."

"But you didn't push her away, did you?"

"Heavens no! I was just taken aback."

"Here's my take on it: You're not an obvious ladies' man, and Connie knew that. She thought she'd have to make the first move."

He sighed. "We loaded the dishwasher. I told her which movies I'd put on my watch list—just suggestions! She asked if I had a TV in my room, and did I have any of the streaming channels."

"Nothing wrong with that," I said.

He nodded. "So we took the wine and went upstairs. She knew the Sox were playing on the West Coast! She wanted to watch the game!"

I said, "Wow. Swipe right!"

He shrugged. "As you know, there's only one chair in my room. I offered it to her, but she said, 'Don't you usually watch . . . in bed?' "

He stopped and asked me if I wanted the oatmeal or that new muesli he'd bought.

"Neither. Keep going."

"The game was called—torrential rain in Seattle. Connie said, '*Now* what do you want to do?' with a smile that told me exactly what she was asking."

"And . . . ?"

Frank said, red-faced to the roots of his short hair, "I'm not made of stone."

I whispered, "Did you ask if she wanted to make love?"

He held one hand up. "Emma, I think that's enough. You're not directing a movie."

"Well, I know she was still here when I went to bed around midnight."

"She was. Amazingly enough, she'd brought a toothbrush." He smiled. "We had pie for breakfast."

"Was it great?" I asked.

"That's not a question a gentleman should answer."

"I know, sorry . . . But didn't this whole conversation start with you saying you owed me an explanation?"

"I didn't mean *this* kind of explanation, not word for word, minute by minute."

"You're right. And I should've already said I'm happy for you. Connie is welcome here any time," I lied.

"We talked about that. I think she sensed it could be awkward."

Were we there, at the crossroads of Frank and Connie and Luke and me? "She doesn't know I went out with Luke, does she?"

"That never came up. We had much to discuss, and a few concerns."

"Concerns you can tell me about?"

"One is obvious: Ginger died quite recently. How long does our relationship have to be kept secret? We talked about future stays—here versus her house." He sighed. "If I stayed at her house, it would be the first time she'd be having relations in her marital bed."

Now I was feeling hot in the face. I managed to say, "There must be other bedrooms."

"There are, but the boys slept in bunk beds. For now, with your blessing, it might be better having our dates here."

I grinned. "So this wasn't a one-night stand?"

"Oh God. I'm the last guy who'd have a one-night stand."

I asked if there was any pie left.

"Yes! We saved you a piece. Connie was flattered that a good chunk had disappeared overnight," sounding relieved to be dealing with something as impersonal as breakfast.

I couldn't help but ask again, "Was it only in the context of pie that my name came up?"

"Well, we heard you come in, and go out again with Ivy. And Connie asked if you were a congenial housemate. I said, 'Yes, it's working out beautifully.' "

"Did she also ask why you live here? I mean, as opposed to having your own place?"

"She knows that Ginger left the house to her daughters, and that I wanted to downsize, that it's overwhelming. Too big, too much, too Ginger. I just wanted a room, no responsibilities, except for what I enjoy helping with." And after a pause, "She also knows it's not a measure of what I *can* and can*not* afford."

"Speaking of downsizing, do your stepdaughters know about Estate of Mind . . . just in case?"

For the first time that morning, he laughed. "That's one recommendation I can make with absolute authority."

"Are they ever coming up to claim the house? From Manhattan, right?"

"They're overdue. I'll give them both a call."

I smiled. "Even if you don't tell them, they'll know."

"About Estate of Mind?"

"No, about you. That you're happy. At least happi*er*. They'll hear it in your voice."

He went to the counter, put the last piece of pie on a plate, and presented it to me, beaming.

After the first bite I closed my eyes and murmured, "Heavenly."

"It was," said Frank.

19

For the sake of discretion, Luke and I no longer arrived, left, or sat together at reunion meetings. The ninety minutes around a conference table brought out the actor in each of us, starting with our formal nods in greeting, me calling him "Chief," declining to serve together on any proposed subcommittees, and keeping our distance during refreshments.

A cover-up made sense, didn't it? We weren't in any way official. Without rehearsing, it was easy enough for Luke and me to revisit our unacquainted high school selves. During the post-meeting social half hour, we could be overheard wondering what teachers, classes, and classmates we had in common while at HHS. Band? Debate? Yearbook or newspaper staff? In clueless fashion, I asked him about siblings. Three brothers? Wow. Were they in law enforcement, too?

He asked if I was related to the Lewis in the math department.

Which led to a friendly scold from Annette the co-chair—"Of course Mr. Lewis was Emma's father. Everyone knew that!"

After a few sips of my watery decaf, I bid goodnight to everyone with equal warmth, and left on my own with no fond backward glances.

Mission accomplished. Still, our forced detachment gave me something of a pang. Might Luke send a text when he got back to his quarters, something that reinforced it was all improv? Maybe a simple "That was fun," or "Bravo, us."

I told myself I was being needy. There were plenty of meetings ahead when our classmates would catch on—not that we'd make an announcement; maybe we'd just arrive or leave in one car. I'd need a green light from Luke first. It was early. In man hours, it was one minute.

20

On speaker with my parents, driving back from a second inventory of the Mankopf house, I described a fraction of what I'd seen. The rugs and runners, oil paintings, appliances, cashmere throws, armchairs, boudoir chairs, ladies' desks, fainting couches, and a sparkling new industrial espresso machine.

"We'll come up at least a week before the sale," Beth volunteered.

Where to put them? Frank slept in my old room. I'd moved into my parents' room. I could almost hear the future debate, every one of us insisting that the spare room's sleep sofa would be fine, just fine.

"Who gave you the tour?" my dad asked.

"Vanessa, the daughter."

"Do we know her?" Beth asked my dad.

He said no; she'd gone away to school.

I told them that Vanessa had been completely unfazed and unself-conscious. Blasé even.

"About?"

"That it was a brothel, for real."

"No euphemisms?" my dad asked. "No embarrassment?"

"None. It was like . . . here's where the bed-and-breakfasters sat by the fire, and here's where the prostitutes plied their trade."

"I assume you took pictures," said Beth.

"Some, but I have to go back. I was amazed by the amount of . . . everything. You wouldn't know her mother had taken a single thing to California."

"The paintings?" my dad asked. "Worth anything?"

"Maybe. There are brass plaques under each one with the name of the artist. That means something, doesn't it?"

"We'd better get up there," Beth said again.

Sensing she meant my inexperience was showing, I said, "I'm not going to give anything away."

"Do you *want* us to come up?" Beth asked. "You're sounding a little defensive."

I knew I should counter with "Of course I want you to come up," but I couldn't muster the enthusiasm. There was no question I'd need the extra hands, but would I still be in charge? We looked at things differently. What they saw as an ugly avocado-green blender from the 1970s, tagged at a giveaway $10, I labeled "vintage juicer" and priced at $50. I said, "Sorry if I sounded defensive. I'm driving, so just distracted."

"And you wouldn't want to get pulled over!" my dad said a little too jovially.

Beth shushed him.

Pulled over? I said, "Was that a police reference?"

Beth said, "We heard."

"From Frank, I assume?"

"No! From the Greensteins," said my dad. "Just in passing."

The Greensteins were acquaintances, but not close friends. "I didn't know you were in touch with them."

"They were having a drink at Beardsley's," said Beth. "Linda said it looked like you were enjoying yourselves."

"He's a nice boy," said my dad. "I had him for something. Probably algebra."

I said, "Of course you did."

"Your father has a big mouth," said Beth, "but we're not going to be asking about future dates or future anything." Followed by a pregnant pause that I knew meant: *Is* there a future date?

"Keep us posted!" my dad piped up nonetheless.

Neither Frank nor Ivy was home. I texted him Back from Quail Ridge! Lots to tell!

Leaving the house now, he wrote back.

Which house?

My ex-house. Needed a few things.

Not unusual. Frank often went back to retrieve things he'd left behind, tools and cleaning products the stepdaughters wouldn't miss.

It was noon. I made a cheese and pickle sandwich, cut it into quarters for easy handling while I worked, and took phone, laptop, notebook, and clipboard to the dining room table.

Where to start? I'd made notes about the most startling finds, but hadn't logged everything due to being in and out of shock. Maybe I'd start with the ad copy and its all-important headline. Beth had enjoyed doing that for Finders, Keepers, and bouncing the first attempts off me. She had a good eye for phrases that called out from community bulletin boards, but mine had to be louder, catchier, sexier. It had to be press-release-worthy.

I'd known since Luke assured me that Mrs. Mankopf was in no legal jeopardy that I could call a spade a spade. Synonyms for *whorehouse*? The "cat" in *cathouse* could be misleading, and a turnoff to some. "Nunnery" in quotes? Too subtle, and too British. "House of Ill Repute"? Possible, as long as "ill" didn't sound an unnecessarily negative note.

Frank's car pulled into the driveway. I could see from the dining room window that he was carrying a bulging garment bag and a shoe box. Ivy was bounding happily up the stairs. As soon as I heard the back door open, I yelled, "In the dining room! Tons to tell you."

Frank peeked in and said, "Let me give Ivy her reward. Be right there."

When he returned, he explained without prompting, "I went over for my gray suit, but when I was going through my closet, I thought—Quail Ridge Road! What if I greeted customers in a tux? It would say, 'Welcome to the swankiest sale this town has ever seen.' "

He pulled out the closest chair and sat down. Ivy joined us, strategically lying under the table where all four human hands could reach her head. "Do we have a date?" Frank asked.

"Labor Day weekend, if all goes well. I'll double-check with the family as soon as I get the contract."

He looked up. "You don't have a signed contract?"

"I'm told it's in the mail."

He put his pen down. "Told by whom?"

"Vanessa. And during the tour, there was never any question that it was my sale to run; never a sense of 'If we choose Estate of Mind.' "

Shaking his head, he said, "We're dealing with people who ran an unlicensed bed-and-breakfast until they were slapped on the wrist. And need I point out—a brothel D.B.A. an escort service?"

"I know, but—"

"Do you want me to call her?"

"Vanessa?"

"No, her mother." He stood up. "Ivy, stay," he said, then went to the kitchen and came back with his phone. "Number?" he asked, still standing.

I found L. Mankopf under "recent" on my own phone and hit it. "Here. Use the company phone. You're on speaker."

As he was saying, "If she doesn't pick up—" I heard a woman's suspicious "Hello?"

"Mrs. Mankopf! This is Frank Crowley with Estate of Mind . . . Emma Lewis, our CEO, spent the morning at your house."

"I know."

"We're eager to get your sale on the calendar, but we can't move forward until the contract's been signed."

"Who are you again?"

"Frank Crowley."

"Crowley?" she repeated. "Why do I know that name?"

He sat down again and said with an unsure smile, "I used to be head of the math department at Harrow High."

A pause, then: "The Crowley whose wife got struck by lightning? What a gruesome way to go. Her husband was devastated."

"Um, yes, I was."

"No, no. Sorry. I meant her ex. Anyway, my condolences."

"Thank you . . . As for the contract—"

"I signed it, and I mailed it back."

"Then you kept a copy? The pink carbonless sheet?"

"Hold on. It's somewhere."

We waited. It sounded like walking, then rustling, then swearing. "I'm going through my desk right now. . . . Found it. Estate of Mind. I mailed the top sheet to Emma Lewis. Or Vanessa did."

"Do you remember when?" Frank asked.

"Um . . . okay. I signed it on July eighteenth . . . probably mailed it the next day."

"Excellent. Thank you. We look forward to its arrival, and of course the sale." Frank gave me a not very jolly thumbs-up, then asked in emcee fashion, "Emma? Any other questions for Mrs. Mankopf?"

I might as well. I said, "Hi, Mrs. Mankopf. Emma here. It's

about publicity. I remember your saying you had no problem with us . . . telling it like it is. Or was."

"Didn't we cover that? I was the housemother, and my girls were professionals? Use any words you want—whatever moves the stuff."

Frank whispered, "Ask if the sex workers have to be referred to as 'girls.' "

Lois heard him and snarled, "I can't be arrested for what went on there a decade ago, so I don't really give a shit."

"I wouldn't want you to suffer any embarrassment," I lied.

"It won't look good for Vanessa's father, the cop, but he won't know what words you use. He's in Florida."

I said, "I saw his artwork on several walls."

"And that's what he's doing now in Fort Lauderdale—painting. He thinks he's a genius. It's all abstract crap."

Frank and I exchanged matching looks: *Charming, isn't she?*

"Are we done?" Lois asked.

To my great surprise, Frank said, "We have a mutual friend. I understand Connie Winooski used to bake for you?"

"Among other things."

I froze. Should one of us ask for particulars? Frank didn't look worried, but I wasn't going to let "among other things" go unexamined. "What else did Connie help you with?"

"Housework. A lot of beds to strip. We sent the sheets and towels out, but still a hell of a lot of laundry."

Whew. Laundry.

"Do you know she lost her husband a year ago?" said Frank.

"I *did* know. You're friends with her? I remember she used to be a very attractive woman, even after a bunch of kids."

Looking sorry that he'd ever spoken any word other than "Have you signed the contract?" Frank said, "She still is."

"How old are you?"

"Me?" asked Frank.

"Yes, you, Crowley. That wife of yours was struck by lightning, for god's sakes. Life is short. Ever heard of going for the gusto?"

Poor Frank. I said on both our behalf, "Thank you. You've been very helpful."

"I wasn't a professional matchmaker for nothing," she said.

21

A text from Luke: Did you hear?

Coming from the chief of police, it could be anything from a lost dog to a robbed bank. I wrote back, Give me a hint.

Answered in the time it took to type it: My mother is "dating" your Frank.

Did that "your" sound accusatory? I had, after all, pushed Luke to send Frank's condolences to his mom. And did the quotes around "dating" suggest that he knew the full story and was being polite? I texted, True. He cooked her dinner on Saturday.

When there was no reply after a few minutes, I wrote back, R U upset?

My phone rang. I answered with a worried "Luke?" then heard, "Not upset with you."

"Not with Frank, either, I hope."

"Frank? Hardly."

"Which leaves your mom . . ."

"You mean Miss No Stone Unturned? Miss True Confessions?"

Was this about his mother having sex? Was Luke narrow-minded and/or religious, and it hadn't come up? "When did she tell you about"—aiming for pseudo-biblical—"*being* with Frank?"

"Five minutes ago. I called to remind her to turn the sprinklers on, and she's all 'Do you want to hear about my date?' "

"And you said . . . ?"

"I said I was at work, had to get off. Hope she had a nice time . . . but the dam broke anyway."

His agita aside, I couldn't help appreciating that I was the one he confided in when rattled. "And what did you say?"

"Something like 'Great. Another notch in your belt.' " He lowered his voice. "Can't talk. I'm at the station."

"Talk maybe when?"

"I was going to get to that. How's Wednesday?"

"Wednesday's great. To do what?—just so I know what to wear."

"The Sox have a Triple-A team in Worcester. They're playing the Buffalo Bisons on Wednesday."

Worcester. I asked a less-than-enthusiastic "Do you already have tickets?"

He laughed. "Not keen on Triple-A ball?"

"Not especially, but I don't want to be that kind of woman."

"Which is what kind?"

"The fussy kind who has to dine at the town's fanciest restaurant."

"I'm not worried. Do you like miniature golf?"

I did, well enough.

"And then we grab a bite to eat?"

Before I could say "Perfect," or anything at all, I heard a female voice calling, "Sir?"

"Be right there," Luke answered.

I said, "Not a crime in progress, I hope."

"Someone's public defender just got here. *Finally.*"

"And now you interview the criminal?"

Luke laughed. "The criminal stole a neighbor's potbellied pig because he thought it was too noisy—then put it in a sidecar and drove it around. Not as hilarious as the thief thought."

"Wow . . . more like this on Wednesday, please," I said.

*

Frank was firm: No more time spent on the Mankopf sale until I had the signed contract in hand. I noted that I was experiencing a more self-assured, even assertive Frank, practically overnight. He knew what I was referencing: Connie's attentions. I told him that she had given Luke the rundown.

"Rundown of what?"

"Your date."

"Everything?"

"I don't know word for word, but he got the gist." Unquoted, the disdainful "another notch in her belt," which a son wouldn't pull out of thin air. What if Saturday night had meant nothing to Connie? What if she was going to break his newly hopeful heart?

We were outside, walking Ivy together. It was unusual to be paired up, since the job was almost always Frank's alone. But we'd been midconversation about the Winooskis when Ivy's needs could no longer be ignored. It was a steamy day, the sidewalks scalding, requiring her silicone booties. A few hundred yards from the house, Frank stooped to bag the poop. I was chatting about who knows what when Frank stood partway up, then crumpled. Panicked, I yelled his name and insisted he put his head between his knees. "No, no," he was saying. "I'm fine. It's nothing."

"Are you having chest pain?" I cried. "Can you move all your limbs?"

It took him longer to answer than I liked. "I'm fine," he kept repeating while looking dazed. "I didn't faint."

"I'm getting the car!" I said, then, "No, I'm not leaving you. I'm calling nine-one-one."

"Please don't. This happens. I have low blood pressure. Sometimes I get lightheaded when I get up too quickly . . . I didn't eat lunch. And the heat . . ."

"Maybe you're dehydrated."

He blinked a few times, signaling yes or no or probably.

I helped him up, my hands clutching one forearm. I said, "We're going home." What if he'd been walking Ivy alone? Would I ever know? Would Ivy do a Lassie? The dog was licking Frank's closest hand, looking worried. "She knows something happened," I said. "She knows the difference between lightheaded and falling down."

He said, "She's a genius"—a relief to hear. Didn't a person need all his wits to be ironic?

We walked back to the house, me pretending to take it slow on my own account, Frank faking a normal stride but soft in the legs. Inside, I led him to the closest kitchen chair. "I'm getting you some water. Sit!" The command made Ivy drop to the floor instantly.

"Good girl," Frank said.

I poured two glasses of water, then joined him at the table. "Are you going to tell your doctor that you fainted?"

"I didn't faint."

"Okay, okay—that you get dizzy when you stand up too fast."

"I did mention it to him—remember, Danny Kellogg? He says I'm in great shape."

"Can I feel your pulse?"

"Which will tell you what?"

I didn't know. Fast might be bad. Slow might be bad, too. Nonetheless, I put four of my fingers on his wrist, then checked it against my own pulse.

"It's sweet of you to fuss over me," he said, "but this isn't anything to worry about."

"Fine! I won't worry that it'll happen when you're alone with Ivy, or when you're driving or . . . or . . . I don't know—running a half marathon!"

"We can put a list of emergency numbers by the phone."

"Your PCP, for sure, and next of kin . . . which would be who?"

He shrugged. "Last emergency contact was Ginger."

"Then we have to work on this. And the next time you fill out a form, put me down as your emergency contact, okay?"

"I appreciate that, but—"

"But what?"

"I have a sister."

"I've never heard about a sister!"

"She lives in Oregon."

"No good. What about the stepdaughters?"

"They're busy."

"I'm it, then."

"HIPAA rules won't let them tell you anything—not that there's anything to tell."

"What about Connie?"

"What *about* Connie?"

"As someone to call if I can't be reached."

His expression was too neutral for a newly anointed paramour.

"Too early?" I asked.

He shook his head in a way that could've meant no, not too early, or no, not Connie. I refilled his glass, sat down again, and, changing the subject with false brightness, "When was the last time you saw either of the stepdaughters?"

"Sadly, not since the funeral."

"But you're not estranged, are you?"

"We talk. They know I check the house regularly."

"Were you the one who broke the news to them about their mother's accident?"

The topic seemed to revive him. "Picture this," he began. "I'm in the car. My phone rings. I'm driving, so I don't answer it the first time. When I get to the parking lot of the Big Y, I answer. It's Luke, who identifies himself as Chief Winooski. He tells me Ginger's had an accident, and to meet him at the hospital. As soon as I hung up, I saw a text from Ginger's stupid, witless golf partner, who couldn't resist—that idiot!—telling me Ginger was struck by lightning. They're trying to resuscitate her. Can you imagine being that thoughtless! Writing to someone's husband without going through the proper channels?"

"Idiot," I said, while hoping I wouldn't have made the same witless call.

"You realize," he continued, "if she'd died almost any other way—a heart attack in her bed, an automobile accident, drowned in the bathtub—I'd have been investigated, given the timing and her well-known infidelity. But no one can be blamed for lightning—well, the victim can! You don't stay out on a golf course when there's thunder and lightning. It was a kind of arrogance, wasn't it?" He followed that with an apologetic smile. "I've become quite the windbag, haven't I?"

Where had this unbosoming started? Oh, right—a stepdaughter as possible emergency contact. I tapped my phone again. "What are the daughters' names?"

"Juliet St. Pierre and Francine St. Pierre."

I pointed to his phone. "Let's call them."

"What for? To tell them I got lightheaded after skipping lunch?"

"I'm a stepdaughter, too. If Beth fainted, I'd want to know."

"That is the worst analogy I've ever heard. She raised you! You refer to her and your father as your parents. Nothing but!"

I decided to give it a rest—well, the emergency contact part of it. Returning to what had sounded like some diminution of enthusiasm for Connie, I asked how the previous weekend was sitting with him now.

He sighed. "I don't love hearing that she told her son about our date, presumably in some detail. It raises the question, who else did she tell?"

"Would that be so terrible if she told a friend? It means she's excited. And smitten."

He might've smiled at that; he might've said that he was smitten, too. But all I got was second thoughts made visible.

Had I knocked him off cloud nine by telling him what Connie had overshared with Luke? I asked when he was seeing her again.

"I guess . . . this weekend."

"You know you always give it two or more dates."

He asked what that meant. I said, "That's the common wisdom. Always give the person a second chance. Date 'em till you hate 'em."

Thankfully he smiled.

"Call her." I refrained from saying "life is short," given my earlier scare.

He said he would. He should. Tonight. He'd suggest a movie. Out, at the cinemas in Hadley. Was that too obvious?

I knew what he meant: as opposed to Netflix, upstairs, watching from bed.

22

Lois's exclamation points and question marks dotted the contract. Were they actual challenges or merely doodles? No parking on the lawn. Chamber music. I knew this much: Defaced or not, the contract was signed, dated, and mailed back.

I texted Vanessa. Home today? Can we drop by?

WE? she wrote back.

My associate & I.

Man? woman?

Man. Frank Crowley.

There was a long pause, long enough that I sent a red question mark. Finally: Nope.

Nope, he can't come w me?

No, hes not in our books. Bring, fine.

In their books! *As if!* Was that her worldview—men were either johns or not johns?

What time? she wrote.

Noonish?

A thumbs-up emoji appeared. I answered with same.

On the ride over, as Frank drove, I read Vanessa's texts aloud.

"I hope you're keeping notes," he said. "And I don't mean notes like 'four wingchairs and three floor lamps.' I mean notes for the book I'm going to insist you write."

Oh, Frank. Such faith. As ever, moonlighting as my guidance counselor.

If she expected us at a set time, why was Vanessa answering the door wrapped in a towel, cleavage escaping? She managed to offer her right hand to Frank, apologizing for her state of undress.

The smile he returned was nervous and half-hearted. One seduction doesn't make a sixty-two-year-old man a player. He said, "We can come back later when you'd be able to—"

I said, "No. We have an appointment."

Vanessa said, "You're the experts. I'm just the . . ."—which provocative job title to choose?—"manageress."

I had to ask, "May we come in?" because she was still posing in the doorway.

"Be my guests," she said, barely turning sideways so we had to squeeze past her and the lingering scent of musk.

Frank rewarded me with a look that said *As billed—and then some*. In the front hallway I pointed left and right, silently introducing Manny's mood-setting murals.

Next stop: the dark green, decorous, fireplaced study. Without Vanessa, we could voice our appraisals: good, better, best, no market value, awful. I took pictures of the paintings and emailed them to my auction-house buddy. He wrote back immediately, asking to see the backs of the paintings and close-ups of the artists' signatures, if any. It took us a while, lifting paintings off their hangers, photographing them, putting them back.

Groaning midheft, I said, "I used to do this by myself."

"No more of that," he said.

On to the next room. "Prepare yourself," I said, leading him through the arched mahogany door into another world.

"Wow. Day and night," said Frank. Here were the pale peach walls and dove-gray carpeting. The black velvet tufted banquette would've been a big-ticket item if only it weren't built-in and unmovable. Frank was pointing at a painting of a full-length nude propped against pillows, a flower behind one ear, with the smile of an unapologetic woman of the night. "It's a famous Manet," Frank said. He took out his phone, searched for something, did some scrolling. "Here it is: *Olympia*. Quote: "It scandalized people when shown in 1865. Visitors to the exhibition sobbed and fainted and scuffled. Armed guards had to be hired.'"

I said, "We'll write all of that on a sign."

Enter Vanessa, now in a lilac slip dress, barefooted, matching nail polish on her toes. "Here you are! It's lovely, isn't it? Sets the mood, my mother thought." She turned to Frank, who'd taken out his reading glasses and was examining or pretending to examine *The Birth of Venus*. "Did Emily prepare you for what our trade was, I mean, in addition to the bed-and-breakfasting?" Raising one hand, she flicked the air. "Poof. Gone but never to be forgotten. Bed-and-breakfasts are a dime a dozen. *This* is our legacy, the most interesting part of our history; surely the most commercial part—for us and now for you."

Frank asked when the Quail's Nest shuttered its doors.

She curled her lip. "Since a new sheriff came to town."

I said, "Frank knows that your father was the former chief of police." Of course he did; Manny Mankopf's brazen scofflawing was one of my favorite topics.

"I wouldn't want you to get the wrong idea," Vanessa said, touching Frank's forearm.

"About what?" he asked.

"Me. I only worked here summers when I was in college."

"And after college?"

"Did I return here?" She smiled. "It was my home, wasn't it? Where's a girl to go?"

Poor Frank. "I meant career-wise."

"What I do now? I'm in development. I raise money for good causes."

He might've asked anyone else, "Such as?" but all he said, moving away, was "Good to hear."

I asked Frank if he wanted to sit down, which made Vanessa ask, "Why?"

"No reason," I said.

Frank surprised me by saying, "I fainted yesterday," which he'd been denying for twenty-four hours. It wasn't strictly speaking true; he'd never lost consciousness. Was he trying to appear older and infirm to stymie the flirting?

She gestured around the room, sweeping in the gallery of nudes. "Copies, of course. I hope all of this is going to be worth your while."

"Emma's the CEO," Frank said. "I chip in when and wherever she needs help."

"Are you two related?" Vanessa asked.

"Associates," I said.

"I thought I saw a family resemblance," she said. "Or maybe it's just the expressions."

That was true: expressions blending discomfort and annoyance. She'd been businesslike to the point of curt with me on Monday, and now: Put a man in the beau parlor, and she was beyond charming. I let her narrate, busying myself inspecting the soft pink throws, three of them, woolly and fringed. Vanessa noticed and said, "They're cashmere. Nothing but the best." With yet another smile directed at Frank, she explained, "They weren't just decoration. Sometimes a patron needed to cover his lap."

"I'd like to see the kitchen," said Frank.

*

She made both of us a double espresso and noted that it would be hard to part with this beauty. "I might take it back to Boston before someone snaps it up," she said, patting the water funnel.

That prompted me to say, "You and your mother have to decide what you want to keep. Once it's listed, you can't change your mind."

That earned me a look best described as *Says who?* Next, and rather mopily, she began opening and closing cupboard doors. "Mugs. More mugs. Bowls. Plates—we gave the B-and-Bers breakfast. Had to. The champagne flutes and the hardball glasses were for the LLs."

Of course that was an invitation for Frank to ask, "LLs?"

"Lola's Ladies, patrons thereof."

Frank said, "I do recall seeing the term 'Lola's Ladies' somewhere."

"We were listed in the Yellow Pages under escort services."

He winced. "I meant in the context of the upcoming sale."

Maybe it was time to show what an enlightened operation Estate of Mind was. I said, "We're looking forward to using the house's colorful past for promotional purposes, even if a little risky—"

"Risky?" Vanessa snapped. "Because some Goody-Two-Shoes will stay away? I'm proud of what we offered here. Mom's escort service was completely legit and incorporated. We paid taxes. If some think it's prostitution, that's their problem. And as I'm sure you know, prostitution is legal in some less uptight states."

Not true; only in Nevada, and not in every county there, but best not to contradict my biggest client. I helped myself to four white mugs bearing green-and-gold Quail's Nest crests, made a grouping on the counter. "How's this? And paired with a sugar bowl and creamer, or an unopened bag of coffee beans in the freezer . . . voila! It'll be grabbed by the first customer who walks into the kitchen."

Vanessa frowned, distinctly unimpressed. "I'm looking forward to it . . . though it could be heartbreaking. The end of an era."

I reminded her that the contract states that family members are strongly discouraged from attending their own sale.

"I'm in development! I'm an excellent saleswoman! I know how to reach into trouser pockets and come up with a bigger endowment every year." She smiled. "Figuratively speaking, of course."

Frank exhaled. He slid one of the stools out from under the table and sat down.

You okay? I mouthed.

He nodded, and I could see an uncharacteristic flash of annoyance at my ongoing solicitudes.

"One reason we discourage the homeowners from attending is because so many dispute the prices we set," I said, hoping that would inspire a "We'd never do that," but what she said was "Are you known for underpricing the merch?"

"Well, you wouldn't want us to be known for doing the opposite—pricing things unreasonably."

She raised her espresso cup. "I'll make a deal with you: I'll come to the sale. I'll answer questions and, when appropriate, give some historical perspective. But I will *not* challenge your sticker prices."

I said, "I can work with that."

But even as I was agreeing to her deal, I was thinking, *appropriate?* Did Vanessa Mankopf know the meaning of the word?

23

What to wear that would look offhandedly attractive while miniature-golf-appropriate? I decided on a denim skirt and, after much experimenting, a camisole under a sheer white blouse. Earrings, yes. Necklace? Just the tiny gold letter E.

When the doorbell rang at 6:01, Frank called upstairs, "Want me to get it?" I said yes, be down in a minute. After a quick check of my hair, I paused at the top of the stairs to eavesdrop. Frank welcomed Luke, who returned a quiet thank-you and undoubtedly a handshake.

"Did I hear miniature golf?" Frank asked, cheerfully paternal.

Luke said, "That's the plan, as long as the rain holds off."

"Good point; I'll take Ivy out now. She hates the rain—stops every two yards to shake herself off." A pause, then, "I'd ask you to send my regards to your mother, unless that's too awkward."

"Awkward?" Luke repeated.

"I meant awkward if your mother doesn't know you're seeing Emma," Frank quickly explained.

I was hoping for "I've told her all about Emma," but he said, "No problem. She'd assume you saw me around town, like everyone else does."

After another pause, Luke said, "I'm glad you want to send your regards," which I was hearing as: *Glad you* still *want to send your regards after she seduced you.*

I decided I'd better unfreeze myself and join them before either died of discomfort. When I was halfway down the stairs, they both looked up and smiled.

Luke was in jeans and a white polo shirt. "Ready," I said. "Just have to grab my bag."

Frank followed me into the kitchen under the guise of getting Ivy. He whispered, "Did I sound okay? I was tongue-tied."

"You did fine. Not to worry."

Luke smiled when I rejoined him, but at the same time panto-mimed a swipe of relief across his forehead.

The ticket guy at Monster Mini-Golf greeted Luke with "How ya doin', Chief?" adding one elevated eyebrow that even I could trans-late as *Here with a date, I see.*

I told Luke it had been a while since I'd played.

"Should I give you a handicap?" he asked, writing with the standard-issue stubby pencil, listing me as Tiger W. and him as Arnold P. I said, "No handicap. I want to win fair and square."

I thought I was making decent-enough bogeys and double bo-geys until I hit one of the windmill's rotating blades on the ninth hole, sending my ball onto the adjacent green. The neighboring team of two teenage boys tossed the ball back to me—condescendingly, I thought.

I dropped it where it had jumped out of bounds, but Luke nudged it with his foot more charitably in line with the hole. I putted, then walked around to the other side of the windmill to find that my ball hadn't made it through.

"We call that a dribbler," Luke said.

"I seem to be getting worse instead of better."

Luke said, "What's the goal here? A par score or a fun time?"

"No question, a fun, humbling time."

He took his shot, making par. Passing me, he gave my hip a bump with his. For the town's chief of police, it seemed like a public display of affection.

It was my first visit to the Two-Faced Liar, one town north of Harrow. The owners were brothers who'd moved from Limerick to Boston, then west to here. We learned that Declan and Eoin had an American da, so were dual citizens. Both were tending bar, both chatty, their brogues delightful. All the whiskeys on sale were Irish, and tastes were offered. Luke said one ale was enough; he was driving.

"Good lad!" said the taller one. "We don't hear that often enoof."

When we moved to a corner table, Eoin followed with the portable blackboard listing three menu items and three sides. "Our hamburgers are famous," he said. "Organic. From free-range cows," which made me laugh.

"No? Most people believe me when I say that."

I said, "I'll have one, medium-rare."

"We do them one way. They're smashed. It's the latest thing."

"Fine," I said.

"Same," said Luke.

I asked if he'd share the fried pickles with me.

"Ahh, the lass has good taste," Eion said.

"Pickles? Sure," said Luke.

"Am I mistakin' that this is your sweetheart?" Eoin asked him.

"No, you're not," said Luke—such a welcome answer, as long as the double negative meant *Yes, she is*.

*

On the drive back to Harrow, I asked if making small talk with Frank would always be excruciating. I was hoping for, "I wouldn't go *that* far," but what he said was, "Probably. As long as, you know . . . my mother and him."

It was 9:10. Frank would still be up. "Then not a great idea to come back to my house to watch a movie?"

He said, matter-of-factly, "We'll go to my place."

We did. His quarters were indeed above the station, one flight up, through a separate entrance. At the top of the stairs, a daunting army-green steel door was labeled "Private."

"Welcome to my barracks," Luke said. I stepped into a skylit living room, its wide pine floorboards polyurethaned to a gleaming finish, the walls painted a dark red. Though I didn't ask, he volunteered, "Three coats. I had to cover the previous resident's murals."

No need to ask: Manny's artwork. "I hope you took photos before painting over them," I said.

"I didn't. Believe me, they weren't photos that a chief of police wants on his phone."

"Good thinking," I said.

He asked if I'd like wine? Beer? Tea?

I said yes to the wine, as long as he'd be joining me, adding, "I can always Uber home."

"Or not," he said.

Those two words seemed a significant leap forward, relationshipwise . . . unless he meant merely that he'd stay under the legal limit and could drive me. While he was at the fridge, I sat on his tweedy couch, wondering what might be ahead and who'd get the ball rolling. He returned with the wine, said he hoped Chardonnay was okay—a generous pour in glasses etched with bunches of grapes that I was almost positive came from a sale on Old Tuxedo Circle.

Luke noticed the appraising and said, "From my mother, a housewarming present, a set of three."

"Sorry. Occupational hazard."

We clinked glasses. After a few sips in what felt like a fond, contented silence, Luke said, "Speaking of the elephant in the room, aka my mother, I need to explain something."

I nodded, borderline worried.

"When I was ranting on the phone to you about my mother's love life, I wasn't blaming Mr. Crowley. I know you think very highly of him, and I do too. It's just . . . big picture."

Did he mean *our* big picture—him and me and his mother and Frank? Too close for comfort? Incestuous because my housemate was dating his oversharing mother? "I'm not following," I said.

"Sorry. I meant big picture as in her track record." And then, grimly, "You might've guessed . . . she cheated on my dad."

Not guessed; only suspected. It would've taken some serious prudishness for him to be so judgmental about his mother's love life without some history and injury behind it. "How did you find out?" I asked. "And when?"

"I was living at home, waiting to hear about the Worcester job. I confronted her. She's a terrible liar."

"Do you know who—"

"A guy she met in some stupid adult-ed course."

"An affair? Or just . . . dates?"

"You mean, dinner and a movie? No! He had a couch in his one-man, loser law office."

"Did she confide all of that—the who, what, and where?"

Finally, a rueful smile. "As opposed to me hiring a private detective? Correct. We had it out."

"Did your dad know?"

"I hope not."

"When was this?"

"After his first heart attack. *Because* of it, she claimed. She didn't want to strain his heart. I asked if it was doctor's orders, and she said she didn't want to take any chances. Such bullshit. And this when he was back at work, full-time, lugging around appliances."

"I know this is outside your comfort zone, but how old was she that she had to . . . go elsewhere?"

A slight wince. "Fifty?"

"And the boyfriend?"

"Younger."

"Married?"

"She claimed divorced."

"Name?"

"No one you'd know. His office was in Holyoke."

I said, "And when your dad died . . ."

"Did I get her boy toy as a stepfather? No. It ended. The second heart attack happened in his sleep, fatal, next to her. . . . She was heartbroken, and it wasn't an act. She had a bad time with it. All four of us moved back home for a couple of weeks, in shifts. She wore black for a whole year. Finally we said, 'You're not an elderly Italian widow from the old country. Enough is enough.' "

I asked if he thought the deep and extended mourning was . . . guilt.

"Pretty sure. But I'd like to think it was love."

Love. If I squeezed his hand, would that seem as if I were underscoring the word in a personal and applicable way? Hoping to move on, I offered a wrap-up: "So she went all celibate for a respectable amount of time. And along comes Frank, just when she thought it was okay to get back on the horse, especially with such a nice man. True?"

As he seemed to be considering my tidy, virtuous summary, I added, "She got a good read on Frank—that he'd be taking it slow and easy, if ever, so she'd have to make the first move. Not that you have to rewrite history, but maybe those notches on her belt could be viewed as water under the bridge."

He groaned. "Will I ever live that down? Have I hoisted myself with my own petard?"

I put my glass down on the coffee table. "Wait! Did you just quote Shakespeare?"

He crossed his arms in hammy indignation and said, "I get it: a future cop wouldn't have taken Senior Honors English with Miss Flugle? I think I'm offended."

I slid closer and kissed him on his fake pout. "I'm so sorry. Is there anything I can do to make it up to you?"

It took only a few seconds of pseudo-deliberation before he stood up and reached for my hand. "Would you like to see the view from my bedroom? It looks out on . . . the DMV parking lot."

"Dying to," I said.

24

Seven thirty a.m. Luke was crisp and uniformed, driving me home in his squad car. When we reached my house, he leaned across the paraphernalia for a quick kiss.

"Be in touch," I said with a squeeze of his nearest thigh.

"Thank you for coming over," he said, but with a wry smile that meant *etcetera, etcetera.*

Ivy was, as ever, ecstatic to see I'd come home alive. Frank was up. He said he hadn't worried. No, not at all. He'd fallen asleep around midnight, figuring . . . I'd had a very nice evening.

I said, "We did. After mini golf I had my first smashburger."

I could see there was another question lurking—surely a personal one, judging by the look of imminent embarrassment.

"Anything else?" I prompted.

"No." And then, with pauses between words, eyes averted, "As you know, I coached the girls' team, too."

I laughed. "Were you going to ask if we're being careful?"

He closed his eyes. "Forgive me. You're not teenagers."

"I totally get it. Not to worry, Coach. Just in case, I went prepared."

I didn't add, *Good thing one of us was.* Luke had apologized profusely: Not that he was famous, not that he was recognized by every CVS clerk and every pharmacist, but he liked to keep his private life private. Hence the lack of provisions. He said he'd brave it next time or use self-checkout—murmured, as best as I could process while intertwined.

Frank had Ivy's leash clipped to her collar when I returned to the kitchen, showered and changed. He'd postponed their walk to say, "Forgive me for asking such a personal question! I'm not your parent or your doctor!"

"You didn't ask it. I read your mind. And don't forget that our main topic of conversation has been personal since the sink swallowed your wedding ring."

He didn't contradict me, because it was true. With Ivy whimpering and straining toward the door, I said I'd come with them.

"Not because you think I need a minder?" he asked.

"No! Because I feel like a walk."

It wasn't until we'd reached the end of Montpelier and were halfway up Dover that Frank said, "After you left last night, I scolded myself for being cowardly, for sending regards to Connie through Luke. I felt I owed her a call. So we're going to an early movie, then take-in. She likes Indian, too. Her place."

"You know that my house is your house."

"I know that. Thank you. But with your parents coming up for the Mankopf sale, the topic of Quail Ridge Road would inevitably come up, and there are things Connie would just as soon not revisit."

"You're not saying she was involved in . . . Lola's Ladies?"

"Heavens no! Emma, really!" His raised voice made Ivy stop, ears at attention, and emit a rare growl. "A mother of four? She baked, and she helped around the place when her boys were at school."

"Sorry! But she must've known what was going on there?"

"She had her suspicions. But don't forget—the so-called escorting happened after hours. She was there mornings."

"Then what doesn't she want to revisit?"

"That she ever crossed paths with Manny Mankopf—as crude as they come, and a man who was all hands."

"Hands? As in . . . ?"

"If you were a woman working there, in any job, upstairs, downstairs, he thought he could get away with pinching and stroking."

"And who was going to slap the hand of the chief of police, right?"

Though we hadn't passed a soul on our walk, he looked both ways before lowering his voice. "Connie did, a figurative slap, but better than that. She quit, and she talked to a lawyer."

"And then what? Did she file a complaint?"

"She couldn't because she was getting paid under the table, in cash, not an employee under the law . . . but she sent an anonymous letter to the mayor."

"Naming Manny?"

"Naming Manny. . . . The mayor figured out who wrote it—in a town this size?—and called Connie herself. A letter like that from a respectable married woman? It did the trick."

"Got Manny fired?"

"Got him to resign. Of course he denied everything. The mayor, the superintendent, every city councillor knew he was covering for his ex-wife's whorehouse. The pawing hardly came as a surprise. You can't fire someone for being an obnoxious blowhard, but you *can* fire him for sexual harassment."

"Her letter must've been a masterpiece."

"I suspect her lawyer polished it—he knew what phrases to use that meant laws were broken. Unwanted attention and all that."

Was it the Holyoke lawyer? I wondered. I asked if Manny had ever done more than pinching and groping Connie.

"He tried."

I stopped him with a hand on his elbow. "He didn't rape her, did he?"

"As much as she would say was 'He followed me into the pantry and unzipped his fly.' She told him to get lost, and shoved him away. That did it, the coup de grace."

I asked when he'd learned all this.

"Last night. A long conversation. I'm no psychiatrist, but I think it was her way of telling me she was a woman of high scruples."

I said, "Wow! Hats off to Mrs. Winooski . . . You know who has to hear this? Dad—union president, filer of many grievances. He'll love what she did."

"She doesn't brag about it."

"She should!"

"She doesn't want anyone to think that she helped get rid of the chief of police so her son could step into the job. Luke applied. Everyone liked him. He was named chief on his own merits."

Good for him. And most of all, good for Connie.

25

Everything was the same: oatmeal on oatmeal day, English muffins by the toaster, eggs waiting to be scrambled, poached, or fried . . . So who was this stranger sitting at the kitchen table, deeply engaged in peeling a hard-boiled egg? She was about my age, with cropped white-blond hair and fashionably dark roots. Her arms were extensively, florally tattooed.

"Sleep well?" Frank asked me.

I said I had, thank you. And did he want to introduce his guest?

"I'm his stepdaughter," said the woman. "And you are?"

Who *was* I? Seriously? This was my house, my table, my egg. I said, "I'm Emma Lewis. I live here."

Frank said, "This is Rain, Ginger's younger daughter." He hesitated, then said cautiously, "I may have once or twice referred to her by her given name, Francine."

Rain asked if we had sea salt. Frank handed her the saltshaker and said, "This will have to do."

Which left me with several questions, uppermost being, *She's not staying here, is she?* He must've gleaned from my annoyed silence that I was waiting to be clued in.

He began with, "Rain has things to take care of at her mother's house."

How much was I supposed to know about the terms of her

mother's will? I said, "I'm sorry about your mother's . . . passing."
I collected what I needed for a bowl of cereal and joined them at
the table. "Are you thinking of returning to the house—I mean to
live there?"

"Are you kidding? It's a mausoleum. No, worse than that.
It's like a nursing home for old furniture. She was practically
a hoarder. I can't live there. And I certainly don't want to live in
Harrow."

Was I hearing a distant whimper? "Where's Ivy?" I asked.

"Outside."

"By herself?"

"On her run."

She hated the run; considered it punishment, incomprehensible
time out. I asked why.

"Not a fan," he said with an almost imperceptible nod toward
Rain.

She held out her cup, signaling *refill*. Frank got up.

I asked him, "Could I borrow you for a minute? I need a hand
with that . . . stuck window."

"Of course."

When we were out of earshot, I asked, "When did she show up?"

"Last night. Late. She called me from the train station."

"Did she stay here?"

"No, no. Of course not. I dropped her off at the Harrow Inn.
I'll drive her over to Greenough after breakfast."

"And this morning? She just showed up?"

"Uber'd over. Not to worry. She knows it's not my home; not
my place to invite guests."

"Why didn't she stay at her own house?"

"Ask her." Then, with a faint smile, "You might enjoy the answer."
He opened and closed a random window for effect, then a loud,
"That did it. Just needed a little elbow grease."

I followed him back and checked on Ivy through the biggest

kitchen window. She'd found a patch of sun and was lying in it, seemingly resigned.

When I sat down again, Rain asked Frank, "Does she know?"

"Ask her."

Rain said, "My sister and I inherited the house when our mother died. You probably know about that nightmare, right? On the golf course, on her birthday? You know what the odds are of being struck by lightning? Less than one in a million."

I said, "I never knew that she died on her birthday . . . I know it was terrible for all concerned."

"It was a horror show. I have PTSD because of it."

I asked if it helped or hurt to come back to her childhood home.

"I don't know. I haven't been there, and I'm not sure if he'll let me in."

"I'm sorry," I said. "I don't understand—"

"My father's squatting there! I came back to evict him."

Frank said calmly, "Stefan moved in with a woman."

"And her teenage kids!" said Rain.

I asked, "Is he not allowed to be there?"

She repeated, "The house belongs to me and my sister. I'm going to give them the weekend to pack up and leave, or I show up with the police."

"Weren't he and your mother reconciled at the time of her death?" I asked.

"You mean because they were sleeping together? That didn't mean anything."

I looked at Frank. It had meant plenty to him, such as the end of his marriage. I said, "If I might play devil's advocate: As long as you and your sister aren't living there, couldn't your father and his girlfriend stay there as caretakers?"

"No! It doesn't work that way. They're trespassing."

"Did they break in?" I asked.

Rain said, "Ask your friend Frank how they got in."

Frank shrugged. "This is Harrow. The key's been under the same flowerpot forever."

I offered a weak, "Would they be homeless if you evicted them?"

"He has a house! He's Mr. Airbnb now. I don't know about her."

Frank said, "Emma and I know the chief of police. He's going to ask questions. You'll end up saying, 'He's my dad, and no, actually, I don't need the house—' "

"Until we do!"

I asked Frank, "You're back and forth over there all the time, but you didn't run into Stefan and company?"

"This is new. And sudden."

"Someone wanted his place on the first of the month!" said Rain.

"And you found out how?" I asked her.

"He texted me. He couldn't remember the Wi-Fi password."

I'd devoted enough time to this ungracious stranger, and I'd finished my shredded wheat. I said I had to get to work.

"Doing what?" Rain asked.

"I do estate sales."

"You give them, or you go to them?"

"I run them."

"You make a living doing that?"

The easiest answer was "Yes, I do."

"Do you need a license to run estate sales?"

"No. But it takes experience. And good stuff to sell." I smiled. "And good staff."

"She means I help," said Frank.

"Not just his consummate math skills, either."

Rain looked puzzled. I said, "Frank and my dad taught together."

"Which sort of brings us to the here and now," Frank said.

"Emma's parents knew I was looking for another place to live, and she was moving back—"

"From?"

Rather than naming the untrendy Framingham, I said, "West of Boston. They wanted me to take over their business because they were retiring."

"Did you have to buy in?" Rain asked.

"No. They handed me the reins. I'd been helping out since I was a kid."

Frank stood and said to Rain, "Shall we?"

"Shall we what?"

"Go over to the house."

"What time is it?" she asked.

"Ten fifteen. We won't be waking anyone up." And then Coach Frank spoke: "If I can have a civilized discussion with him, so can you. You'll settle things. If the police come, it'll be on the record, and it'll be a screaming headline in the *Echo*: 'Daughter Throws Father to the Wolves.' "

"Do I care what the local rag says? I don't live here."

I asked if her father and mother had jointly owned the house.

"Is this the third degree? Our mother left it to Jules and me. We'd sell it right now, but we can't unless we contest the will. We were surprised that we were getting it. We assumed it would go to the husband du jour."

"In other words, me," said Frank.

"It's no better than some bum who finds his way into an abandoned building and eats up whatever canned goods the last bum left behind."

Frank said, "Your position would be somewhat understandable and forgivable if you or Juliet wanted to move into the house now."

"My sister wants me to. But Stefan has to die before we can sell it."

"Not imminent," said Frank. "He's what . . . seventy? Seventy-two, three?"

I said, "I'd be careful. People ring a doorbell and an angry, confused gun owner opens the door and shoots them."

"I'm his kid!" said Rain.

I wanted to say, *Yes, you certainly act like it, Miss Call the Cops.*

Frank said, "Something's not lining up. Something's missing from this picture."

"No, there isn't!"

"Who's the woman?" I asked.

Rain hesitated, then whispered, "Miss Eliopoulos."

"*Athena* Eliopoulos?" asked Frank.

"Yes! My fossilized father has taken up with my kindergarten teacher."

There was math to do, and Frank beat me to it. "Wouldn't that be at least twenty years ago? She's very likely age-appropriate now."

"Was she a bad teacher?" I asked. "Because it sounds as if you hated her."

"I worshipped her! She had long, shiny dark hair. And she used to wear big, clunky necklaces. We all thought she was beautiful! Like Wonder Woman."

Frank asked, "Rain? May I say something?"

She smirked, slouched down farther in the chair.

"You're being bratty. He's your father. She's a teacher that you loved. Wouldn't most daughters be happy for them? I think this is displacement. You're calling it a property dispute. I think it's personal."

"Like . . . like I'm jealous that he's in love with my kindergarten teacher?"

I said, "Frank's a good psychiatrist. All those years in the classroom—"

"Like algebra makes him a psychiatrist?"

I said, "It makes him logical."

"My mother would turn over in her grave—him living in her house with another woman! I think he was fucking her when she was my teacher!"

Well, there it was.

Frank asked calmly, "What proof do you have of that?"

"He chaperoned a field trip to Plymouth Rock! It was a whole day, and he was the only dad."

"That's it? He chaperoned a field trip?"

"Something was up! I remember my mother asking me questions when we got home. Was Daddy extra nice to Miss Eliopoulos? Did they sit together on the bus? Did they eat lunch together? Why would she be quizzing me if she wasn't suspicious?"

I gave Frank a look that said, *I'm no longer interested and even less entertained. She needs a shrink, and you deserve a medal.* He took his keys and his Red Sox cap off their respective hooks. At the back door he said, "Just go over there, for godssakes, Frankie. Bring some doughnuts. Smile when someone comes to the door. Give your father a hug. Tell him if he's going to be there for a while, turn the sprinklers on and restart the trash service."

She finally stood. Over gym shorts, she was wearing a long, transparent skirt in pink tulle. Motion detector Ivy barked the bark that asked, "Am I coming with you?"

What to say to Rain as a farewell? I couldn't go as far as "Nice to meet you," or "Drop by any time." Luckily, a sympathetic truth floated up from somewhere. "I loved my kindergarten teacher, too," I said.

26

Why wait around for Frank to return? He could be mediating at Greenough for hours, and I had notices to pin up all over town. They were beautiful: black and silver text in a Victorian font over a washed-out photograph of the Venus de Milo, my first attempt at subliminal messaging. Keys in hand, Ivy in her crate, I was already at the back door when a cruiser pulled into my driveway and honked. Luke! Maybe a quick, unplanned hello just because he was passing by Montpelier. I checked my face and hair in my phone, but when I opened the door, a deflated Frank was trudging up the steps.

"Are you all right?" I asked.

"I'm okay," he said. Then: "One thing led to another."

"Sit. I'll be right back." I ran outside lest Luke drive off without a hello or goodbye. He was waiting, his window down.

"Where's Frank's car?" I asked. "Was there an accident?"

"No accident."

"Did he faint? Is that why you drove him home?"

"He didn't faint. He'll give you his side of the story. I figured you'd drive him over to Greenough to pick up his car. Give him some time, though." His window was on its way back up, but I heard, "I'll call you tonight."

I blew a kiss with my fingertips, and he nodded, mostly all

business, but with enough of a smile to reassure a nervous entry-level girlfriend.

Inside, I found Frank in the study, drinking beer—rare for him at noon. I joined him on the sofa and asked him what happened.

"I don't know why I even went in with that brat! I should've just dropped her off."

"But?"

"But she wanted to give me some things for safekeeping."

"Because she thought the sons might break stuff? Pawn it? Flog it?"

"They're not even home! One's in college, and the other one is a lifeguard at that lake—" He gestured, vaguely westward.

"So you went in with her . . ."

"She marched in and told them—her own father, for god's sake, and her favorite teacher—that they had to be out by the weekend. To which Stefan said the equivalent of 'Make me.' That didn't stop her. She said she and Juliet were going to challenge the will—'the stupid will,' 'the fucking will'—because they wanted to sell the house, immediately! Then she turned to poor Athena, the teacher, and said, 'My mother wanted him back after her second divorce. But nooooo! He had to punish her for her nothing of a marriage that lasted a minute. Just because he screws someone doesn't mean . . . that it means anything!'"

"So cruel," I said.

"All the time I'm saying, 'Rain, that's enough.' But she kept it up, yelling, practically spitting. And finally, as if he could shock her out of it . . . he slapped her."

His raised, shaky voice brought a worried bark from Ivy, who I'd forgotten in her crate. Freed, she ran into the study and immediately ministered to Frank.

"Did Rain slap him back?" I asked.

He looked away and mumbled, "Thankfully, no."

"Is that it?"

"Not quite."

Silence, then: "I pushed him away from her."

"Knocking him over?"

"Not quite. Unfortunately, his flailing arms caused two lamps to fall over." He winced. "Milk glass and stained glass."

"And broken glass was enough to get the chief of police there?"

"Athena called nine-one-one. I was in the kitchen, the only one who knew where the dustpan was."

"And Luke found *what* when he got there?"

"An earsplitting argument about a will." Frank was stroking Ivy's whole body with two hands, strenuously, unhappily. "Luke was as annoyed as I'd ever seen him. At least Rain quieted down for ten seconds—probably due to the appearance of a handsome police officer. Athena was asking Luke the names of his brothers because she'd had half the kids in town for kindergarten."

"Just now . . . what did Luke mean by 'your side of the story'?"

"My side of the story was a speech; okay, a harangue, directed at the room in general. 'Name a commandment short of murder that this man hasn't broken! Bedding my wife, in my own house, while I was at school; yes, I was a classroom teacher, too! They didn't even have the dignity to sneak off to a motel in Springfield'—on and on I went. Stefan was listening, looking smug and proud. Luke had me by the elbow, saying, 'That's enough, Frank. I don't need this to escalate. Let's go. I'll drive you home.' I told him I had my car, but . . . here I am."

"And Rain? Did she stay?" I asked.

"Presumably, and still on the warpath. She wouldn't let go of 'They're squatting, they're trespassing.' Luke asked, playing dumb very effectively, 'Am I not getting this right? This man is your father. If he moves out, you'll be moving in?' She didn't answer. Instead, she started a new rant, that her father and probably his girlfriend were going to make a ton of money selling her mother's collection, all these valuable antiques! So Luke asked Stefan: 'Are you planning to seize or sell the contents of this house?' Stefan said, 'Valuables? Ginger didn't know shit from Shinola.'

"Then Luke said, 'Okay. We're done here. Mr. Crowley and I are leaving. This is a family matter.' So that's how it was left: me being led away by Luke, effectively for disorderly conduct—"

"For real? He arrested you?"

"No! Thankfully, no one wanted to file a complaint. He didn't want me driving. Did you ever tell him I have low blood pressure?"

I might have. I patted his closest forearm. "You got it out of your system. Some adulterers get killed by the angry husband, and all he got was a tongue-lashing. I think it was way overdue."

"Unfortunately, Luke had to hear it all. I'm not going to sound very stable if he tells his mother about my rant. Thankfully, he missed the shove."

"I'm sure he won't say a word . . . professional confidentiality."

"I'm not proud of this. I'm going to offer to pay for the lamps."

"You probably did Miss Eliopoulos a favor."

"She has a married name now, which I can't remember. She was the most reasonable person there."

I smiled. "She and Stefan are probably having an interesting conversation right now."

Frank seemed to be considering that, stroking Ivy absentmindedly. "When you drive me over to get my car, maybe you could check to see if Rain's still there? I can't go in, but you can."

Into the house whose contents were begging for an estate sale? It could all be junk, but junk with a Brimfield Fair provenance.

Frank said, "I'm thinking I should call Juliet and tell her what happened today. I think she needs to be here."

"Juliet, the sane sister?"

"San*er*," said Frank.

27

I had to ring the doorbell several times. Finally a woman, undoubtedly Athena, her hair a gorgeous gray with streaks of white perfectly framing her face, opened the door, looking pleasantly inquisitive.

"I was wondering if Rain needed a ride somewhere," I said.

"And you are?"

"Emma Lewis."

"A friend?"

Without mentioning Frank by name, I said, "She's my housemate's stepdaughter. He asked me to check on her."

That produced an analytic squint. "He made that request from *jail*?"

"No! He wasn't arrested! The chief of police is a friend of ours. He was only giving Frank a ride home."

After a too-long pause: "I see. Can you come back another time? Francine is resting."

I said it would only take a minute. Mind if I came in?

She said, "Of course. Sorry. Wait here," then whispered, "She has bad cramps, and left her meds in New York."

I murmured some sympathetic syllables and said I'd wait, thank you.

It took two paces and one glance inside Frank's marital

home to diagnose his late wife as crazy. I'd heard "stuffed" and "jammed," and "mausoleum," but what I'd been picturing was merely too much furniture, too close together.

Athena saw me gaping. "I know, hideous. But it's less crowded upstairs. We're pretty much living in the east wing."

East wing? How sprawling was this big brick house? I said, "I do this for a living, and I see a lot of houses . . . but wow."

"Do *what* for a living?"

"Estate sales." I fished out a business card.

She studied it, handed it back to me, then asked if I'd been Emma Lewis in kindergarten, or was that my married name, and had I gone to Coolidge Elementary.

"Same name. Not married. But I went to DeWitt."

"Then you had Maryanne Kelleher! We student-taught together!"

"That's nice . . . Can you tell Rain I'm here?"

She whispered, "I'd tell you to make yourself at home, but who'd want to set one foot in there?"

I would. This was beyond crowded, beyond jam-packed to psychotic. This wasn't collecting for one's own sake. This had to be a future business venture, Ginger Crowley Vintage Valuables, Inc. I squeezed my way through the bad and the really bad, phone in hand, photo app at the ready.

I could say this much: Two banquet-sized mahogany dining-room tables held lamps, rolled-up carpets, and bulging cardboard cartons labeled in black Sharpie: "Life," "Look," "Playboy," "Reader's Digest," "Pop. Mech." "Gourmet," "Bon Appetit," "yearbooks," "pic. frames," "costume jwrly," "paperbcks." I counted three sofas. Chairs were everywhere; Ginger seemed to favor Louis XVs, with curved frames and dramatic feet. The oak partners desk had potential, even with the cigarette burns. Ornately framed mirrors and sports posters hung on walls. How many more rooms were packed to the gills like this one? Frank would know. Luckily, I wasn't snapping pictures when I heard a stern "Excuse me?"

Had no one told me that Stefan was shockingly handsome and fit? Seventy-what? The family's social history instantly made sense, except for Ginger's taking up with another man while still married to this specimen. Dressed for golf in salmon-pink trousers and a black polo shirt, he was holding a half sandwich, very likely tuna fish. "We're eating," he said. "Not a good time."

I asked if I could have a minute with Rain.

"Rain," he grumbled. "Ginger and I named her Francine, which I use out of respect for her late mother . . . And you want to collect her on whose behalf?"

I said, "I'm Frank's housemate. I drove him back here to get his car—"

"Housemate," he repeated with a smarmy smile. "Interesting. Care to define?"

I considered returning a cold, offended stare, but instead said calmly, "Frank rents a room in my house. I've known him all my life," then threw in as corroboration, "He was the best man at my parents' wedding."

"Renting a room like an itinerant salesman when he could've stayed here after Ginger died? No one was kicking him out."

Frank's noninheritance notwithstanding, I said, "He wasn't comfortable here. He found it somewhat"—I gestured around me—"congested." Then, another try: "I'm here to give Francine a ride back to the inn or the train station or . . . wherever."

"We have a car. In fact, we have three. My partner has two sons who both drive."

"Her sister's concerned," I fibbed.

He took a bite from his sandwich, then called out a mayonnaisy "Francine! Someone's here who'd like an audience with you."

I said, "She knows me. She had breakfast at my house this morning."

"After arriving with guns blazing, no doubt."

Why dignify that, even though true? Before I could confirm or deny, he said, "Her sister got all the manners."

Francine still hadn't answered her father's summons. "Are you sure she's okay?" I asked.

"Why wouldn't she be?"

Was that a challenge? I said, "Because you slapped her, and the police had to be called."

"She was hysterical. Someone had to bring her down to earth."

Like on television, I thought; like a soap-opera slap that instantly brings the hysterical ex-wife back to her senses. Just as I was about to call out Rain's name myself, she appeared, with a few garments, still on hangers, draped over her arm. "What?" she asked.

"Do you need a ride somewhere?"

She seemed to like that question. "Not if you can get my stuff at the inn and drop it back here. Do you know when checkout time is?"

"Probably noon," said her father. Pointing to the clothes over her arm, he said, "You don't have to switch rooms. Theo can take the blue room. Nico's in Juliet's old room." And to me, proudly, "Six bedrooms."

I asked if I could speak to Rain alone. When she nodded, Stefan retreated, walking backward with some overly theatrical bowing.

I was sick of this mission, and sick of Rain. I said, "This isn't complicated: Frank wanted me to check on you and see if you needed a lift somewhere. Yes or no?"

"No. But maybe later? Or tomorrow?"

Without endorsing that, I said goodbye, opened the front door, and left.

"Do I have your contact info if I change my mind?" she called after me.

I said, "I'm in the phone book," even if I wasn't; even if there was no such thing anymore.

Back on Montpelier, Frank was in the driveway, washing his car with a giant sponge. He asked what took me so long and who I'd spoken to over on Greenough. Instead of answering, I retrieved a large, grease-stained brown bag from the passenger seat and held it up. He smiled. He loved fish and chips.

I went inside for knives, forks, plates, and malt vinegar. Back at the picnic table, food unpacked, Ivy sniffing hopefully, I told Frank that Rain seemed to be staying over on Greenough. I hadn't quizzed her. Could we drop the subject?

"Gladly. I've had enough unpleasantness for one day."

I told him I'd seen Ginger's stuff. Ye gods.

"There's no explanation for the hoarding. I might say about another woman that it was filling up an empty nest, but not Ginger. I *do* know she was going through . . . hormonal changes."

I tried to stifle a laugh, but unsuccessfully. He asked what was funny.

"Sorry! No, not funny. It's just . . . your saying 'hormonal changes' like it was no more personal than a toothache. I was smiling at how far you've come."

"Maybe *too* far! If you'd heard me over at the house, warning Athena about Stefan! I don't even know the woman! And why the hell did Rain call me and not her father when she got to town?"

"Because you're a hundred times nicer than he is. Plus, she was plotting to evict him." I asked Frank to pass the tartar sauce and said, "When I asked Lars if he was using haddock, he said 'for you, always haddock.'"

Good. More eating, more compliments for Lars and Fjord Fish Market. When Frank's phone rang, he said, "I'm not letting this delicious lunch get cold." But when it rang again a minute later, he sighed and picked up. I heard a sharp "No. That would *not* be appropriate. . . . No, I don't have it. And for God's sake, that's not what nine-one-one is for."

"What's wrong?" I whispered.

His frown said *Only more foolishness*. Then to his caller, "You can take care of that yourself. The inn is less than a mile away. Walk there. We're eating," And without a good-bye, he ended the call, scowling.

"Rain, obviously," I said. "Is she moving back to the inn?"

"No. She wanted me to get her bag. When I told her to walk over and get it herself, she said 'Walk? With a bag that doesn't have wheels!' "

"But that other thing she wanted to call nine-one-one about? Did she tell you why?"

"She didn't have to tell me why! She wanted the name and phone number of the police officer who'd taken me away."

"Luke."

"Of course Luke."

"Because . . ."

"Why do you *think*?"

Did I have to be delicate? No. I asked, shaking a french fry for emphasis, one eyebrow arched, "Would that be, by any chance . . . to *fuck* him?"

"Oh, Emma," Frank sighed.

28

I emailed press releases to the *Boston Globe*, the *Boston Herald*, the *Springfield Republican*, the *Hartford Courant*, the *Worcester Telegram & Gazette*, and of course the local Harrow paper.

Shouldn't "estate sale at a former brothel" have been a scoop, or at least enough to pique a reporter's prurient interest? After five days of nothingness from the bigger papers, I called the *Echo*.

Marcia Kirshner had given me the name and phone number of the reporter who'd covered the FBI raid that effectively ended her marriage to Gideon, the crypto scammer. She said the guy, Orwell, was smart, fair, and menschy. When he didn't pick up, I left a short but compelling voicemail, saying that a former B and B in Harrow had conducted dual operations, one illegal.

He called me back, sounding bored. "Let me guess: gambling?" adding that he usually covered hard news. Sorry.

"Would this be hard news—that an inn on one of Harrow's grandest streets was actually a house of ill repute?"

"Meaning?"

Meaning? "Meaning men paid to have sex on the premises."

"With . . . ?"

"Women."

"Prostitutes?"

He repeated the word, then asked what my connection was to this house of ill repute.

"It's all in the press release. I'm with Estate of Mind."

A long pause, some clacking of keys, and finally, "You're saying that your state of mind prompted you to go public now?"

"No, Estate of Mind is my company. I'm doing a huge estate sale there over Labor Day weekend."

"So this has nothing to do with your having worked there?"

"Wait! Do you mean as one of Lola's Ladies?"

He repeated "Lola's Ladies" with, finally, some gusto. I said that was the corporate name of the VIP escort service headquartered at 1010 Quail Ridge Road. And please note: I never set foot in the place until it needed deaccessioning.

"Name?"

"Estate of Mind."

"No, your name."

"Emma Lewis."

"L-O-U-I-S? And you found out about this how?"

"L-E-W-I-S. There was a For Sale sign up in front of the house, so I called the real estate agent—"

"No, how you learned it was a whorehouse."

"Firsthand, from the owner, though she never used that term—"

"Name?"

"Lois M-A-N-K-O-P-F. She used 'Lola' professionally."

"Mankopf? Like the cop?"

"Ex-cop. Ex-husband."

"Interesting. Was he involved?"

Though the answer should've been "Pretty much, yes," it wasn't what I was calling about. Returning to his previous question, how I'd learned that the bed-and-breakfast was a brothel, I said, "She was worried about photos left behind in a file cabinet—"

"Photos of . . . ?"

"Women. She wanted me to get rid of them."

"Naked photos?"

"I assume so. She didn't want to embarrass anyone who might be someone's wife and mother now."

"This was what? Escorts on duty? Pick your pleasure?"

Why had I gone there? I said, "I haven't seen the contents."

"What about the johns? Records? Phone numbers?"

Though I was sure the file cabinet's contents would embarrass men and break up marriages all over New England, I said, "No idea."

"I wonder if the feds could've had a wiretap on the phone. That would be interesting. It's how Eliot Spitzer was caught."

"There was no raid. No arrests. Especially with her ex-husband being the chief of police."

"Her ex? Must've been an amicable divorce, if he looked the other way."

We were so off track. I said, "I'm not judging. I'm only bringing up Lola's line of work as a marketing tool. I told Mrs. Mankopf that nudes are art, and I sell art."

"She must've given you the key, if she wanted you to burn whatever's in that file cabinet."

"No, she did not."

Technically speaking, that was true. I hadn't been given the key. But I'd found it.

It was in a chenille bathrobe, discovered during a routine search of all pockets in all closets. I knew by its half-size and its molded plastic cap that it was a key to a mailbox, a strongbox, a jewelry box, or possibly, *the* file cabinet.

I didn't announce my find or run straight to the beau parlor, because Vanessa, who'd hinted at some future gainful use of the X-rated files, was at the kitchen table, frowning at her laptop.

I knew why: She'd announced earlier that she was working on

a list of household items she couldn't bear to part with. "Returning to Boston tonight?" I asked.

"It's Friday, so yes, definitely," with eyebrows raised to remind me of her enviable social life.

Frank was present, too. He'd insisted on replacing burned-out bulbs and cleaning the cellar because we'd be selling the big-ticket washer and dryer. I yelled from the top of the stairs that he should call it a night.

"I need ten more minutes to clean up all the mouse droppings before I leave. If there's more tomorrow, I'll know what's what."

I didn't like lying, or even withholding. My hardest-working, most dedicated volunteer deserved to know what my mission was. I joined him in the cellar, took the key out of my pocket, and said, "Possibly to the top-secret file cabinet."

"Possibly? You haven't tried it?"

"Vanessa's still here. I'll find out when we have the house to ourselves."

"I don't know, Emma. It sounds to me like breaking and entering."

"I wouldn't take anything. I'd just be looking."

"But . . . is it necessary? Or just—you'll forgive me—snooping?"

"It's what we do! Beth once found a vintage handbag in a file cabinet—genuine alligator! Two women were fighting over it at the sale."

When he only shrugged, looking both dubious and unhappy, I asked, "Aren't you curious?"

He sighed. "If you want to look at those pictures, that's fine. But it's not a job for mixed company."

I went back in the morning, Vanessa gone, helped myself to a double espresso, then straight to the beau parlor. When the key slipped right into the lock, I closed my eyes, pausing for a few long seconds before opening the top drawer. *Think this through. There could be regrets and consequences. What if I recognized a friend, a friend's father, brother, or uncle; a neighbor, a teacher, a Winooski?*

But I'd come this far. I slid the top drawer open. The front folder was hot pink and labeled "Tonight," which I took to mean *On duty; take your pick.* Here were eight women, not necessarily beauty queens as billed, but doing their best with makeup, eyelashes, voluptuous hair, and breast augmentations. I sensed that Lois had been behind the camera, asking for what she thought men wanted to see, which was everything.

On the back of the photos were names. Could these women really be Victoria, Elizabeth, Isabella, Juliana, Anastasia, Antoinette, Guinevere, and Camilla? I guessed no, because each name was attached by Post-it, transferable to whoever was on duty.

That was enough of that. I opened the second drawer and took out a bulging green folder filled with receipts, which I took to the velvet banquette for examination. Had her clients really paid by credit card? The vender was an innocent-sounding "The Quail's Nest," but still; didn't these men have wives who saw their credit card statements, or personal assistants who could blackmail them? There were printed invoices for cash payments; the who, what, when, how long, and which escort, filled in by hand.

Hadn't "discretion" been Lois's watchword? Yet here was everything: names, addresses, disbursements—a whopping average of $1,000 for a trip up the stairway to heaven. Once again, I asked myself, what was my goal? If I recognized names, then what? I certainly wasn't going to embarrass or confront anyone. At most I'd reveal a name for gossipy fun over a glass of wine with Luke or Marcia or over breakfast with Frank.

I was about to return the green folder to the cabinet when three names rewarded the snoop I'd become. Though it was utterly predictable, I still let out a yelp when I saw the first of many half-price charges to Werner F. Mankopf. I understood the discounted rate . . . but *really*—in his own ex-wife's house, with his own daughter concierging?

But Manny wasn't the most startling steady customer whose name I found. That honor went to Stefan St. Pierre, proud philanderer and the love of Ginger Crowley's life. Further: on every one of his six invoices, what followed "Hours" was "overnite." And the name after "with" was unfailingly a handwritten "Lola."

29

I was too distracted and agog to do anything but go straight home to tell Frank what Lois's recordkeeping had revealed.

His car was there, but so was the green Subaru I knew to be Connie's. Was I supposed to know about the anonymous letter she wrote that got Manny Mankopf fired? I'd be able to tell by the cautionary look on Frank's face when I joined them.

If they were joinable, and not upstairs.

I called his phone, and he answered immediately. "Would I be interrupting anything?" I asked.

"No, of course not. We're having a nice chat."

"I could come back later."

"Don't you dare! I want a full report."

I whispered, "In front of Connie?"

"Yes, in front of Connie." I could tell he was saying that with a smile for her benefit. She'd been added to the team.

What a pretty woman—petite, blond, and beauty-parlor styled, but not in the extreme; not even dolled up but in a tie-dyed T-shirt and Bermuda shorts. She jumped to her feet when I walked into the kitchen, causing double Ivy excitement over me arriving and this near-stranger's sudden movement.

"I'm Connie," she said, hand extended. "And I know who you are."

I wished I'd looked a little more presentable. Had I even combed my hair when I'd set off this morning? "Lovely to meet you," I said. "Please sit."

While Frank was getting me coffee, Connie was smiling at me in a way that was pleasantly appraising. Was it up to me to bring up Luke? She saved me from further deliberation by saying, "Luke speaks of you so fondly."

I said, feeling my cheeks flush, "You have a very nice son."

"Four nice sons," Frank piped up. He delivered my mug along with a bulging muffin on a small plate. I asked Connie with mock wonderment, "You didn't bake on such a hot day, did you?"

"I start early, before it gets too hot."

"Would you believe apricot muffins?" asked Frank.

"Apricot oatmeal, to be exact," said Connie.

"Tell me everything," he said.

When I hesitated, Frank said, "Connie knows why you went there this morning. I didn't think you'd mind."

Was this time for a little lighthearted joke? No, because it brought the conversation back to Luke and his job if I alluded to possible unlawful possession of someone else's key. I broke a piece off the muffin, chewed, swallowed, and complimented it. I began with, "You know about everything? I mean what business went on under the guise of a bed-and-breakfast?"

"Girls turning tricks?" she said. "Sure. It was hard to miss—the comings and goings."

We hadn't referred to the escort service as turning tricks before, and probably that wasn't technically true, since no one was soliciting out on the streets of Harrow. Where to start? I asked her if she knew the role of the red file cabinet.

Frank explained, "By 'role,' I think Emma means what its contents were."

Connie said, "I know it was locked all the time, and only Lois had the key."

"Until now," I blurted out.

"She gave you the key?" Connie asked.

I explained how I'd learned from experience—well my *parents'* experience—that women often hid jewelry and things in pockets.

"Did you open it?" Connie asked.

I said I did, out of pure nosiness. Lois and Vanessa had made such a fuss about me burning its contents . . . meaning, what if there was something in there that needed to be reported to the police?

"Like children, God forbid," said Frank. "Or what if Lois was blackmailing her customers?"

Connie said, "It sickens me."

"The whole enterprise?" asked Frank. "Manny? The memories?"

She answered with one word: "Vanessa."

"Of course, if you helped out there, you would know her."

"Vanessa was behind everything! Who do you think those girls were?"

I looked at Frank. Vanessa, the daughter who helped out during her school vacations? I squeaked, "Could you explain what you mean by 'She was behind everything'?"

"It started with one girl! You know how school chums talk. She had a friend—how to put this politely?—who was the most sexually advanced, sophisticated, whatever, in Vanessa's clique at school."

Frank asked, "How old was this school chum?"

"She must've been a senior, because she was graduating and needed a job."

"Tell me you didn't mean a *high school* senior," he pleaded.

"No, college." Her sad expression said *Unfortunately, of legal age*.

"Are you saying that it was Vanessa who turned it from B and B to brothel?" I asked.

"Brothel first, B and B simultaneously as a cover."

"One girl doesn't make a brothel," I said.

"It wasn't one girl," Connie murmured.

I asked, "Vanessa, too?"

She winced—a wince I thought was more about Frank's delicacy than ratting Vanessa out. "I don't know. Why else would she be so proud, so approving of the family business? So *into* it?"

Though I knew the answer, I asked anyway, "And Lois?"

"In a pinch," said Connie.

Was this the time to confess how much I knew? If she hadn't been there, I'd have blurted everything out to Frank the minute I'd returned, but I had a lot to weigh: Connie was Luke's mother. Connie might disapprove of my detective work, of going through records and photographs without Lois's permission. I started with "Did you know Stefan St. Pierre?"

"Of course. He was one of the few overnighters. He liked to linger over a cup of coffee in the morning."

I hadn't told Frank yet, hence the look of fixed, angry astonishment. I said, "I was going to tell you, first thing."

"Stefan was a customer?" he asked. "A john?"

I said, "A regular."

"When?"

Of course he would ask when. "Connie knows I have a history with that man," he explained.

She reached across the table and squeezed his hand.

I said to Frank, "I was too startled by the Lois part of the invoice to look at the dates."

"The Lois part?" he repeated.

I said, "I don't think you'll be shocked to hear that's who he was with every time."

"*With?* As in he paid to have sex with Lois?" Frank asked.

"They deserve each other!" Connie said.

Was I supposed to know about how she'd rebuffed Manny, had

repulsed his unwelcome advance and the anonymous letter that followed and got him fired? She asked, "What are you going to do with this information?"

I said, "Nothing."

Frank said, "I can think of a use."

Connie and I both turned to him and waited.

"Evidence. What if any girl was coerced? What if there was sex trafficking? Emma has an aunt—I'm very sorry to say—who was on the roster."

I said, "A step-aunt, famous for marrying her customer."

"It had to be . . . I forget her name . . . from some eastern European country? She was a sweet girl, always hoping—" But she shook her head, a retraction of whatever the rest of her sentence was going to be.

"Hoping to marry an American citizen?" I asked.

"As if," said Frank.

"As if what?" Connie asked.

"As if she was going to find a husband among the married men who paid to have sex with women of the night. She was lucky that a nice guy like Paul showed up."

Connie and I shared a look that was a meeting of the minds. We were asking each other: *Was there a kinder man in all of Harrow than Frank Crowley?*

30

As soon as Luke and I walked into Noodle Dynasty, I heard my name. Marcia Kirshner, sitting with a man I didn't know, was gesturing *join us!* I did, just for a quick hello, or so I thought.

"You've met telephonically," she said. "This is Jeff Orwell . . . from the *Echo*. He interviewed you."

I said, "Thanks, but Luke's on duty, taking a quick supper break, so maybe next time—"

"It's going well, I see," said Marcia.

I motioned to Luke, who was not only in uniform but fully equipped. He knew Marcia, the high school valedictorian who returned to teach at Macmillan despite offers elsewhere.

Unsmiling, Luke said, "Orwell, right?"

The reporter finally stood up, shook Luke's hand, confirmed he was Jeffrey Orwell, then shook mine. He was younger than the middle-aged cynic he'd seemed on the phone, maybe mid-thirties, with curly black hair beginning to gray and appraising eyes behind round wire-rimmed glasses, defiantly wearing a Yankees T-shirt in Red Sox country. "Nice to actually meet you," I said, and to Luke, "Jeffrey is going to write something about my upcoming sale."

That wasn't exactly true. I'd been hoping for a tantalizing feature; his version of that was names that he could Elliot-Spitzify in an exposé.

"Sit, sit," Marcia instructed, pushing and pulling the next table closer to make a foursome.

"Okay?" I asked Luke.

He said, "Sure," with a look I translated as *Do we have a choice?* Marcia waved to a waitress and pantomimed something that resulted in menus being delivered.

How to ask Marcia the nature of their get-together? She must have recognized the inquisitive look on my face because she volunteered, "Jeffrey covered Gideon's arrest."

"I know," I said. "It's why you recommended I pitch my story to him."

I thought I was seeing Jeffrey smirk, as if he'd been misidentified as a reporter who covered yard sales. Smiling nonetheless, Marcia continued, "Jeff thought there might be a follow-up piece to Gideon's fall from grace, about the unknowing wife of the Bitcoin Bandit."

"À la Ruth Madoff," said Jeffrey.

"I disabused him of that theory in about two minutes," said Marcia.

"Two minutes where?" I asked.

"I'll back up. We'd talked several times by phone. Jeff figured out that we could talk in public without me dissolving into tears. We met in person at the Over Easy. I was determined *not* to be Ruth Madoff; not to skulk around town in a baseball cap and sunglasses. I knew nothing about what Gideon was up to! You'd have to be a forensic accountant to know what he was doing! The smartest thing I ever did was to keep our money separate, my mother's advice—Emma knows my mother. Three marriages! Gid and I had one small joint household checking account, and that was it."

Just as I was wondering how to stem this narration, Luke said, "I'm not sure we should be discussing this. I might be called to testify."

"You and me both," said Marcia.

I asked Luke why he'd be called to testify.

Suddenly looking and sounding official, he said, "They sub-poena everyone."

"Were you there?" I asked.

"Pro forma. It was my town, as backup, if someone needed handling—"

"Such as the wife?" Marcia asked.

"The wife, associates of his, overnight guests, visiting parents, a dog . . . but"—finally he smiled—"I knew she wasn't a section twenty-one."

Jeffrey picked up his phone. In seconds he read aloud, "Transporting the mentally ill. Section 21 of Chapter 123."

Marcia said, "I froze! I didn't do a thing. You can imagine— the FBI breaks down my door at five in the morning. I might've looked like a crazy woman because I was screaming at Gideon, 'What the fuck did you do? Why are they taking you away?' I had an eight o'clock class! What time could I call a lawyer? I think Luke stayed. Did I offer you coffee?"

"You did. I declined."

I said, "I must've missed the piece Jeffrey wrote about Marcia."

Jeffrey shook his head. "After a certain point, after so many interviews, I couldn't. Not without full disclosure. Of course I covered the raid and the arrest."

"On the front page," said Marcia. "Not great for a tenure-track associate professor. God, his parents. They're still in shock."

I sensed Luke had heard enough. Barely changing the subject, I asked him how he knew Jeffrey.

Luke said, "He hangs around the station. We're the crime beat."

On cue, Jeffrey asked, "I saw on the log that you were called to a domestic disturbance on Greenough. Anything there? Anyone arrested?"

"No."

"A misunderstanding," I said. "Not that Luke told me anything."

"Greenough," Marcia mused, shooting me a look that said *You'll tell me later.*

Did Jeffrey ever take a night off? Apparently not. While I needlessly studied the menu I knew by heart, he startled me by asking, "That file cabinet you told me about. What's happening there?"

"What file cabinet?" Luke asked.

"At the whorehouse." Jeffrey was speaking loud enough that a man across the narrow aisle looked up.

I whispered, "Maybe we could refer to it as the B and B."

Why had I brought up the file cabinet in my first conversation with Jeffrey? I remembered: I was trying to pique his interest in the risqué aspect of the estate sale. I said, "The file cabinet is still locked." That was true; I had indeed locked it when I'd left, and put the key back where I'd found it.

Luke, behind his menu, was shooting me a quizzical look, and for good reason: I hadn't yet told him about my trespassing, let alone what johns the invoices had outed. I was saving that confession for Saturday night or Sunday breakfast, in private.

"Could you get a search warrant?" Jeffrey asked Luke.

"For what?"

"The contents of the cabinet could be evidence in a criminal case," said Jeffrey.

"No, I'm not getting a warrant," said Luke. "And that's without me even knowing what you're talking about."

"Aren't you the reason the operation shut down—a new, upstanding chief comes to town?"

"Maybe," said Luke.

I was tempted to say, "Besides, the statute of limitations on prostitution, which by the way is only a misdemeanor in

Massachusetts, has run out." Instead, I raised a finger to my lips to stem further public pronouncements as the waitress approached.

With a smile, Luke said, "The usual," then recited, "Sesame noodles, Kung Po chicken, Salt and Pepper Shrimp," adding, "I don't have much time."

I poured tea all around. Sensing that the nearby couple was still all ears, I said in my best promotional pitch, "So! I hope I'll see everyone at the estate sale at the former Quail's Nest B and B over Labor Day weekend. My biggest ever."

"With an intriguing past," said Marcia, in her lecture-hall voice. "The word is, sale of the century."

I was rewarded. The neighboring woman asked, "What's the address?" I fished out a business card and a pen, and wrote down "1010 Quail Ridge Rd."

But we weren't done with the one-upmanship. Jeffrey apparently had to say, "A cathouse, right in the middle of Harrow, Massachusetts. Not one arrest, right, Chief?"

Luke made himself busy separating his chopsticks, then finally said, "Before my time."

Marcia said, "I don't think Jeffrey was implying that you were derelict in your duty—"

I said, "Especially since Mr. Orwell has surely read up on Mankopf and knows about his pimping and the overall shadiness that led to his removal."

"He wasn't fired," Luke said quietly. "He resigned." His walkie-talkie squawked. Had he keyed the mic himself?

Marcia wailed, "Does that mean you have to go? I hope we didn't ruin your date."

I let Luke answer. He said, "Of course not. Always nice to see you."

"Time enough to eat, at least?" I asked as the platters arrived.

"Sure. If I inhale it."

"In which case, let's get you a knife and fork."

That prompted Jeffrey to inform us that he'd spent his junior year in Shanghai. He trapped a single grain of rice with his chopsticks, then ate it triumphantly.

I looked at Marcia. We knew each other so well. "A man of many talents," she said.

31

Who'd said Manny Mankopf was in Florida, retired and disgraced?

Everyone.

It was Luke who spotted his return, in the form of a business card, which he photographed and thoughtfully texted to me.

Werner "Manny" Mankopf
Nationally recognized master
of the brush & sponge

Of course it boasted two phone numbers, his website, and a compliment from someone identified as "art critic, blogger & influencer."

I texted back, Where'd you find this?

Stuck in my door.

That was enough for me to abandon texting and call him. He answered with "I thought you'd appreciate that."

"He's back?"

"Unless someone else is leaving his business cards around town."

"Are you going to call him?"

"No."

"Kind of creepy that he came to your apartment, don't you think?"

Luke said, "He's a creepy guy."

I said, "Still, 'Nationally recognized master' made my day." Then straight to: "Do you think he's back because of the estate sale?"

"No idea. Would that matter?"

"It *would* matter if he's opposed to it, or just wants a piece of the action."

Luke said, "As you know, ma'am, I don't deal with hypotheticals. Just the facts."

I said, "I love when you talk like that."

I was driving back from an unexciting split-level on Bridge Street. It had nice views of the Holyoke Range, but scenery doesn't move contents. I'd told the widow that Estate of Mind would send a contract. I had to, after letting my marketing slip, too comfortable living rent-free, and with "the manse," as we'd started calling the Mankopf house, putting stars in my eyes. And after losing the Duggan sale to Goldie's Oldies.

When a call came from my own 413 area code, I answered with a professionally brisk "Emma Lewis," which earned a gruff "Chief Mankopf here."

First impression: liar. He wasn't chief here or anywhere. I said, "I'm driving—"

"Call me back," he ordered and hung up.

I pulled into a small plaza (nail salon, hair salon, weed and wine shops), took a pen and notebook from my newly silk-screened Estate of Mind canvas bag, and hit his number.

I could hear voices in the background. "Who's this?" he barked.

"You just called me. Emma Lewis."

To someone other than me, I heard a jauntier "C'mon. You can do better than that."

The woman he must've been addressing said, "It's weighed. See—in portions."

I said, "Mr. Mankopf? Can you talk?"

"I'm at the Big Bagel, begging for a decent amount of smoked salmon." Then, "Thanks, doll. I used to be chief of police in this town."

There was only one bagel place in Harrow, and it wasn't called Big Bagel. He must've found a table, because I heard a chair being scraped along the linoleum, and the clap of a tray hitting Formica. He said, "I didn't have breakfast. I'm doing that intermittent thing where you don't eat till noon. It's a killer."

"How's that working?" I asked.

"I lost three pounds the first week. I can't even put half and half in my coffee when I get up." A pause, and then with his mouth full, "I want the key."

Oh God. Good thing I wasn't driving. I asked, "To what?"

"The house!"

Whew. I said, "If you're referring to the property at ten-ten Quail Ridge Road, it's standard operating procedure for the purveyor—"

"Not at my house, it isn't."

Does one challenge the likes of Manny Mankopf? Trying the born-yesterday approach, I said, "I'm sorry. I didn't realize you were a party to this sale. Lois Mankopf is my client."

"Lois Mankopf? Did you notice her name? *Mankopf*?"

I waited a few polite seconds before saying, "My understanding is that you and she are divorced."

"Ha! Convenient, isn't it?"

I said I wasn't sure what that meant.

"Shacking up in California with that gold digger she met on a cruise! I don't know what she told him. He probably wouldn't give a crap anyway if she was married; even if she was cheating on"—his voice rose—"a goddamn chief of police!"

Was he showing off for the neighboring tables? I said, "I'm going to call Mrs. Mankopf now."

"What for? How old are you? Who's in charge of this sale?"

I repeated, "I'm going to call Mrs. Mankopf and set this straight, because from everyone's testimony—"

"Testimony! What testimony? My case never went to trial! She filed for divorce. So what? I never signed the papers."

Is that how divorces worked? I'd call the attorney who fine-tuned my contract template. Though I said, "I'm not sure why you're calling me," I *did* know. He was going to rip up the contract, or—who knows what else?

"Can you meet me here?" he asked.

"No, sorry—"

"C'mon. I want to pick your brain. I can be very very nice when I want to be. Emily, right?"

"Emma." I asked who gave him my number.

"My daughter. Why does that matter?"

It mattered because it meant that father and daughter were conspiring to the detriment of Estate of Mind. "The contract's been signed," I said, "and it's airtight."

I heard more loud chewing, then a gulp. "Coffee's crap. Have Lo-Lo send me a copy," he said.

Did I really need to talk to Lois? I was disinclined to call Vanessa, her father's ally, but surely a daughter would know if her parents ever divorced.

Vanessa answered her phone with, "What now?"

"Just a heads-up that I'd be coming by this afternoon. There are a few things I still need to price."

"Is it necessary? My dad's visiting from Florida."

Did I have to be tactful with the graceless Vanessa? "One legal fine point: "Are your parents still married?"

"They're as good as divorced. Why?"

"I'm asking because if the house is jointly owned—"

"You mean, is he fine with my mother selling it? They had no choice. Who was going to pay the real estate and school taxes on an empty house?"

"If the house is jointly owned, there could be issues over who wants what."

Her voice lowered. "He's here. I can't really talk."

I didn't say *That's funny, because two minutes ago he was at Best Bagel.* Instead I said, "Can you tell me what brought him back to town?"

"It's over a hundred degrees in Fort Lauderdale. And me—I'm his only child. He misses me terribly."

Her voice went suddenly wobbly. I could hardly bring the conversation back to what could threaten my potential blockbuster of a sale. I said, "I'm an only child, too. My parents will be coming up for the sale. They lived in Harrow forever . . . I'm sure they know your dad."

"Yours probably weren't ridden out of town on a rail—for nothing! He kept Quail's Nest brochures at the station! So what! Do you ever see the bulletin board there? Business cards, taxis, restaurants, home health aides, support groups, Catholic masses. People stop in the station all the time for directions—out-of-towners. It made perfect sense, and all legal!"

Like a cowardly capitalist, I said, "I know he was proud of such a beautiful house . . . and its murals." Then, ever helpful: "I'm sure you remember that we made an official list of what's for sale. We can't have random relatives showing up and saying 'I love this. I'm keeping it.' Believe me, that *does* happen."

"You're worried that he'd swoop in and grab something out of a customer's hand?"

"I just meant he might not have had the chance—"

"He's not someone you can push around," said Vanessa. "He's a big guy—and he's not afraid of a bunch of teachers."

What did she just say? I breathed in, and I breathed out, once, twice. Clearly she'd seen my website's bio boast about my father's distinguished career. Add Frank Crowley—the very man she'd greeted in various stages of undress—to the honor roll of math teachers emeriti. What hypocrisy. What nerve.

Though I usually tried not to call our current chief of police during working hours, I did. "A quick question: Is Manny's return a violation of a restraining order?"

Luke laughed. "If only."

"You'd think someone would've said, 'You're a sexual harasser and an embarrassment to this town. You're fired, and we don't want to see your face in Harrow ever again.' No?"

"Probably in executive session. I wasn't here yet. Oops. Gotta go. Duty calls."

"Be safe!" I said.

Later, presumably walking his beat, Luke sent a photo: the window of Frangella Fine Arts, advertising a show titled *Colossal Formats by W. M. Mankopf.*

My phone rang as I was gaping at the image, my eyes popping. "What is wrong with Mike Frangella?" Luke demanded. "Nobody liked Manny! Who's gonna want one of his paintings? They don't even have frames!"

Besides, they were awful. They featured foul words stenciled over muddied backgrounds in different clashing hues. One had local zip codes interspersed with the swears. I said, "Maybe Mike is hoping to sell it like celebrity art, like Sylvester Stallone's or George Bush's." More enlarging showed me the date and time of the opening. Should I go? I went to most of Mike's openings as thanks for his appraising the occasional paintings I thought could be worth something.

I asked Luke, "Want to come to the opening? August twenty-second, six to eight."

"I don't want to be in the same room with Manny Mankopf *or* his paintings. No way. I'm sure there's an important game I need to watch that night."

I said—a test, flirty and disingenuous—"I totally understand. It's not as if we're exclusive or anything . . ."

"Speak for yourself," said Luke.

32

Frank's was an unusually abbreviated text: Cd u pick up Juliet St. P @Peter Pan bus Spfld, arrvg 10:05? Still waiting 4 crown. Sorry!

Though it sounded urgent, I wasn't worried; he was at the dentist. Nor was it totally out of the blue because I knew he'd summoned Juliet, his more reasonable stepdaughter, to Harrow for the possible rescue of her sister.

It was 9:20. I texted back OK, leaving now.

As my satellite office, my van always needed decluttering. The mess was mostly notices waiting to be circulated, the paraphernalia needed to tack, staple, or tape them up; clothes meant for the dry cleaner, and a blanket that protected the passenger seat from Ivy's shedding. I did a quick cleanup but left my latest Estate of Mind brochure within reach, should conversation turn to my line of work, reinforced by the new, custom E. of M. T-shirt I'd quickly changed into.

Would I know Juliet? The woman who jumped to her feet in Peter Pan's waiting room, smiling hopefully, was close to six feet tall, with the kind of long-limbed skinniness that high school coaches recruit the first day of freshman year. She was wearing a long, peasanty floral-print sleeveless dress and a necklace that looked like shellacked cherry pits. Her reddish hair was long, pulled back, messily clipped up. No suitcase, just a backpack.

I introduced myself and explained the substitution of drivers.

"I didn't give him any notice! Thank you! Not just for this—for your house! He's so happy there."

I freed myself from her hug and led her to the van, apologizing for it not being a car. As soon as we were both buckled in, I asked, "Straight to Greenough Street?"

She winced. "Rain isn't answering her phone, and her stupid mailbox is filled. I texted her but so far, nothing."

"And you can't just drop by?"

"I'd rather not . . ."

How much was I supposed to know about her dysfunctional family? I hadn't witnessed Stefan slapping Rain, or Frank shoving Stefan, but I had firsthand knowledge of Frank arriving home from the fracas in a police car. I said, "Frank probably told you that things got out of hand, and someone called nine-one-one?"

"He gave me the blow-by-blow. It's all ridiculous! Suddenly Rain is charging up to Harrow to evict Dad and what's-her-name."

What's-her-name? Athena, the adored former teacher of Rain? I glanced over to check Juliet's expression, which struck me as sincere and genuinely uninformed.

I said, "Athena was Rain's kindergarten teacher. She's living there—"

"Miss *Eliopoulos*?"

"Yes," I said. "Her maiden name—I don't know her married one."

"We both had her. It's unbelievable that she'd be with him." A pause, and then, "She had to know we were his daughters. I mean Stefan St. Pierre, Juliet St. Pierre, Francine St. Pierre . . . not even a birthday card or email that said, 'I'm dating your father. Hope you'll visit'?"

"I'm surprised Rain didn't tell you. She claimed she was rushing up here to evict your father, but maybe it was to save Athena from him."

Obviously unaware that I knew the stipulations of Ginger's

will, Juliet explained, "If Rain and I don't want to live in the house, it goes to our dad. Just like that! We can't just sell it like normal beneficiaries could. Rain wants to contest the will, but how much is that going to cost?"

I asked if anyone had talked to the lawyer who'd drawn it up.

"I should! I want to ask, 'Didn't you say to my mother, "Stefan St. Pierre is *not* your husband. You're leaving the house to your daughters, period, end of sentence. If they want to sell, it's their prerogative'"?' Mom *knew* we wouldn't be moving back to Harrow; she knew she was handing the house over to Dad. I think he exerted undue influence on her."

After a pause she added, "In bed—that lovely piece of ongoing adultery."

I said I did know about that. Frank and I talk . . .

"My mother was an idiot! She lucked out meeting Frank, and she blew it. He'd have divorced her if she hadn't died."

Given Juliet's "idiot" designation of her mother, I thought it was okay to skip the condolences. "I never met your mother, but from what I've heard . . ." Did I need to be polite? I finished with ". . . forsaking all others just wasn't in her DNA."

"Same with him! And now he's with, of all people, Miss Eliopoulos. I can't get my head around it."

I, who had proof of Stefan's ongoing overnights with Lola, added, "Your father hasn't slowed down, from what I hear."

"He's a pig," she said, so matter-of-factly that I laughed.

She asked if I thought Frank would be home from the dentist yet. Could we stop by my house?

"Probably. Text him." After a pause I said, "If you're hoping he'd go over to Greenough with you as backup, I think his last visit was quite enough."

"I know! They almost got him arrested. Frank—of all people!"

Only a few seconds after her fingers were flying over the keys, her phone pinged. "He's home! How much longer before we get there? What should I tell him?"

"Tell him we just passed the 141 exit, so ten/twelve minutes. He'll know." I glanced over. She was texting with a half smile.

"Can I ask why you and Frank haven't kept in better touch?" I said. "You're obviously so fond of each other."

"I have no excuse! Time just flew since Mom died. Plus, the shock of it."

"Rain calls it PTSD."

She checked her phone again. "She's probably still sleeping."

"It's your house, your sister, your father. Can't you just show up?"

"I might have to," she said.

Stepfather and stepdaughter hugged for a long time. When they finally moved apart, Juliet was wiping away tears.

I said, "I'll give you two some time alone."

They both said versions of "No, no, you're joining us!"

"You did us . . . *me* a huge favor," Frank said. "I made a fresh pot. I warmed up Connie's muffins."

"Connie?" asked Juliet.

I raised my eyebrows. For the first time since I picked her up, Juliet grinned. "Excellent news," she said.

It was slow going: morsel, sip, morsel, sip, review of what Frank had last seen over on Greenough and their worries about Rain's instability and anger. Hoping to speed things up, I said "I could go in with you, if that'll make it easier."

"I'd appreciate that," said Frank. And then, with an indulgent smile, "If I know Emma, she wouldn't mind another look at your mother's so-called collection."

"Ugh," said Juliet. "Another reason I want out—who'd live in that junkyard?"

Frank pointed to my T-shirt. I'd designed the image, which was the top half of a head, its brain filled with furniture and knickknacks.

Leaning closer, Juliet read "Estate of Mind" aloud, picked up her phone, and snapped a photo of my chest.

"I help Emma with the sales," said Frank. "It's my second career: retail."

"I can't deal with it, can't stand being there. Mom always claimed she had valuable stuff, but that's what you say when you call yourself a collector."

"If she had valuable stuff, I'd have known about it," said Frank.

Ivy had been snoring in her crate until Juliet asked in just the right, bright tone, "Can I meet your pup?"

Ivy answered with eager pants and wiggles. Frank opened her crate, led her back to the table, and sat down again, beaming.

Juliet, stroking Ivy's head, said, "I always wanted a dog."

"Me, too," said Frank.

After much checking of her phone, seeing nothing, Juliet finally turned to me. "Let's go. Unless they've changed the locks, I have a key."

"Keep your phone on," Frank said. "Both of you."

Juliet said, "You'd think we were going into a war zone."

I said I hoped Athena would be there. When I'd gone over to collect Rain, Athena seemed a calm voice in the storm.

Juliet closed her eyes for several long seconds. When she opened them, she said, "I'm not Rain. I'm not going to obsess over when or why or how Miss Eliopoulos got together with my father." She stood up. "If she's there, I'll introduce myself graciously as the adult Juliet."

Frank smiled. "Ju-Ju without the braids, twice as tall."

Juliet moved behind him, leaned over, put her arms around his neck, and kissed him on one cheek. He looked at me apologetically, embarrassed that his eyes were filled.

It was a short drive to Greenough. When we passed the park, Juliet said, "I went to a lot of birthday parties here. Every one of them had a bouncy castle. Do they still have the paddleboats on the lake?"

They did, I said. Lately they'd started charging to rent them.

That was the end of reminiscing, because as soon as we tried to make a right turn onto Greenough, we saw a cruiser blocking the street, blue lights flashing. A gray-haired uniformed cop was signaling *Street closed, turn back*.

Juliet yelled, "Let me out!"

I lowered the window, smiling. "She lives here," I explained.

"What number?" he asked.

"That's my house!" said Juliet, pointing down the street, where an ambulance, a fire truck, and a police car were parked. "Forty-four."

He nodded grimly, walked around to the passenger side, opened her door, and gestured, *Go. Now*.

Juliet jumped down from the van and ran. I asked the cop, who seemed to be radioing ahead, if he knew what had happened and who was hurt.

"Are you family too?"

"Friend of."

"Not at liberty," he said.

33

It was Stefan.

Athena had heard the thud and run toward it. She screamed for Nico, her lifeguard son, who couldn't get a pulse. Someone called 911 while Nico and Athena switched off doing chest compressions. Also of no help at all: Rain screaming "Daddy! I'm sorry!" on repeat.

The EMTs with defibs and Luke had arrived only minutes apart. By the time Juliet rushed in, a body under a blanket, presumably Stefan's, was on its way down the front steps. I waited. What I found, after the cop unblocked the street and the ambulance was gone, was Luke with notepad and pen, and Athena standing between her two sons, looking exhausted and defeated.

Luke's questions, cleverly rephrased as to sound *help-me-out-here*, produced the same answers from everyone: Rain and her father were fighting when he collapsed.

"Physically fighting?" asked Luke.

"No! That's crazy! I didn't touch him! He got this shocked look on his face, then clutched his chest"—Rain demonstrated—"and whoosh, he collapsed."

"An argument, then. About what?"

"What they were always about," said Athena's younger son, shirtless, in boxers, who I would soon know to be Theo.

"Whether he had a right to be living in this house," Athena

finished. She traced their circle in the air. "Plus the three of us, not welcome here."

Luke was nodding and writing. I wondered if he was acting, trying to give the impression that he was buying "natural causes."

Ever helpful, I told Luke, "Juliet is Rain's older sister. . . . She just got off the bus from New York. I picked her up in Springfield."

Luke said, "My condolences."

Athena held out her arms. "Ju-Ju," she said softly. "You're back."

Though she stood her ground, Juliet emitted a single, quiet sob.

"What happens now?" asked Rain.

"You cuff her?" muttered Nico.

"Not funny!" wailed Rain.

"An autopsy. It's an unintended death," Luke said, while avoiding eye contact with Rain, who was wearing baby-doll pajamas and nestling herself against Theo.

"Do we call a funeral home?" asked Juliet.

"A funeral home!" yelled Rain. "How could you ask that, like two minutes after Daddy drops dead? As *if*!"

"As if what?"

"As if you're in charge!"

I volunteered that I was on a committee with an undertaker.

"Keohane Funeral Home," Luke said. "Ask for Joe."

"Athena? Could *you*?" asked Juliet.

"It's not my place. The next of kin does that, or *should* do that." Juliet asked, "When?"

"I think the undertaker picks up the body after the autopsy," I said.

"Who wanted an autopsy?" Rain whined. "Do we have a choice? Do we want him all cut up?"

"It's called for in a situation like this," said Luke. "Besides, families like to know the cause of death for their own health, going forward."

Athena turned to her sons. "We should let the girls have the privacy they need."

"No, wait!" said Rain. "Do you mean you're moving out?"

"Not this minute."

Juliet, heretofore the mature diplomat, asked, "How long ago did this start, you and my dad?"

I gave her a look: *Now? Really?*

"I mean, when I was in kindergarten? Or Francine?"

"No, hon, not even a year ago."

I didn't want to walk away from this give-and-take, but I could see that Luke was finding it excruciating. He expressed a general "I'm very sorry for your loss. I'll be heading back to the station now. If you need any further information, call me. And if I get any updates, I'll call you." Then: "Miss Lewis?"

Did I have any agency here? I asked Juliet if she wanted to come back to Montpelier, but she was shaking her head.

"She can go," said Rain. "As long as I'm not left here alone."

"I'm leaving," Luke repeated. "The coroner's office will contact me if we need to do follow-up."

Rain, who'd come from Manhattan to banish her father, to reclaim the house, and to sue if necessary, was now pleading with Athena, "You don't have to leave! Theo doesn't want to leave!"

Was she right? Theo's expression didn't exactly say *Save me from this scantily clad woman.* Quite the opposite.

"If we can help, we'll stay. But we are fully aware of whose house this is," Athena said firmly.

Juliet asked, "Do you have a place of your own to go to?"

"We do," said Athena. "I've been going back and forth. I don't have that much to pack up."

Touched by how she'd greeted Juliet, I said, by way of a fraternal goodbye, "My father was also a teacher in Harrow, and for years president of the HTA. John-Paul Lewis? You probably knew him."

"Um, sorry . . . not at this moment." She managed a thank-you while looking newly bewildered.

Once outside, before Luke could scold me for crashing the debriefing, I asked, "There was nothing the EMTs could do for Stefan?"

"Apparently not."

"Thank goodness this didn't happen when Frank shoved him! You might've had to arrest him for manslaughter!"

"Very true."

"Do you think he was murdered?"

"I do *not* think he was murdered, Nancy Drew." He gave me a careful, on-duty smile. "But then again, I'm only the chief of police."

"Sir!" It was Rain at the front door, now wearing a man's shirt over her baby-dolls. "We hope you'll come to the funeral!"

"Oh brother," I muttered from the safe distance of the sidewalk.

"Coulda seen *that* coming," Luke said.

I called Frank from the van, and without preamble said, "Stefan had a massive coronary incident . . . and he didn't make it."

"He died? Stefan's dead? When did this happen?"

"Like, half an hour ago. There was an ambulance, a fire truck, and a cruiser in front of the house when we got there. Juliet ran in, but he was already being taken away."

"To the emergency room?"

"No! To the morgue! He died!"

Frank said, oddly clinical, "I never heard anything about a weak heart or clogged arteries or high cholesterol or high blood pressure."

"Who would've told you? Not Ginger."

"The girls," he said. "They should be seen."

"By?"

"A cardiologist!"

Strange emphasis, quite off-topic. I said, "I'll be home in two minutes."

"I was on my way out to get some kibble. If you can believe it, we've gone through the twenty-pound bag. Do we need anything else?"

Kibble? Now? Then again, what was Frank supposed to do? His attachment to a piffling errand told me he was either in shock or carrying on with normal life—and why shouldn't he? Because a person he despised had died? A grudge-holding man of lesser character would not just be heading soberly to PetSmart, he'd be doing so gleefully.

I said yes, totally understandable. Ivy needed food, no matter what life delivered. Maybe check if we needed eggs?

He was gone long enough after I got home that I called his cell.

"I lost track of time," he said. "I stopped at Connie's to tell her the news. We were supposed to go out tonight, but if the girls need me . . . Well . . . she understands completely."

"You don't have to rush back here."

"I have eggs in the car. I was just about to leave."

"Give her my best." I hesitated, not wanting to sound pre-sumptuously girlfriendy, but forged ahead, "Tell her Luke was called to the crime scene, and was extremely dignified, which wasn't easy—a bunch of people in shock, Rain hysterical. I mean, didn't everyone there have a gripe against him? It reminded me of *Murder on the Orient Express*."

"Let's save that, okay?" Frank said.

"They're orphans now," he said, our lunch of leftover pizza ig-nored. I told him how much I liked Juliet. We'd do what we could.

If she wanted to stay here, we had the sleep sofa in the third bedroom.

"Thank you. I'll offer."

"She said such wonderful things about you on the drive up from Springfield. About how her mother was an idiot to cheat on you."

He asked if I'd told Juliet about Stefan—he winced—paying for overnight visits with Lois.

"No. I didn't see the point."

"Good," said Frank. After a pause he mused, "I wonder if Ginger knew? Would Stefan have bragged to her about his tom-catting outside the bounds of whatever she thought the two of them had?"

I said, "We'll never know. It's over. Ginger's gone. Stefan's gone. I might be the only one left in Harrow who knows about his overnights with Lois Mankopf—and I'm not saying a word."

Frank was nodding, his eyes closed. "Thank goodness she's out of the picture," he said.

34

Since when did hard-news ace reporter Jeffrey Orwell write obituaries?

His byline, the full Jeffrey George Orwell, was above a wordy front-page feature on Stefan. The choice of details was perplexing, as was the photo of him manning a booth at the 1998 Three-County Fair. I learned that Stefan's legal name was Steven, that he'd drove a 2022 Harley Davidson Sportster Iron 883, that he'd played baseball for Cambridge High and Latin—to which was added in parentheses, "now Cambridge Rindge and Latin after merging with Rindge Technical School in 1977."

Apparently Jeffrey couldn't leave unreported that the deceased had violated a local law requiring owners to obtain a permit before renting their property on Airbnb. Plus: "The office issuing the cease-and-desist order could not be reached for comment."

Was that necessary? I dashed off an email scold to Jeffrey, my subject line Slow News Day??? which he didn't answer except to run it in the *Echo*'s Letters to the Editor section. Had I known it was for all of Harrow to read, I wouldn't have written, "Though no fan of the late 'Stefan' St. Pierre, I don't understand why you felt the need to mention some rinky-dink violation of a stupid town law in his obituary."

That earned me a sweet email from Athena, forwarded by Juliet, thanking me for writing to the *Echo*. She'd been offended, too. There was no mention of his degree from Rensselaer, his consulting business, or his various awards. Might we get together for coffee? She felt she had some explaining to do.

Consulting business? Awards? Hoping that "some explaining" would also explain her romantic history with Stefan, I wrote back immediately, proposing coffee the next day or the day after that.

She wrote back, Better for me after the memorial service.

I didn't have to ask how Juliet and Rain were doing, because I knew: Juliet had returned to Manhattan, planning the funeral by phone, text, and email. Rain was co-mourning with Theo on Greenough, and doing not much else. Frank reported, after bringing her bagels and Connie-baked cookies, that Theo had greeted him with an apologetic look that said, *She threw herself at me, and . . . I'm a guy.*

The forensic autopsy found no external or internal injuries; no drugs, needle marks, ligature marks, petechiae in the eyes or whites, or anything that a murderer could inflict or inject. I expected to read that a shouting match between father and daughter contributed to his collapse—maybe a reference to social and familial factors—but no. The cause was sudden death by ruptured extrapericardial aortic aneurysm.

The funeral could go on.

I went as moral support for Frank, who went as moral support for his stepdaughters. Luke and the officer who'd closed off Greenough Street, attended, both in uniform, a nice municipal gesture, I thought. There was a printed program with a cover photo of the young Stefan, handsome and solemn in his ROTC dress whites.

First up, music: "Candle in the Wind," "Bridge over Troubled Water," and "Fathers and Daughters (Never Say Goodbye)" with Mrs. Selvaggio, Harrow High's voice teacher, on piano and vocals.

The first speaker was Ron of Ron's Reliable Repairs, where Stefan had his motorcycle serviced. He said they chewed the fat, liked the same music, grabbed lunch a coupla times a month. Both were ex-pack-a-day smokers who quit the same month. Once a customer gave him Sox tickets he didn't want, and he invited Stef, who caught a foul ball, then gave it to the kid sitting next to them.

Next up was Chuck Mendez, the fellow teacher and neighbor who'd squealed to Frank about Stefan's assignations with Ginger. But for these purposes he spoke of the early days of Stefan, when Juliet and Francine played with his daughters and the men jointly invested in a swing set, which Stefan generously let the Mendezes put in their backyard.

Juliet, from her seat, rose and asked if anyone else had memories they'd like to share before she closed with a selection of poems.

A woman stood and walked to the podium without raising her hand, notebook between bicep and ribs. She was tall in stiletto heels and hugely bosomed, wearing a black sleeveless tunic, shiny black leggings, and a black fascinator in her burnt-orange hair. She introduced herself with a catch in her voice: She was Lois Mankopf. She'd flown in on the red-eye from San Diego to honor and speak about Stefan.

I nudged Luke on my right, as Frank on my left was murmuring "What the hell?"

With a deep sigh and a wobbly nostalgic smile, she began. "We met in a long line at the DMV. He kept letting people go ahead of him until I was right behind him. We talked and talked; he put the new plates on my car. He asked me out for a drink, but I had to get home—my guests would be arriving at six. 'Can I be a guest, too?' he asked, sincerely . . . innocently. He followed me in his beloved Harley. It was summer; I made us G and Ts." She looked up from her notes. "Please know we were both divorced. Still, we had to be discreet. My ex-husband, as many of you know, was the chief of police. The divorce wasn't an amicable one." She scanned the audience. "He isn't here, so I can say he was not only underfoot but possessive. He thought he had ownership . . . had privileges. Some of you also know that I was the proprietor of the Quail's Nest bed-and-breakfast. Stefan was living in a studio apartment. My house was large, light-filled, welcoming . . . he loved coming over. If I had other company, he'd wait patiently. He always brought his laptop.

"But I'm getting off track. I've been talking about *us*, not about Stefan, the man." She took several deep breaths before whispering, "We were in love!" She looked up. *"Did* any of you know?"

She scanned the silently horrified half-filled room. "I thought so. We were careful. For a long time, there were jealous ex-spouses who didn't want to release us. No wonder we called each other our guilty secrets. If we'd been younger, we'd have married." A slight, proud smile. "He proposed every time we were together. I wanted him to move with me to California, but life intervened . . . other people. Was he the love of my life? Is that a cliché? Maybe I can say he was the *secret* love of my life. Since I moved away, we've been in constant touch, as much as the three-hour time difference and new partners made that workable."

She started, stopped, started, stopped, then finally, "When my daughter called to tell me that Stefan had passed, I cried and cried until I had no tears left. I asked myself, 'Why did you *not* marry him? Be honest, Lois! Tell them how two roads diverged, and you were afraid to take the bumpy one.' He had no job, no savings, no 401K. What does that say about my character? Please . . . if you take anything away from my remarks today, it should be this: In the end, only three things count: love, love, and love."

Just when I thought she was ending with that message, she demanded of Athena, stone-faced in the front row, "He was magnificent, wasn't he?"

Who would put an end to this? Athena stood up, and with great dignity and with the son who wasn't propping up Rain, walked out.

Lois asked the room, "Did I do that? If so, I apologize. I thought this was a safe space for me to stand up and say, 'I'm Lois Mankopf, and I loved Stefan St. Pierre.' I wanted to confess and to honor him. If my house weren't in escrow, I'd invite everyone back to ten-ten Quail Ridge Road to celebrate his life."

With head high and mascara running, she took her seat.

Now what? Was anyone else speaking? Yes, Juliet. Thankfully, when she reached the podium, she shook her head, and, like a wry moderator getting back on track, eyes comically wide, said, "Well! That was fascinating. Thank you." She read poems about death by Emily Dickinson, Maya Angelou, and a poet I'd never heard of but for the credit in the program.

When finished, she looked up and said, "Francine and I thank you for coming. Burial will be at Bridge Street Cemetery. Everyone's welcome." She took a step back to her seat, but returned to the podium. "I did love him. And our mother never *stopped* loving him, which is nice for their daughters to know."

Was it over yet? It seemed so. The two-person recessional was leaving the hall. Luke squeezed my hand and said he had to get back to work. Frank and I had driven over together, and he certainly wouldn't be going to the cemetery. Who *would* go, I wondered?

There was a tap on my shoulder, and a male voice said, "Text me the Mankopf woman's contact info?"

It was Jeffrey Orwell, reporter's notebook in hand. Who was I to withhold Lois's phone numbers? Besides, I was dying to read whatever he was going to write.

35

L uke called me at 7:25 a.m.

"Well, hello, you," I answered.

"Please tell me you didn't tell Orwell what you found in the file cabinet," he said.

"Why would you think—"

"The *Echo*—it's a full-page story about the funeral and the surprise speaker."

I heard "Eggs benny, no sauce," in the background, so I knew he was at the Over Easy, as ever reading the local newspaper over breakfast. I asked if he'd be there for a while. I could join him.

"Sure, come."

I jumped out of bed and threw on a rumpled cotton sundress. I'd gone to bed with wet hair and woken up with waves that I usually tamed before leaving the house. No time. I grabbed my keys and drove to the diner.

I didn't kiss Luke upon arrival due to our cone of public discretion, and because Trudy, the tiny, seventyish owner, was approaching with a coffeepot in each hand.

"I thought so," she said. "He's been looking happier than usual."

Luke groaned—hardly the confirmation I would've liked.

I slid into the booth and said good morning with an extended fond gaze, taking in the whole picture: Luke in uniform, creases sharp, straight from the dry cleaners.

"What?" he asked.

I gave his foot a nudge with mine. "You know," I said.

He gave the open newspaper a jab. "Have you read it? . . . What a dick."

"Not yet."

Before he could ask again if I'd told Jeffrey about Lola's invoices, I said quietly, "Only you and Frank know what I found in that file cabinet. I locked it and put the key back where I found it, in a bathrobe pocket . . . if you can call something that transparent a *bathrobe*."

I smiled at my own negligee joke; Luke tried not to. I turned the newspaper sideways so we could both read it. Why did Lois's soliloquy qualify as news? I skimmed. With a liberal use of "allegeds" and "probables," Jeffrey gave himself permission to characterize the Quail's Nest as a house of ill repute. Another takeaway, implied not stated, between the lines: that Lois was a self-employed hooker, and Stefan was her favorite john.

Trudy returned with Luke's sesame bagel and scrambled eggs. I ordered my eggs over easy, with the turkey sausage and sourdough toast, the diner's proud new bread option. Trudy told me that she and her husband—that good-looker at the grill—had gone to Luke's induction. In fact, the Easy had operated on a skeleton crew that afternoon.

"I'd have gone, too, if we'd been friends back then." I gave Luke another nudge under the table. He nodded, eyes closed—*Got it. Hilarious. Breakfast with a comedian.* Trudy added that her Lisa used to babysit for the older Winooski boys, but was already out of high school when Connie had her fourth, this guy.

Alone again, Luke read aloud, " 'Mankopf repeatedly alluded to a love affair with the deceased, noting that she and St. Pierre were both divorced, as if underscoring that their dalliance did not constitute adultery.' Dalliance! Who cares! Manny's probably on his way over to the *Echo* now, waving the Glock he never turned in."

I said, "I know you're not supposed to speak ill of the dead, but I have my own case against Stefan. You know he was sleeping with Frank's wife, his ex—"

"I didn't know that."

"While Frank was at school! And Lois? She brought this on herself, showing up uninvited, marching up to the pulpit in her stiletto heels."

He pointed to a line in italics at the end of the article. " 'Part two tomorrow, an interview with Lois Mankopf.' I don't know what's left for her to say."

"Maybe she'll name names."

"You mean other customers? Great. Just what this town needs."

"Would you have to arrest them?"

"No. Whatever she says is hearsay."

"I do like this phrase: 'Operating out of a grand, ten-room Victorian on Harrow's most high-status street.' As far as I'm concerned, when it comes to an estate sale, there's no such thing as bad press."

Trudy returned to top off our coffees. Pointing to the headline "Elegy for a Casanova," she said, "Lois was married to Mankopf, you know, the old chief. What a horndog. I hated to see him come in. I had to wait on him because the younger waitresses didn't want to go near him. And passing out his wife's business cards. An escort service! Are you kidding me? He was as subtle as a truck."

I asked, "You mean everyone knew what really went on at his wife's B and B?"

"You didn't have to be a detective. Guys in expensive suits, out-of-towners, showing up here, sports cars and Mercedes out there. She ran a bed-and-breakfast? What happened to the breakfast?"

When another customer called her name, she excused herself with a wink, as if to say, *I can't play favorites all day, can I?*

Alone again, I said, "See?"

"See what?"

"Jeffrey isn't breaking any news. He's only been in town a year, so he thinks he dropped a bombshell."

"Either way, I don't have to like the guy."

I ran a finger down a column and up to the next one. "He must've recorded Lois's whole eulogy. He quotes her about their great, guilty love . . . and how quote-unquote life intervened, meaning Stefan took up with Athena, and she took up with a guy she met on a cruise."

"So much for true love," Luke said.

"You don't think true love is still around?" I sipped my coffee, hoping to hear *I know it is*, or a smile that said *Ask me when we're alone*. But he checked his watch, then said he should get to work.

I only had myself to blame. Too eager. Love was too big a topic for the Over Easy, and too soon. "Okay," I said. "I'll see you at the reunion meeting."

He asked if something was wrong. I could hardly say, *You clammed up when I stupidly asked about true love, and now you're leaving before I got my eggs*. I said I just had a lot on my mind, with Lois showing up, and how she might screw up my sale.

Luke was chief of police, a public figure, and an eligible bachelor. Unlike Manny Mankopf, he wouldn't want to be seen flirting at the Over Easy. And unlike Emma Lewis, he couldn't wear his heart on his sleeve.

36

I was back from the Over Easy before nine to find Frank at the open fridge and Juliet at the kitchen table. She'd been staying in Harrow since returning for the funeral, dropping by daily, always with something—doughnuts or berries or a baguette from the Big Y. "Sorry," she said as a greeting. "I hate my house. Yours is so . . . clean."

"Happy to have you," and I meant it. "How's things over there?"

If only they could agree, Juliet said. She wanted to sell their white elephant; Rain wanted to keep it, for reasons that were boy-crazy-personal.

"I don't know how it reached this point," said Frank. "Well, yes, I do. Your mother had a disorder, I think—the hoarding she justified as collecting." He shook his head. "I tried."

"It isn't just the overload. It's a pigsty. No one's cleaned out the refrigerator since who knows when? Rain is useless. The milk's sour? Ever heard of a *store*? And Theo? He never comes out of the bedroom."

"How old is he?" I asked.

"Eighteen. Rain doesn't care."

"Won't he be going back to school in the fall?"

"Yes and no. He's starting his freshman year, but living at home. Rain, of course, is offering ours."

"Where's he going?" Frank asked.

"Springfield College, majoring in exercise science or sports psychology or coaching philosophy. Something like that."

"What is she doing for money?" Frank asked. "Doesn't she *need* to sell?"

"We both do!" Juliet said. She added that she was getting by, freelancing; had applied to do marketing for a food festival that was coming to TriBeCa.

I asked if their father had left them anything, which made her expel a loud "Ha!"

That inspired Frank, who was scrambling eggs at the stove, to say, "Hon, he must've had a will, and every will has an executor. You'll be hearing from him or her, I'm sure. And you don't have to spend your money bringing us anything when you come by." He held up the grater. "Cheddar or Swiss?"

"Cheddar. That's so sweet of you, but my mother wouldn't want me to come empty-handed."

"Don't I know," Frank murmured.

"Didn't Stefan have a consulting business?" I asked.

"He *wished*. If you asked what he consulted about, he'd say something like 'I solve problems that keep CEOs up at night.' "

"Did you think Stefan and Athena were . . . anything?" I asked.

Her answer was delayed by the delivery of her breakfast. After a few bites, a sprinkle of salt, and a thumbs-up, she said, "Here's my theory: When she was my kindergarten teacher, he was twenty-five years younger and the handsomest dad in the whole school. He chaperoned field trips." She shrugged. "It could've been a crush that started then."

Would it be self-centered and insensitive to say what was keeping *me* up at night: business in general, and the next sale in particular? I could almost hear Beth reminding me of the long winter, my off-season, stretching out ahead. Wouldn't she take the initiative, right here, right now? I started with what I hoped was a vague, bereavement-appropriate question: Had she and her sister discussed what was next, propertywise?

"Only on the night Daddy died . . . We were high, so not sure where we left it."

"Just weed, I hope," Frank said, which made me laugh at the ex-teacher's cannabis nonchalance.

I said, "Here's a thought: The house could be made livable *without* selling it." I paused; I wasn't great at this, and I knew it. "Okay. Let's say Estate of Mind conducts a sale, *not* because the house is going on the market—just so it's no longer bursting at the seams."

Frank quickly added, "Which means getting rid of nine-tenths of what your mother accumulated."

"People would buy all that shit?" Juliet asked.

Sales enthusiast Frank said, "Trust me. Cars pull up an hour before doors open. They buy the oddest things. Emma, can you think of anything that *doesn't* sell?" I could, many things—snow tires, cassette players, cassette tapes; I could go on and on—but for this crusade, I said, "Whoosh! Out it goes."

"There's plenty of time to decide," I said. But was there? Juliet was hoping to do PR for a mere three-day festival, and who knew how Rain was even paying for her takeout. "You've heard about the sale I'm doing at the ex-brothel? We're going all out on that. If you're still here over Labor Day weekend, you'll come as our guest and see how it works."

I could see Frank digesting *You'll come as our guest*—as if there weren't notices on every bulletin board and telephone pole in town.

"That woman!" Juliet cried. "Did you see her looking at Rain and me during the funeral? Like, 'I'd have been your stepmother if I'd accepted one of his fifty proposals.' Dad would be on the phone with a libel lawyer already. Or slander, whichever. What's wrong with that guy?"

"The reporter?" Frank asked.

"Jeffrey Orwell," I said. "He thinks he's a one-man *Globe* Spotlight team."

"The whole thing, from start to finish, was in very bad taste," said Frank.

"I'm going to write a letter to the editor," Juliet said.

"Saying?" I asked.

"Saying . . . that woman crashed the memorial service! How did you know she was telling the truth about a long-term affair with my father? What proof did you have?"

Frank and I exchanged quick, queasy glances. He said, "Imagine when all your mother's stuff is gone, and you'll be living in a clean house!"

"Clean?" Juliet repeated. "I wouldn't know where to start."

"You'll get a cleaning service," I said. "They'll come in for a few days—"

"Wouldn't that be, like, hundreds of dollars?"

Frank said, "I can help with that."

"Knowing Frank," I said, "he probably means he's going over there with his Swiffers and a gallon of ammonia."

Juliet's eyes filled. She turned around to the fleecy bed in the corner and asked Ivy, "Is Frank the best stepdad you could ever have imagined?"

Thrilled to be included, Ivy stretched to her full length, then joined us, her tail at ecstatic maximum wag.

Wiping off Ivy's kisses, Frank said, "Bring Rain over and we'll paint a picture of an uncluttered life."

"Another thought," I said. "When the house is empty—well, empti*er*—and there are clean sheets on the bed, you could get an Airbnb license. Parents' weekends, graduations, reunions—you'll never have a vacancy. Six bedrooms, right?"

"I'd have to get Rain's okay." Juliet's lip curled. "I'd also have to get bathrobes for her and Theo."

"She shouldn't run the show!" I said. "All she's done is throw herself at the first guy who came through the door. Even Saint Frank has called her a brat—"

"Bratty," he corrected.

"She's having a harder time with it than I am," Juliet said. "All their yelling, the fighting, right up to the moment Daddy dropped dead. Did you see her at the funeral? She was bawling the whole time."

Frank said, "I did."

I had, too. I'd wondered how much of it had been for show, for the benefit of Theo, as she slumped against his shoulder and impressive biceps.

Frank asked, "What's your living situation in New York?"

"Crap."

"Can you get out of it? Did you sign a lease?"

"No lease. I'm an illegal fourth in a supposed one-bedroom."

"That's that!" Frank said. "You're moving back."

At last I had some genuine professional inspiration: *Get the house uncluttered so Juliet, who Frank loved, could imagine moving back.* "We'll get the ball rolling," I said. "And next thing you know, you'll be living in a house fit for human habitation."

Frank patted Ivy absent-mindedly, sounding dreamier than usual. "Sometimes I wonder why I didn't take on the project myself. I mean, it was my legal residence. I could've gotten rid of so much . . ."

"Really?" I asked him, with a wide-eyed stare that said, *NOW you're telling me this?*

"Why didn't I?" he continued. "No one was kicking me out. I was Ginger's widower. We lived on my salary. I paid those bills. I had a perfect right to get rid of what was making life impossible there."

"What about now?" I asked. "Can you make the same argument?"

"No argument with me," said Juliet. "If Rain objects, I can say, 'Too bad; it's two against one.' I'll tell her I checked with a lawyer, who said a widow or widower can sell the contents of the house that was their last legal domicile."

"I'd rather you didn't lie," said Frank.

Juliet patted his free hand. "I know you wouldn't."

37

Even Marcia hated Jeffrey's coverage of the funeral. She thought the whole piece was cringe-worthy, misogynist, and blatantly anti-sex-worker. It provoked her to send a text to me, asking if I'd I read the article. Had I heard Mrs. Mankopf's eulogy in person?

I called her and said, "Yes and yes."

"Is she 'flame-haired and statuesque'?"

"Pretty much."

"Did people actually walk out in protest?"

"Only two. Athena, the current girlfriend, and one of her sons."

"Why did Jeffrey even go? What was he looking for? I wonder if she tipped him off that she was coming."

"Ask him . . . but I doubt it. She made it sound like she jumped on a plane as soon as she heard Stefan died. Her name wasn't on the program, and it wasn't like an open mic. She stopped the show."

"He thinks this is his ticket out," Marcia grumbled. "Next stop, *New York Times*. Well, good luck, Clark Kent."

Was her disdain journalistic or personal? I asked the awkward question—she and I were fine with awkward questions—"Are you breaking up with him?"

She didn't answer, just continued deconstructing. "Why did

this great love affair have to be a guilty secret, if both parties were single?"

"Because she was a madame and everyone in town except us knew it. And maybe because she and Manny were still having sex, if that's what she meant by 'privileges.'"

"Exes having sex," Marcia mused. "Hmmm. Imagine that."

I knew that tone, and I knew what she was telling me. "Is Gideon back home? Has he been paroled?" I asked.

"Well, not back home with me . . . at his parents'. Just until the trial, wearing an ankle monitor."

"You've seen him?"

"He wanted to talk in person. He's heartsick. He couldn't be more remorseful. And . . . he's been working out in prison . . ."

I asked if this meant they were back together.

"How quaint," she said. "Well, we're still married. And I'll be going to the trial. It looks good to have the wife there."

"But what if he's sent back to prison? Didn't Madoff get hundreds of years?"

"A hundred and fifty. But Gideon's no Madoff. He thinks that if he pays whatever fines the jury comes back with, his sentence could be just house arrest and community service, like helping poor people get loans and doing their taxes. I mean if ever there was the whitest white-collar crime, this is it."

"What about you? *Your* money? Does the divorce protect you?"

"The divorce is on hold. His lawyer thinks me divorcing Gid looks like I found him guilty without a trial."

"Does Gid know you're seeing Jeffrey?"

"No . . . Well, maybe. He knows that Jeffrey stopped reporting on him, on *me*, due to personal reasons."

"I always liked Gideon . . ."

"As opposed to taking an instant dislike to Jeffrey?"

"Not 'instant' . . . More like a gradual immense dislike."

She said flatly, unenthusiastically, "He's smart, and he writes well. Or *did*."

"Have you told him what you think of the article?"

"Not yet. I'll tell him in person." She paused. "That's the polite way to break up with someone."

"This article is already coming back to bite him on the ass. There's you, there's Stefan's daughters, and then there's Manny Mankopf. Luke thinks he'll go batshit when he reads it."

"Wait. Wasn't Mankopf run out of town? Jeffrey's article says Lois could speak freely about the great love of her life precisely because Manny was gone for good."

"Walk by Frangella Fine Arts. The window's filled with Manny's artwork. He's having a show there, and an opening, which I have to go to."

"Why?"

"Because Mike helps me with appraisals. I go to every one of his openings, good or bad. It's how you do business in a small town."

"When is it?"

I checked my phone. "Thursday, six to eight."

"How's the artwork?"

"Hideous."

"I'm coming with you," she said.

38

Hideous" didn't tell half the story. Every painting inside was as huge, blotchy, muddy, and abstract as the giant canvases in the window of Frangella Fine Arts, with numbers and obscenities stenciled in white. "Pigeon shit," to quote Luke. I made the rounds, pretending to study every painting. Mike introduced me to Manny, who said, "At last we meet."

Mike pointed to the back gallery. "Also Manny's," he said. I nodded and smiled like the good fellow businessperson that I was, and moved on. There hung life-size charcoal drawings, all of naked women, all smiling, their eyes closed as if transported.

With no one watching me, I didn't have to pretend to be interested. As I was returning to the front room, I heard a woman yelling, "Take it down! Take it down, you sonofabitch!" A crowd had gathered. Moving closer, I saw a small, dark-haired woman, forty-fiveish, with a perfect, shiny pageboy, face-to-face with Manny.

I called Luke, who answered with "I thought you were going to Manny's opening."

"I'm there now! A woman's having a fit over—"

"A literal fit? Do you mean a seizure?"

"No! She's screaming at Manny."

Luke sighed. "Is Mike not handling it?"

"Mike's pretending to be otherwise occupied. Manny looks like he's enjoying it."

"Is anyone with the woman? I mean someone who can take her by the arm and get her away from him?"

"No one's stepping forward."

"Aren't you there with Marcia?"

"She's not here yet."

"Just lead her away. Tell her everything's okay. Ask if there's anyone you can call."

I was embarrassed that he had to tell me to render assistance to another woman, especially one with a gripe against Manny Mankopf. I said, "Okay, I'm hanging up—unless you think you should stay on the line in an official capacity."

"You'll be fine. I'm deputizing you—just don't say that."

The woman was now crying while still yelling, "You didn't have to put my name on it! I live here!" I put my arm around her waist and whispered, "It's okay. Let's go. He's not worth it. Besides, the drawings are beautiful," I lied.

"No, they're not! They're porn! I never posed for this!"

I said with false cheer, "Then it can't be you, can it?" at the same time Manny was saying, "Well, Miss Lewis to the rescue." And then to anyone still gathered, "She's selling the contents of my house out from under me."

I didn't wilt at that. I said in retreat, over my shoulder to the small gathering, "My business cards are on the bar."

Luckily, backup arrived in the form of Marcia. She came straight to my side, assessed the situation, and asked the woman her name in the soothing, strategic manner of a shrink talking a patient down from a ledge.

"Beverly," the woman moaned. "Bev . . . He had no right!"

Marcia looked to me for translation.

"She thinks one of the nudes"—I nodded toward the back gallery—"is of her."

Marcia turned to Bev. "Show me."

"No! I want it ripped down and ripped up! I don't want my naked body hanging in a museum!"

I didn't correct that. "She never posed for Manny," I explained.

Marcia said, "Okay then: deniability."

"He says he's a memory painter," Beverly wailed.

Was it any of our business when and under what circumstances Manny had seen her naked? She was leaning against me, having accepted the tissue I'd supplied for the tears and snot running down her face.

Marcia said, "I'm Marcia, and this is Emma. We hate Manny, too."

I tried another variation of *no one will know it's you*: "The women in the drawings all look alike. The faces aren't even detailed."

"It has my name on it! He named it Bevy."

I said, "Bevy could mean a lot of different things."

"No, it couldn't! He painted all of the girls!"

"All the girls, as in . . . your coworkers and friends?"

"That's a nice way of putting it," said Bev.

I asked, "Have you had dinner?"

"I'm not hungry."

"C'mon," said Marcia. "I'm starved. You'll keep us company."

First question I asked at Buena Comida after a round of margaritas was "Bev, were you and Manny in a relationship?"

"No!"

"But you were having sex?" Marcia asked.

"*He* was."

I didn't ask her to clarify. "He wouldn't have drawn you if he hadn't greatly admired your body—"

"And wanted to memorialize it," added Marcia.

Bev leaned across the table and whisper-shouted, "I wasn't some girlfriend he wanted to memorialize. I was a paid escort, okay? How's that? I mean my job was 'escort,' but we never went anywhere except to bed."

She must've been expecting us to gasp and recoil, because she added almost triumphantly, "That's right. Upstairs on Quail Ridge Road. Did you know it was a whorehouse?"

I said, "Actually, I did. I'm doing an estate sale there over Labor Day weekend."

"Bev," Marcia said, "please tell me you're not apologizing for the work you did in another life, and under duress."

Bev returned to, "As if no one would know that Bevy was me? That Dawn wasn't Donna? That Polly wasn't Paulina?"

"Paulina?" I repeated. *Our* Paulina? Uncle Paul would die. A charcoal drawing of his nude wife would tell the world she wasn't just an overlapping guest he met on the bed-and-breakfast side of the Quail's Nest.

Marcia clearly wanted to get back to Bev vis-à-vis Manny's sexual overreaching. "Did Manny *pay* to have sex with the escorts?"

"At a reduced rate. Or maybe it was some kind of blackmail, like 'I get favors or I shut you down.' Neither one of them had any scruples. He had a rotation—one or two a week. And he bragged about not playing favorites."

"Could you refuse?" Marcia asked.

"No one did."

"No one *dared*? Or no one minded?"

"We minded," Bev said.

"Yet you came tonight to his art opening," said Marcia.

"He invited me! I wasn't expecting to find myself on the wall in all my glory!"

The waiter came to make guacamole tableside, so we switched to the slightly more neutral topic of Manny's awful paintings. "Some had Harrow's zip code," Bev said. "What's that about? That he used to live here? Big deal."

Marcia asked Bev whether she had a husband, a boyfriend, a girlfriend.

"Husband! Thank God he didn't want to come tonight."

Marcia and I exchanged glances that meant, *Do we ask?* She did. "Does your husband know about your past?"

"*He* does. His mother doesn't, though. It was bad enough that I wasn't a Roman Catholic."

"Kids?" I asked.

"No! I did a stupid, ignorant thing."

Marcia seemed to know what she was talking about, because she clasped Bev's hand.

"I think I missed what the stupid thing was," I said.

Bev said, "I had my tubes tied. I didn't think I ever wanted children, and at the time it was a plus."

"For the men, maybe," supplied Marcia.

"As long as I've known Marcia," I said to Bev, "which is forever, she's always way ahead of me. She knows the way the world works."

To that Marcia added cheerfully, "My husband's a felon. The FBI came for him one morning at five a.m. Poof! Off to jail."

"But they've patched things up," I said, smiling.

"You don't seem like someone who'd be married to a felon," said Bev.

"She's a college professor," I bragged.

"What was he arrested for?"

"White-collar stuff. Cryptocurrency."

"But you stuck with him," said Bev. "That's nice: for better or for worse." Then: "My husband reminds me that I was lucky that Lola's house never got raided, and I never got arrested."

More glances passed between Marcia and me. "It wasn't really luck," I said.

39

Another reunion committee meeting, Luke and I still romantically undercover, this one at the co-chairs' house, a turquoise ranch a block from Harrow High. Host Annette opened the front door even before I rang the doorbell, looked me over, said she liked my hair up. Down was nice, too. But this was fine . . .

I'd brought our co-chairs a baker's dozen ears of corn. "It's my favorite," I said, handing her the bag.

"Let's put these in the kitchen," she said, then, rather pointedly, "Would you like to see it? We put in all new appliances."

I followed her through the living room, where the rest of the committee was milling and chatting, Luke included. I smiled and nodded to all with equally token enthusiasm.

"We'll get started in a minute," Annette announced. "Chris? Everyone around the dining room table? Emma and I will be back in a sec."

But there was no tour of the shiny new appliances. Annette motioned me to the pantry, then whispered, "I have an idea."

I waited, sensing it was on the topic of—

"You and Luke," she whispered. "It must've occurred to you, but you don't even sit next to him at the meetings! Is he attached? We don't think so."

"It would be awkward."

"What would?"

"Coming on to someone I'm serving on the committee with."

"I'm not talking about flirting! I'm talking about . . . well, Chris and I say all the time, 'Luke Winooski and Emma Lewis. Duh!' Wouldn't it be adorable if they became a couple, fifteen years after graduating, because of this?"

I was tempted to say, "We've been sleeping together since June," but we'd agreed to keep it to ourselves for exactly this reason: Annette. Her class newsletter had a section called "Social Notes," and we'd be the lead item, with kudos to the reunion committee for putting the idea in our heads.

"We have a plan," she continued. "When tonight's meeting is over, you say, 'Anyone want to go out for a drink?' I'm sure Luke will say yes, so it'll just be the two of you."

"How do you know that?"

"Because everyone else is going to say they have to go home."

Oh god. "Everyone's been clued in?"

"Well, not Luke. Everyone else is married, and they're all rooting for you."

I said, "I think these things have to happen organically."

"What's more organic than being on a committee together and going out for a drink afterward?"

This was a pickle. We'd be outed soon enough just in the course of living and dating in Harrow, then found guilty of feigning platonic nothingness.

"Email him. Ask him over to dinner, for god's sake. There *is* life outside the committee, you know."

"We should join the others," I whispered. "They'll wonder what we're talking about."

"No, they won't," she said.

*

First on the agenda, the budget. We didn't have one because we didn't collect class dues and couldn't sell tickets that hadn't been printed yet. How much should we charge? That took a calculator and a prolonged debate. We settled on $50 per person to cover the nibbles and one drink. After that, a cash bar. The VFW Hall could be rented for just the cost of paying the guy who cleaned up and locked up. And who did we know among our classmates who could provide such-and-such goods and services? Bartenders? Musicians? Bakers? Door prizes?

Next up: the list of classmates we'd lost track of. Melissa said she'd put those on the class Facebook page. Also, who'd be willing to cut up his or her yearbook so we could put graduation photos on the nametags? I volunteered.

When Chris gaveled the meeting over, Annette shot me a look, then a second more urgent one. I shook my head.

Patting her belly, she said, "I can't join you for obvious reasons, but who'd like to go out for a drink?"

"Another time," said Melissa.

"Promised to go straight home," said Joe. "We have a wake tonight."

Brooke's and Keith's wives were expecting them.

"That just leaves you, Luke," Annette said.

"I'd love to," said Luke, "but I promised to take my mom out for a late dinner."

I said, "Oh well. Maybe next time."

When Luke left with the others, I caught his nearly invisible nod to me, which I returned.

A deflated Annette thanked me for the corn. I offered to shuck it so it wouldn't take up so much room in their fridge.

"No thanks. We microwave them unshucked," she said.

"He had a good excuse," I pointed out.

As soon as I was outside, I checked my phone. Luke had texted: The usual plan?

Be there in 10, I texted back.

*

We had a morning ritual: coffee delivered to me in bed, early, Luke already in his uniform, badge gleaming. I always smiled at this version of him, which generally made him say, blushing and grinning, "Cut it out."

I said, "I'm getting up. Do you have time to join me for another cup?"

"Sure."

I put on his Harrow softball league T-shirt, one of my favorites, a surprising pink, and met him in his tiny kitchen. I groaned. "Ten more days."

He knew I was referring to my main dread, the Mankopf sale. "It'll be fine. You'll pull it off."

"But still so much to do! And there's Manny threatening to cancel every time he doesn't like the price of a saltshaker."

"You could be singing a different tune in thirteen days, laughing all the way to the bank."

"Doubt it," I said.

"Worst-case scenario? Manny cancels. No sale. Not your fault. Would that be catastrophic?"

"Yes! It would look like I pulled out at the last minute. I'd never get another client after this buildup."

"Do you *want* another client? Another sale?"

I said, barely audible, "Maybe not."

40

I'd driven over to Quail Ridge with a to-do list: vacuuming, dusting, airing out the third-floor rooms, cleaning the guest bathrooms.

All present: Lois, Manny, and Vanessa. "We're expected to do this ourselves?" asked Lois.

"You could hire a cleaning service," I said. "And a window washer would be great."

No confirmation or comments. Vanessa asked what I'd be wearing to the pre-sale gala, taking in the faded T-shirt and gym shorts I'd worn for walking Ivy, who was alone on their back porch, contented with the rawhide knot I'd brought to occupy her.

"A cocktail dress," I said, and described its color and fabric, quoting its description on Rent the Runway, which I'd joined just for this occasion.

"Sounds quite delightful," said Manny. "You looked very smart at my opening, too."

Ugh. "Thanks."

"Did you like the show?"

Oh god. Did anyone? "Those huge canvases . . . I don't know how you did them. On a ladder?"

"No." He smiled. "I'm a big man. With long limbs."

I turned back to my to-do list. No more cigar smoking inside for several days before the party, I suggested. The grass would need to be cut, and, ideally, bushes trimmed. Maybe put some clothes on the pink statue—Frank and I were thinking a Macmillan tee or scarf? And we'd make a nice arrangement of the garden tools. I looked up and said, "They always go. Husbands head straight for the garages and barns."

Manny said, "We haven't discussed pricing."

Eyes on my list, I said firmly, "Estate of Mind makes those decisions."

He said he'd been studying the Sotheby's website for imported pottery just like theirs, the bowls and tureens in the shape of lettuce and cabbage. Did I know what they went for?

Here it was, the chronic estimates challenge. I said, "If they're in a Sotheby's auction, then we're talking about another level of—"

"Sixteen thousand bucks for a pair of cabbage tureens!"

I took out my phone and went quickly to eBay, where I found Lois's cabbage tureen for $49.99 or best offer; no bids yet.

"Fake, fake, fake," he said.

"Trust me: Tureens that sell for sixteen thousand bucks are French, antique, and previously owned by Jackie Onassis."

Vanessa asked, "Can't you say, 'One like this sold at a Sotheby's for sixteen K'?"

"Leave her alone," said Lois. "She knows what she's doing. You can't just slap a ridiculous price on something because the owner's ex found the most expensive one ever sold."

I thanked Lois, adding, "I've been doing this my whole life," which earned a loud hmmph from Manny.

I said, "I'd better take my dog home. Any other questions?"

"We like the idea of tours," said Vanessa. "Guided ones. Have you ever been to the Mark Twain House in Hartford?"

I said no, yes, other house tours. The Emily Dickinson Museum in Amherst . . . did they mean, guided, as in narrated?

"By someone who isn't ashamed of our line of work and knows what he's talking about," said Lois. Mother and daughter both looked toward Manny.

"We have a lot to be proud of," said Vanessa. "We have a compelling story: My mother started her own business from scratch, made a success of it, paid taxes, gave her girls health and dental."

"She put Harrow on the map," said Manny. "What else does this town have to crow about? Macmillan College for Women? Pie Tuesday at the Over Easy?"

I said, "Would the point of a tour be the house's history, or to increase sales?"

"Sales," said Manny, "guaranteed."

He had gone one braggadocio note too far for his ex. "You can't guarantee that!" Lois snapped. "You think if you tell stories about what went on here, people will fall all over each other to buy our sheets and pillowcases? Would they be the same art lovers who fell over themselves buying your paintings?"

"I can still stop this," he growled, "so don't test me."

Stop what? My biggest sale ever? I said, "Guided tours sound quite doable."

Frank and I were walking Ivy and sharing our worries about everything Mankopf-related: the gala, the sale, the weather, the turnout, and what Estate of Mind had on the calendar going forward, which was negligible.

"Traffic flow?" he asked.

"You mean parking?"

"No. Inside, at the gala. I'm picturing that guests will congregate in the room where the refreshments and drinks are, but it should operate as an open house. I could draw up a floor plan, which we'd hand the guests as they arrive."

"*Or,*" I said with great emphasis. "*Or* . . . someone gives tours."

He seemed to be considering that for a whole block. Finally he said, "I don't know . . . wouldn't a tour guide have to spell out what business was conducted in those third-floor rooms? I remember my first visit—the walls covered with kisses. I was stunned."

"Would the guests be stunned, though? I didn't hold back in any of my press releases."

"I suppose . . ."

"The real purpose of a tour would be pointing out the good stuff, the high-value stuff—the fireplace tools, the silver, the supposed antiques, the vintage clothing"—and, saving his favorite for last—"the brass *Downton Abbey* bells on the kitchen wall."

"True," he said, "a conversation in themselves."

"Which is why you'd be the best tour guide."

He smiled and thanked me, unaware he was being recruited.

I said, "Let me rephrase that: I'd like you to give the tours."

"Me? I'd be terrible. I wouldn't know how to handle the questions about the ladies, the commerce, the adult toys."

"I disagree. You'd be perfect. You're dignified. You wouldn't offend anyone. You wouldn't make off-color remarks about the escorts. I can picture you saying, 'This was called the stairway to heaven, where Mrs. Mankopf's customers began their journey' . . . using whatever nouns and verbs you'd be comfortable with."

"I can't, Emma. It's one thing to pour the prosecco and answer general questions, but leading people through that warren of rooms, bed after bed . . . What if they're ex-students of mine?"

"First of all, any ex-students who showed up would be adults now. They'll still be seeing Mr. Crowley, *Coach* Crowley, conducting a tour with dignity."

"Have you considered the logistics? You can't say to people, 'Please gather in the kitchen. The next tour starts in ten minutes.' People will want to wander around, look at price tags, open closets and drawers at their own pace."

"But here's the thing—here's what I'm up against: Manny is throwing his weight around. He's hinting that he could pull the plug on the sale if he doesn't get his way. He's insisting on tours, and he wants to give them."

"That bully. His name's not even on the contract. What nerve."

Ivy, who'd done her business, had found a patch of grass in the shade. It was hot, even at nine in the morning, and getting hotter. Frank gave her a drink from her doggy water bottle. I suggested we turn back. As ever, she sped up when we reached Montpelier, envisioning a biscuit and cool linoleum.

From a few houses away, I spotted a third car in the driveway. Two bicycles strapped to the back distracted me, but not for long.

My parents had arrived.

41

They hadn't wanted me to fuss; hadn't wanted me to devote one minute to cleaning, straightening up, or shopping. If there were linens to change and towels to wash, they'd do it! Though I'd been shocked and dismayed at the first sight of them, tanned and smiling and days early, I found myself rushing into my father's outstretched arms, with Beth encircling both of us.

Frank stood a respectful distance away, then shook hands all around. I knew them so well; I knew they'd want to impress upon Frank that this was his house, too. Whatever sleeping arrangements were currently in place, so be it! No argument: The guest room would be fine. They loved that room, its viny wallpaper, its view of the Rosens' weeping willow, and of course the state-of-the-art sofa bed, with its sturdy frame and memory foam.

Frank started his next three sentences with, "I appreciate that . . . ," but no—they wouldn't hear of displacing him.

"And who's this!" my father cried, knowing full well it was ideal dog Ivy. Though she'd barked at the sight of strangers in her driveway, she caught on as soon as she smelled them, humans she knew from throw pillows on the forbidden couch.

Frank helped himself to the suitcases in the trunk. Not carry-ons, I noticed, but serious baggage, packed for a long stay. When my dad came inside with a top-of-the line cooler, Beth asked me, "Can you guess what we're having for dinner tonight?"

Yes, I could, easily. "Lobsters?"

"Caught yesterday! We go straight to the wharf where the lobstermen come in!" She looked at the butter dish, still out from breakfast. "Any more butter in the fridge? And a lemon?"

"I'll run out," I said.

When they said they should get these suitcases out of the way, I followed them upstairs. At the door to what was now my room, I stopped and said, "I can't sleep in your bed, with you on the pull-out sofa."

"Tish tosh," said Beth, continuing down the hall. In the guest room, she gave the enraptured sigh of the happy hotel patron. I'd exhausted the one argument I'd had, that I'd appropriated the room that had been theirs for two decades. I offered to get sheets, towels, water and water glasses, extra pillows. What about extra hangers?

"Nope! I only packed work clothes; only brought one dress, in case we have reason to celebrate."

I knew what she was referring to: a history-making sale.

My father was describing the route from Buzzards Bay, how long it took to the minute. They'd wisely chosen a weekday, left after the commuters headed for Boston, taken 495 to the Pike and 91, and here they were!

"How many miles?" Frank asked.

"A hundred forty on the nose! When we were deciding where to move to, we drew a circle with my compass—it had to be within a hundred fifty miles of Emma."

I asked, "Who wants coffee?"

My dad said, "I'd love it! I only had one cup this morning."

"So we didn't have to stop five times on the Pike," Beth said.

She unpacked the half and half—theirs, brought just in case. Frank asked my dad if he'd like to have the honor of giving Ivy her treat, which she always got after her walk. Ivy barked at "treat," and at my father's sudden leap to his feet.

"Wait," I instructed Ivy, just to show off one of her best tricks. She lay down again, a body length closer to the treats cupboard, looking sheepish. "Stay, stay, stay . . . go."

"She's so great!" said Beth. "Why didn't we have a dog?"

I said, "None of us knew what we were missing."

"Ginger didn't like dogs," Frank said. "I should've negotiated better."

My parents said nothing, silently acknowledging the suffering under his authoritarian nympho wife.

I said, "But then you wouldn't have Ivy! You'd have moved in with some less wonderful animal that had been a compromise. Or a cat."

Frank returned his gaze to Ivy. I could compliment her all day long, and he'd nod proudly at every adjective.

Beth asked what other sales we had on the calendar besides the Mankopf's.

The truth? None buckled down. I said, "The Mankopfs have turned into a full-time job."

Frank looked at Beth. "And who knows better than you and John-Paul how much diplomacy it takes to land a job, with Goldie underbidding at every turn."

"When can we see it?" she asked.

I said, "Tomorrow. If it's okay with everyone."

"Who's everyone?"

"Lois, Manny, Vanessa. I don't want them to feel invaded."

"Manny's here? Manny's back?" they simul-asked.

"Adding to an increasing list of complications," I said.

"Did we come too early?" Beth asked. "Because I'm sensing something."

"Beth, we just got here," said my dad.

"We can go home, and come back for the sale if you'd prefer."

I said, "You're *not* going home. What you might've been sensing was just me wishing I had a lemon, and half and half, and clean sheets on my bed." I walked my mug to the sink and said I was running upstairs to check on the bathroom and straighten up whatever needed straightening up. "You know how immaculate and house-proud I am," winning a chuckle from my dad and an eye roll from Frank.

In the master bath I moved my bulging cosmetic bag to a lower shelf and wiped the toothpaste-streaked basin. What else? Replace the towels, or just refold? I Windexed the mirror, scrubbed the toilet, unwrapped a fresh bar of soap.

My bed was made, as I hadn't slept in it. I smiled as I picked up the clothes and underwear I'd worn last night, recently recouped from Luke's bedroom floor.

Muted conversation was drifting upstairs. I whistled on the way down to warn of my imminent appearance.

"No one will judge you," Beth was saying.

"Judge who?" I asked.

Frank said, "I told her that I'd met Connie Winooski, and that I was nervous about seeing another woman so soon after Ginger died."

"I'm working on that," I said. I thought he'd appreciate a change of subject, so I asked Beth, "You remember Marcia Kirshner? She's teaching at Macmillan. Engineering science. We've reconnected since I've been back."

"Have you told her about you and Luke?" Beth asked.

Did all roads have to lead to one of the house romances? I

said, "I didn't want to talk about my personal life, given what she's going through."

"Not ill, I hope," said Beth.

"No, personal. Marital. Criminal. You were here when it happened—front-page news, Harrow's first FBI raid. He's awaiting trial. His parents hired a big New York City defense lawyer."

"Are they still married?" Beth asked.

"Still . . . not *un*married," I said. "He's out on bail, staying with his parents. Marcia visits."

"Why are we all standing around," my dad asked, "when we're dying to see what you've got?"

"What *I've* got?"

"Notes, pictures, ad copy, numbers?"

I said, "I don't know what you mean by numbers."

"Expenses, insurance, incidentals."

"*I* take care of all that," Frank lied.

"Good to hear," said my dad.

I was feeling fifteen again, the weekend helpmeet who wrapped and bagged and gave change. I had to speak up, which might earn another injured offer to return to Buzzards Bay. I knew exactly what button to push on the topic of their overreaching. "You trust me, don't you? I mean, that's why you turned Finders, Keepers over to me, right? You trusted my instincts and my judgment—"

"Of course, of course," my parents said, one then the other.

"It's not a trial run. I've done"—how to quantify so little?— "countless sales with Frank's help, and I've ended up in the black on every one."

"What are you picturing our roles to be?" Beth asked.

What I'd been picturing wasn't so much roles as role reversals: the wrapping, the bagging, the directing traffic.

Diplomat Dad said, "No more shop talk. What should we serve with the lobster? A salad? Frank, want to come with me?"

"I'll give you a list," said Beth.

Frank patted my dad's back. "This guy loves running into his ex-students. I swear, every single bagger went to Harrow High."

"Only summer jobs, on to bigger and better things. We'll get corn at the farm stand on Route 9, the one right after the bridge."

"A Sancerre would be great—my treat," said Frank.

"Is Connie free tonight? She'd be *very* welcome," said Beth.

I pointed out that they'd only brought four lobsters.

"Another time then," Frank said, his expression belying his words.

My dad and Beth were astonished that Frank had only eaten lobster in a roll. They demonstrated their newly acquired mastery over cracking the shells and mining the meat, instructing as they extracted.

After several glasses of Sancerre, a bolder Beth said, pointing to Frank and then me, "He's dating Connie, and you're dating her son. What are the odds?"

"Odds? In Harrow? It's not even a coincidence," I said. "He and I are on the reunion committee. A few weeks ago we were talking in the parking lot of the Over Easy, and I asked him out for a drink."

"Good for you," said my dad.

"What about the time he dropped by to tell us we couldn't sell alcohol?" Frank asked.

"What *about* that time?" I asked.

"I saw something like a spark that morning."

I said, "That's interesting, because I didn't think I was very nice to him, and vice versa."

"You were selling alcohol?" my dad asked.

"More or less accidentally, just a giveaway with some stemware," Frank said.

Beth said, "That could've earned you a whopper of a fine."

"He must've known you weren't operating a liquor business," my dad said, "wholesale or retail."

"His crooked predecessor looked the other way about everything," Frank said. "I'm guessing Luke wants to dot every i and cross every t."

"He let us off with a warning," I said. "And since then, any booze left behind goes home free, drinkable or not."

"I like that," said my dad. "Word can get around. 'Come to a Lewis estate sale and you may go home with a free bottle of vintage port.'"

As if it were the logical next question, Beth asked, "Is being chief of police in Harrow Luke's career goal?"

I said, "Do you mean, would he be making more money in Springfield or Hartford or Boston?"

"I think you know me better than that. I wasn't asking a salary question. It was an ambition question. Is this job a big enough challenge for him? Does anything happen here?"

I said, "Harrow needed someone with scruples who wouldn't be pimping his ex-wife's escort service on the beat—"

"To any adult male in a nice suit," added Frank.

Beth said quietly, "My ex had nice suits."

This was new. I'd been too young to have learned the particulars of Beth's divorce. I poured myself another half glass of wine, added a few ice cubes, and sat back. "Is it possible that your brother heard about the Quail's Nest from your husband?"

When she didn't answer, I said, "Uncle Paul's meeting Aunt Paulina there? I know it's not your favorite topic."

"I take the long view of it: He has a happy marriage."

"One more question: Do you know if he just googled

'bed-and-breakfasts in Harrow, Massachusetts,' and then got led up the wrong stairway?"

"What does that mean?" my dad asked.

"There were two stairways," Frank said. "One had kisses painted on the walls. The other went up to the beautifully furnished guest rooms on two."

"My brother was, still is, the sweetest man in the world," Beth said. "He was in his forties, alone and lonely."

"I'm on their side," I said. "I love how they met. In fact, I got a slap on the wrist from junior house mom Vanessa when she thought I was being judgmental."

"She remembered Paul?" Beth asked.

"Vividly. I'm sure it was the only marriage that came out of there."

Beth said, "They wanted to host the wedding! I said no fucking way my brother was getting married at a whorehouse!"

I'd never heard Beth say fuck or fucking or go as far as "whorehouse." I said, "Well that must've settled that."

"It was at the Harrow Inn, a lovely event," my dad said.

I said, "I know. I was there."

"Is there any reason this has to be discussed?" Beth asked me.

"It fascinates me, that's all. It's like our own version of *Pretty Woman*."

Frank surprised me by asking Beth, "Has your brother ever acknowledged, in confidence, how he met his wife?"

"The most he'd ever say that had the slightest negative ring to it was about her getting a green card by marrying him. He's utterly devoted to her. Shall we warm up the pie?"

"It's been in the oven at two hundred since we sat down," Frank said.

I said, "I wish they lived closer."

"How far away are they?" Frank asked.

"Chicago," Beth said. "She had relatives who immigrated there."

"Chicago's an easy flight from Bradley," said Frank. "Not even two hours."

"Are you thinking Thanksgiving?" I asked.

"We could do Thanksgiving here, if I wouldn't be intruding," said Frank.

"Or sooner," I said. "Maybe they'd want to own something from the house where they met."

"No, they would *not*," said Beth.

"We've always let sleeping dogs lie," said my dad.

"Why would they come all the way from Chicago for an estate sale?" asked Beth. "We can't even get them here for Thanksgiving."

"Let's call them!" I said.

"Now?"

"Yes, now. Isn't that how life used to work before texting? People sat around reminiscing, and somebody brings up a relative they haven't talked to in a long time, and someone else says, 'Let's call him.' "

Beth still looked torn. I said, "You must miss him."

She sighed. "Maybe later tonight. I don't want to interrupt their dinner."

"Do you have his cell?"

She said she had both cell and landline in an actual address book that required a trip to her suitcase. She came back downstairs, still looking reluctant to make the call. With encouragement, she hit the numbers. We waited. Then: "Paul! It's Beth . . . no, no, everything's fine. We're all fine. We're here with Emma. In Harrow. We drove up this morning. We're going to help her with a big sale. . . . Yes, she's in charge now. . . . Thirty-two . . . and you're both good?"

She was nodding, smiling, bigger and bigger smiles, then happily, "When were you going to tell me?"

"What?" I whispered. "Tell us what?"

"Paulina is looking at a job here!"

"When?" I asked.

"When?" she asked Paul.

More nodding and listening, but more and more glumly. "Would you move here?" she asked, then winced at his answer. "I see . . . a scouting trip?" Then "I didn't know Paulina had a brother. . . . You okay? . . . Good. Keep us posted. Love you."

As soon as she'd hung up, my dad said, "Paulina has a job interview? Is that such a tragedy? You look so depressed."

"It sounds like an excuse," said Beth.

"For what?"

"A separation. She's coming here with her brother? When did he pop up?"

"Did you ask what the job is?" I asked. "Where? Doing what?"

"Emma! I don't know! He was sounding more and more heartbroken."

"Are you sure a new job means a separation?" my dad asked.

Beth didn't answer. Frank had served the pie and added scoops of melting ice cream. Beth was the first to take a bite, and then another, in agitated fashion.

"Beth?" asked my dad.

"Once a whore . . . ," she muttered.

Frank shooed us away from the dishes and the kitchen. That's what he was here for, he said. Go discuss whatever you have to discuss. He rejoined us, postcleanup, with cognac in cordial glasses as my father was saying, "A job interview could be just a job interview."

With a nod of mild thanks, Beth took a glass. "My mother never blessed their union. She threatened to disinherit him." That made my father fake a cough, which I interpreted to mean *Disinherit what? Nonexistent money?*

"Did she come to their wedding?" I asked.

"She boycotted it. And maybe she was right."

"What are we missing?" my dad asked. "Did he say where the interview was, or with whom?"

"Some place that hasn't opened yet. It has to do with hospitality."

"It could be all on the up-and-up," he said. "Paulina lived here. She liked America. She thinks Harrow is her hometown, with all due respect to Bratislava."

Beth's glance in my direction said *Isn't that your father all over?*

"Can we change the subject?" I asked.

"To what?"

"Tomorrow. What you'd like to do."

I was expecting "Go to Quail Ridge Road," but instead Beth said, "I'm thinking I should fly to Chicago."

"Beth!" my dad yelped. "That's crazy! Did he ask you to come?"

She picked up her phone, stared at it, then tossed it back onto the coffee table. "Maybe it *was* a half-cocked idea, even if I meant well."

"Would you like to go over to the Mankopfs' tomorrow?" *Consolation prize*, I thought.

It was just the ticket. When her face brightened, I reeled off, "The cellar, the garage, the closets. I know you'll see things I missed."

"Is there an attic? Have you been through what's stored up there? Remember the antique rocking horse we found in what's-his-name's—that ex-dean's—house on campus?"

"This attic was converted to bedrooms for the escorts."

"Emma means where they plied their trade," said Frank.

Beth's smile faded. Surely neither Frank nor I had meant to remind her of Paulina, but apparently we had.

"You love going through closets," my dad tried. "Remember the coat you thought was faux fur, and it turned out to be mink?"

Beth shook her head. "Not mink, muskrat. The lining was in shreds. Nobody wanted it."

Still hoping to distract, I asked if she remembered the sale where she found a wad of cash in a bathrobe pocket.

"A trench coat," she corrected joylessly.

"Which we turned over immediately to the lawyer in charge of the estate," said my dad.

Beth wasn't listening. "A brother," she grumbled. "Wanna bet?"

42

Tell us about you," Beth said to Juliet, who continued to ride over on her old bike, declining breakfast, then cheerfully eating whatever Frank scrambled or flipped. He routinely apologized to Beth, my dad, and me for the intrusion, for treating the Lewis kitchen as his family conference room and therapist's office.

"Don't be ridiculous!" said Beth. "She's lost both her parents. She's an orphan. She obviously adores you."

Juliet seemed equally grateful for Beth's attention. She told her that she'd lived in Manhattan since college. Hoped to return. Worked freelance. Considering graduate school, just not sure for what, adding, "First, we have to deal with the house."

For Beth's purposes, could any summary end better? It took only a few more benign questions before she got to "Hon, Emma told us that the house needs paring down."

"'Paring down' is putting it mildly," said Juliet. "It's uninhabitable."

"I'm sure. So many bad memories . . . where your father died, not that long after your mother's tragic death."

Juliet said, "That's true . . . but it's filled with shit! Frank can tell you—it's an indoor junkyard."

"I'd love to see it," said Beth, retirement forgotten. "I think you know it's what we do. We help Emma help children get out from under what their parents thought they'd want to inherit."

"I was shocked when I came back for her funeral," said Juliet.

"Estate of Mind has a very big sale ahead of us at the manse over Labor Day weekend. But we can extend our stay beyond that, if Emma doesn't mind."

I said, "This is your house." Then, less truthfully, "You can stay as long as you want."

Immediately and predictably, Frank piped up, "I hope I'm not in the way. I hate that you're sleeping on the foldout couch."

"Don't start that again," Beth said, then turned back to Juliet. "Hon—Mr. Lewis and I have more than twenty-five years of experience running estate sales. When I hear that two daughters have—presumably—inherited a house that's overwhelming them, I can't stifle the impulse that says, 'Lend them a hand.'"

Quietly, Frank said, "Their father died two weeks ago, Beth."

But I could see that Juliet was paying attention. "In what order?" she asked. "You get rid of the stuff, get it cleaned up, and then we put it on the market?"

"Yes," Beth said. "And sometimes a customer comes to the sale, looks around, and says, 'I love the bones of this place. Can you tell me who has the listing?'"

I asked Juliet if Rain agreed that it was time to sell.

"I'm the executrix. Besides, she doesn't have a job. She'll get half of whatever the house brings in."

"And half of what *our* sale brings in," said Beth, "which is a full sixty percent of the proceeds."

Frank shot her a surprisingly defiant look.

"Or more," she said.

"I think as long as Rain doesn't have to lift a finger or stop hanging all over Theo, she'll say okay, do it," said Juliet.

"Theo?" Beth said, confused.

"Athena's younger son, who's been consoling Rain full-time," I said. "Eighteen years old."

"Athena," my dad repeated. "Athena Eliopoulos, who taught at DeWitt? She was our union rep over there."

"She was my dad's most recent girlfriend," said Juliet. "Both Rain and I had her for kindergarten."

"I don't remember an Athena being mentioned in the *Echo* piece," said Beth.

"That stupid piece!" Juliet cried. "I wanted to sue, but I'd have to hire a lawyer."

"Everyone hated that story," Frank added.

"And now everybody hates the reporter who wrote it," I said.

"Athena Eliopoulos," my father mused. "How is she doing?"

"She's okay," said Juliet. "It wasn't exactly true love."

"Still teaching?" asked my dad.

"Greek, at the Center for Adult Education. She's fluent."

"She was the only sane one I dealt with when I went over there," I said. "No offense."

"She emails me about the house," said Juliet. "She thinks there could be some valuable stuff there."

We three estate sale professionals exchanged glances that Juliet rightly interpreted as *We've heard that before.*

"No?" she asked.

"It's what everyone who's ever watched *Antiques Roadshow* believes," I said.

"That they own the goose that'll lay the golden egg," said Beth.

My father said, "One of the things we were famous for, and Emma too, of course, is peace of mind combined with expertise. Nothing—no painting, no antique—goes unnoticed. We run anything that could have high value by experts in the field."

Except that we were mostly our own experts. It didn't take an art historian to tell us that a canvas covered in dripped paint wasn't a Jackson Pollock.

"I should go," said Juliet. "I have an interview at ten."

She was in cutoffs and a faded UConn T-shirt. Frank asked, "Here? A job interview *here*?"

We waited. She finally said, "For Amazing Maids. They're hiring."

I knew Frank would worry about her cleaning offices at night, in buildings without security guards.

"Did your father or mother leave you *nothing*?" Beth blurted out. "She must've had jewelry? A car? I certainly remember a fur coat."

"Just the house."

Frank stood. "I'm driving you. I'll get your bike back over to Greenough." And to Ivy, "C'mon girl."

When they'd left, Beth said, "Remind me of the address on Greenough."

"Forty-four, but you're not going over there yet."

"I think we're one conversation away from a handshake," Beth said. "I'd like to get this on the September schedule."

Did I remind her that Finders, Keepers no longer existed; that now I was in charge? But I was sitting at her kitchen table, in a house with no mortgage, effectively sleeping in their bed and watching movies on the Netflix subscription charged to their card.

"September sounds right," I said.

43

Though it had been at least fifteen years since I last saw her, I instantly recognized Paulina when she answered the door on Quail Ridge Road. The hair that had once been yellow was now platinum; maybe instead of a size 2 she was a size 6, still stunning and—it suddenly came back to me—still a statuesque head taller than Uncle Paul. But, but . . . why here?

When I introduced myself with a reminder of who I was—her husband's sister's stepdaughter—she threw her arms around me. "You're a vimmin now! You're good? Do they all still hate me?" —her accent no lighter than I remembered from her vows.

What to admit, as the sole spokesperson for the family? I could be astonished to find her here, but I didn't have grounds to be annoyed. A job interview didn't mean a relocation or the end of a marriage; it didn't even mean a job.

"No one hates you," I said. "Why would we?" And then with a neutral smile, having looked up "brother" in Slovak, "We didn't know you had a *brat* in this country . . . or at all."

"Tomáš?"

"Do you have more than one?"

"Four," she said without elaborating.

I would've asked for particulars, but without warning Manny appeared at her side, putting his arm around her waist and grinning. He asked if I'd seen the drawing titled *Polly* at the gallery.

"I did."

"My favorite," he said.

"Did you know you were going to be part of his show?" I asked Paulina.

"Not surprised. He sketched."

It was easy to fill in that blank, under what circumstances Manny Mankopf sketched the live-in escorts.

I asked how long she was staying. When was the interview?

"It happened. I'll be front of house."

"Which house?"

Manny answered, "She'll be making an announcement at the gala."

The gala? Estate of Mind's gala?

"My new boss will be there," she said.

"The gala is to show off the house and its contents," I reminded Manny.

"She means not to be about me," said Paulina. "We'll do another gala."

To get the conversation back to family matters and firmer ground, I asked, "How's Uncle Paul?"

"He's fine."

"Will you be moving here? Will he?"

"Right now I am thinking I'll be here weekends. We have modern marriage."

"I taught her that phrase," said Manny.

"Beth is worried about that," I said.

"I should talk to her before party. Can you call her and put me on?" When I hesitated, Paulina said, "I will be nice."

I dialed Beth. When she answered, I said, "I'm over at the manse. Paulina is here. She wants to talk to you."

"What's she doing there? What's going on?"

With Paulina at my elbow, I could only answer unhelpfully, "She'll be at the gala."

I could hear a loud exhale. "Okay."

"Give me a minute," I told Paulina, and ducked into the beau parlor, out of earshot. "I think she wants to set the record straight. I haven't seen the brother, if that's what he is. There's some announcement coming, and she says she's moving back."

"To Czechoslovakia or whatever it is now?"

"No, to Harrow. Will you talk to her?"

"Do I have a choice?."

When I rejoined Paulina, another man was standing next to her. He was stocky, gray-haired, shorter than Paulina, eyeglasses on his head, reminding me of an HHS shop teacher I'd had for driver's ed.

"Tomáš?" I asked.

He grunted, then asked Paulina something in what was presumably Slovak. Paulina waved his question away and said, "Is Beth wanting to talk?"

I handed her the phone, Manny and Tomáš still in attendance. "You two," she said, pointing at both men. "Leave." Then, "Beth, it's Paulina. I asked Emma to call you—"

I could hear a few words coming through from Beth, most often *Paul . . . my brother . . . your husband.*

"He'll visit," Paulina said. "He can't just pick up. He has job. We FaceTime." Then she was listening, nodding in a way that struck me as patient, even sympathetic.

I could hear the word *heartbroken* through the phone.

Paulina said, "He always sound like that when he talks about me. It's because of the shame."

Beth must've asked, "For what?"

"He married a *prostitútka*, Elizabeth. Or whatever word you like more. He had to pretend he didn't. And had to pretend he didn't make big mistake. It's very boring. We're fine. I'm going to work here. He'll visit."

I took the phone back and said to Beth, "It's me again."

"Well, if she isn't as cool as a cucumber."

I asked Paulina if she'd excuse me. Back in the beau parlor I told Beth that I had everything under control. She and Dad should not rush over. No need.

"Are you sure? We can be over there in ten minutes."

I was very sure. Paulina plus Tomáš plus Vanessa, Lois, and Manny? Too much.

"You know what would be a huge help? If you went over to Ginger's house. We could start making a dent over there. Ask Frank for the key. He'll let Rain and Juliet know that you'll be looking around."

"Should I bring a contract?" she asked.

"They don't know what our protocol is. If they question you, tell them we always visit a potential client in advance of . . . anything."

I congratulated myself on the assignment: They'd get that one going, start climbing that mountain of brown furniture. Who better, who more thorough, knowledgeable, more sharp-eyed, than Mr. and Mrs. John-Paul Lewis?

44

Beth described it this way, her chin trembling: "It was packed to the gills. We expected that. The second we walked in, we said, 'This isn't normal.' First the two front rooms—sofas, chairs, tables, lamps in multiples. Junk. Games, magazines. Framed garbage. How Frank ever lived here, I'll never know."

"Poor guy," said my dad.

"You've been there," said Beth. "It has a lovely layout. From the outside, it looks like a stately home. It could've had character, if it wasn't a nightmare inside."

They were telling me this at the police station, after giving statements, while Luke was interviewing Frank in a more official capacity.

"Four bedrooms," said Beth. "Maybe five."

"At least," said my dad.

I'd been letting them vent and digress. Finally I asked, "Where was this secret room?"

"Not so secret—I mean, not to us," said Beth. "How many Murphy doors have we seen? A bookcase that's a door? We see a hinge, and we don't think twice—there's a room on the other side."

Only half listening, I had my eye on the closed door of the interrogation room, repeating, "Uh-huh, uh-huh."

"We opened the door and found the light switch," Beth

continued. "We looked at each other, both of us thinking—or maybe we said it out loud—'Are you seeing what I'm seeing?' "

"Two words," said Beth. "Stolen art."

"Or 'art thief,' " said my dad.

They recognized, first, a Childe Hassam from the Macmillan College Museum of Art, its collection known to every Harrowite with even a passing interest in art.

"Her walls were covered," my dad went on. "It was a gallery, perfectly manicured. Every painting, every drawing, no bigger than an ordinary sheet of paper! And the other little stuff on shelves, again beautifully arranged. Small bronze sculptures, a Tiffany box with a scarab on the top—"

"The most charming Warhol shoe drawing!" added Beth. "I was praying they were all fakes!"

"Except they're not," said my dad. "We're talking Picasso, Whistler, Reginald Marsh, Klimt. Beautiful watercolors. Even some books, first editions! A Dickens! We're walking around and thinking this one, this one, this one."

"The Isabella Stewart Gardner heist of Western Massachusetts! She had to be a klepto!" said Beth.

"Hell of a mess in the public rooms," said my dad, "yet a curator at work in the hidden one."

"Frank couldn't have known," I said, for the tenth time since I'd gotten their frantic call from Greenough Street. But did he *not* know there was an art gallery on the other side of a bookcase?

The interrogation room's door finally opened. I could see that Frank had been crying, and Luke was looking as serious as I'd ever seen him. My face didn't know where to go or what to do.

Frank suspected nothing, yet my parents had breezed right in? Not the time to make that point.

"From the moment I moved in," Frank said, "there was a desk in front of the bookcase and a file cabinet next to the desk. Why would I move a desk to examine a bookshelf that looked like a bookshelf? No one knew!"

Still, she must've come home carrying paintings and sculptures, and whatever else made my parents dial 911. I said none of that—I'd ask him in private—but Beth asked unhelpfully, "You never suspected anything? She never asked for your help, for a hammer, to hang up a picture? Or 'Help me get the desk out of the way'?"

"I left the house at seven, seven-thirty! I was at school all day."

"I'm going back over there," Luke said. "I'm meeting the state police forensic team."

I asked Frank if I could drive him home. "Ivy probably needs to go out," I said, to bring him back to life.

"Please," he said.

"Is he out on bail?" I asked Luke.

"He wasn't arrested."

"Can I *still* be arrested?" Frank asked. "I swear—and you know me—I'd cut off my right hand, both my hands, before I'd steal anything, let alone priceless works of arts." He turned to me. "Two of them were from the Wadsworth Atheneum. Bronze statuettes. Ye gods, from the J. Pierpont Morgan collection!"

I took him by the arm and said, "Let's go home," sending a silent, worried goodbye to Luke that meant, *I'm so in the middle.*

45

It was a terrible night for us all. Beth called Connie the minute they got home and asked if she could come over. She told her that Frank had gotten some very bad news—no, not from a doctor, not about his health, thank God. In a word: his ex would've been arrested today for grand theft if she wasn't dead.

"Luke may or may not be coming over," Beth continued. "He had to semi-arrest Frank. No, bad choice of words. He had to *question* Frank, who was at the station for several hours this afternoon. We'll explain everything when you get here."

How someone could arrive in twenty minutes with a huge pot of chicken and dumplings—reassuring us that it was healthy, the dumplings being whole wheat? Sorry, she added; she hadn't had time for dessert.

My parents roundly discussed the subject of whether we should eat or wait for Luke. Frank had gone to his room, tears running down his face as he headed for the stairs.

"We should eat," I said. "And drink."

I'd had an update. Luke was at Greenough with not only the forensic team but the furious yet ecstatic director of the college museum, who'd tearfully offered to resign every time another priceless piece of art went missing. Had the guards looked the other way? How many per floor, per room? Had she damaged canvases with a pocketknife?

No. We would learn that Virginia "Ginger" Crowley had taken everything, piece by piece, under her coat or in her giant, unsearched purse.

Every single thing she'd stolen was listed with the Art Loss Register. Ginger had helped herself, in and out, back and forth, sometimes even in a group on tour, while Frank was at school.

We called upstairs to Frank, "Connie's here!" He came down, pale, red-eyed, and greeted her with, "I'll never live this down."

Was it possible to cheer him up? I couldn't think of one single thing.

My dad said, "If I'd ever known what a can of worms we'd be opening . . ."

But Frank cut him off, sounding impatient, even annoyed. "As if you'd want to be complicit! As if you wouldn't dial nine-one-one when you discovered all of Macmillan's lost art in my house! Certainly you're not suggesting that!"

"Never in a million years did we think you'd be Ginger's accessory," said Beth.

"He is *not* implicated," I said. "I'm sure no one, including Luke, thinks Frank ever knew what Ginger was hiding, or had a secret room."

"I was married to her! This was going on under my nose . . . except that it was behind my back."

One of them had set the table and managed to coax all of us into chairs. "Around this table are"—I pointed—"one, two, three, four character witnesses, and if I may speak for us all, who love you," I told Frank.

Connie said, "I can't remember which movie—I think *It's a Wonderful Life*—where people stand up for Jimmy Stewart and don't take their money out of his bank. It would be just like that— your ex-students show up, a whole pep rally, if it ever goes to court."

"It won't," I said.

*

Luke came over straight from Greenough. We knew he couldn't comment about an open case, but we tried anyway. *C'mon. The suspect's dead. There won't be a trial, right?*

He tried to ignore our questions. He helped himself to a plate, knife, fork, spoon, beer.

"Seconds?" Connie asked the rest of us.

"It's delicious," everyone assured her.

With Luke squeezed in around the kitchen table, Frank was first to speak into the conversational void. "If you have any more questions for me . . . we're all family here."

I was sure Luke would decline the offer, but after a few bites, he asked Beth, "The room on the other side of the bookcase? How did you know it was a door?"

Beth answered. "After all these years, we know where to look"—but quietly, as if their ease in finding a hidden room reflected poorly on Frank.

Luke took another bite from the stew and asked what the beige things were.

"Dumplings," said his mother. "Comfort food."

I had to ask: "The museum didn't have surveillance cameras? I know they have guards."

"Not in every room," Luke said, "and some were Macmillan students."

I asked if the heists started and ended with Ginger. Any other works of art missing from the museum since she died?

"If so, unreported," said Luke.

"Innocent until proven guilty and all that, but imagine what she'd have to face if she was alive," said Connie.

"Prison," said Luke.

"Any chance the museum wouldn't have pressed charges?" my dad asked.

"Zero," said Luke. "They're foaming at the mouth, ready to bring charges against the corpse . . . sorry, Frank."

"I should go to prison for stupidity," he said.

"That's enough," Beth scolded. "You weren't arrested. Ginger stole this stuff when you weren't home and hid it in a house she owned two marriages before you moved in." She turned to Luke. "How did he react when you told him? That tells a lot, right?"

With an apologetic glance at Frank, Luke said, "He fainted. I thought I'd killed him."

Frank said, "The charge would be 'receiving stolen property.' Well, you can only imagine! It hit me like a ton of bricks."

"Frank has low blood pressure," I said.

"I wanted to take him to the emergency room, but he talked me out of it," said Luke.

"Embarrassing now," Frank murmured. "Except it was the worst, most shocking news I'd ever heard in my entire life."

None of us said what we must've all been thinking: *Worse than hearing that your wife was struck and killed by lightning?*

"This isn't tied up in a bow yet," Luke said. "The FBI will be questioning you. They have a special art division . . . and as much as I hate to say it, there's still art missing from houses all over Massachusetts."

"Small art?" I asked.

"That'll be my first question."

"Frank, innocence aside, you need a lawyer," I said. "A criminal lawyer."

"I know. I know. Of course."

"Not some ex-student you had for trig," said my dad. "We'll find you a Boston lawyer."

"The evidence will prove you had nothing to do with Ginger's crimes," a blessed thing for Luke to say. I squeezed his hand under the table.

"But it was my house. How do you prove that I too wasn't the crazy collector who stole paintings and drawings and sculptures and snuff boxes, for God's sake, and took them home to my private locked room?" Frank whimpered.

"Fingerprints, a lie detector test, and DNA. And there were two fur coats with oversize pockets sewn inside. Would I find large pockets sewn inside any overcoat of yours?"

It was Luke's first smile of the day, yet Frank wasn't finding one shiny penny in anything he was hearing.

"Fur coats," said Beth. "No wonder she wore them everywhere." She winked at me in a way that could mean only one thing: *Mink! Stay tuned. Sale ahead.*

Frank asked Luke, "Were the girls home?"

"They were."

"Obviously you told them why you were there?"

"I did."

"Were they horrified?"

"I was vague. I said we didn't know yet if the art had been stolen."

"Thank you," said Frank.

"I can't help wondering if Stefan was in on it," I said.

"Another guilty corpse," said Beth.

Dishwasher loaded, Connie again apologized for arriving without a dessert.

"Ridiculous!" said Beth. "We don't know how you made, let alone transported, a week's worth of chicken and dumplings."

"It's been in my Instant Pot since I heard," said Connie.

"I can't stay," Luke said. "I'm beat." He asked if I'd walk him to his car, prompting a hopeful bark from Ivy, who'd been following our conversations, her attention fixed on forlorn Frank.

"Not you, girl," Frank said. "Emma will be right back. Daddy will take you out soon."

"So will I," said Connie.

At the driver's-side door, Luke exhaled. "Conflict of interest much?"

"I've lost count," I said.

46

Were any one of us in a mood to host a presale gala? No.
Still, my elegant black and silver Paperless Post invitations went out. They showed a woman in a flapper dress flirting with a tuxedoed man, above the caption "Everything Must Go," in Glamore Luxury Display italic.

Beyond my own mailing list, I invited members of the chamber of commerce and city council, Macmillan professors recommended by Marcia, and every homeowner on Quail Ridge Road who might complain about traffic. Frank had worried about the degree to which the Mankopfs would upstage Estate of Mind, and I worried too: The guest list should be mine, and the host should be me. One thought: Should Lois invite former clients?

"Ask her," Frank said.

I called, and she answered. "As long as they bring a checkbook," she said.

In under an hour, she'd sent me a long list of names and email addresses, subject line "Confidential."

I wrote back, "Confidential? But I'm inviting them, right?"

Her answer was an emoji thumbs-up.

"Whatever happened to discretion, discretion, discretion?" I asked Frank as I typed up the finished guest list.

"She's looking for a new beau," he said.

*

Refreshments, yes. Prosecco in plastic flutes, since we'd need a hundred if all invitees came. We'd be displaying the real stuff on a rented table, covered with an embroidered table runner ($25). Beth had guessed, after googling, that the crystal glasses were Waterford, which we'd sell in lots of four ($55) with a question mark after "Waterford."

In fact, everything our customers would need for entertaining was on display: Lois's Portuguese cabbage tureens, a punch bowl short only one cup; silver and more silver: silverplate trays, silverware; silver creamer and sugar bowl, candlesticks, pitcher, serving pieces, salt and pepper shakers, grape scissors, lobster forks, pickle forks.

Foodwise, we had a budget, so nothing more than cheese, crackers, and grapes on some Vermont-made cutting boards ($35) that we'd wash and oil before doors opened in the morning.

I dressed way up in my Rent the Runway flouncy peach chiffon dress. Lois was in black, still in mourning, but floor length and low cut.

People came. The future buyers, the rubberneckers, the old patrons—men of a certain age who seemed overly happy to see Lois and Vanessa.

The reason we were doing this open-house gala preview was what? Beth said it wasn't just about the manse, but to show future downsizers that Estate of Mind knew how to put on a sale. She and my dad were circulating with prosecco, pointing out the sale's leading lights. My business cards were on the display table and every other horizontal surface.

How late would people stay? How soon could I go home?

*

What is a wingman called when she's a woman? Yes, once again, Marcia Kirshner.

She was making herself useful, as both server and conversation starter, in a short red lace cocktail dress. She joined me, surely having noticed that I was having a longer-than-usual exchange with a fiftyish man in a double-breasted seersucker suit. Later she would tell me the cost of his mahogany cap-toe Oxford dress shoes.

"Am I interrupting?" she asked, kissing me hello, complimenting my dress.

"I was asking this gentleman if he'd stayed at the Quail's Nest," I said, my eyes opened wide to signal *i.e., patron/john*.

"And what did the handsome gentleman say?" she asked. That's all it took, one flattering adjective.

" 'Stay' isn't quite the right word. Visit, yes, on my birthday, as a gift to myself. And maybe on a few other holidays. What about you?"

What did he mean, what about us?

Suddenly, Improv Marcia materialized. I would've answered with a straightforward "Mrs. Mankopf chose my company to sell the contents of the house," but she took over. "Do you mean, our connection to the red-light aspect of the house?"

"That's exactly what I'm asking you two lovely ladies."

"When I was a senior in high school, I worked here to pay my tuition," Marcia said.

"Fascinating. When would that have been?"

"Let me think . . . well, I'm twenty-five now," she lied. "So seven, eight years ago."

"And you?" he asked me.

Confident that we'd be confessing in seconds that we were joking, I whispered, "Also to earn tuition."

Marcia exhaled a theatrical sigh. "It was great while it lasted."

Linking arms with me, she said, "We were very popular, weren't we? Barely legal."

"And when you'd earned enough for college—was that it? Your work here was over?"

"I worked summers through college," Marcia said. "I mean, you must know what room, board, and tuition was even then." Then, peering more intently at him: "I'm trying to remember you. Were you famous for something?" She raised her eyebrows. "Some physical attribute? Girls talked, you know, didn't we?"

Could a man look any happier? Could I be any more dumbfounded? What else could I say but "We did . . . talk."

"What do you ladies do now for work?" he asked, hope washing over his face.

I waited to hear what Marcia would come up with. "We've moved on," she said. "Sometimes I think about getting back into that line of work . . . but I doubt if my husband would be on board."

"A husband? Interesting. Were you honest with him—I mean, about your past?"

Marcia grinned. "I didn't have to be honest! It's how we met!"

The man put out his hand, "I'm John Doe," he said with a wink.

At this point I was just watching Best Supporting Actress Marcia in action. "I'm very open about it," she added. "I have no regrets. In fact, I'm something of an activist. I put 'escort' on my résumé. It's always a good talking point at an interview. Ours wasn't the only marriage that came out of this place."

"You, too?" he asked me.

I shook my head.

"I know the *girls* fell in love," he said. "The men . . . well, who is going to bring home—forgive the expression—a working girl to meet the parents?"

I said, "I know a man who fell in love and married one of the escorts."

"And got her green card!" Marcia said.

"Green card," he repeated. "Where was she from?"

"Bratislava," I said.

"Paulina!"

"You knew her?" Marcia asked with a nudge to his elbow that could mean only one kind of "know."

"I recruited her. We hope to open before Christmas."

Recruited her when? Then? Now? Having strained my last acting muscle, I was relieved to be back in real life. "Open what before Christmas?" I asked.

"A home away from home," he said, eyebrows arched. "Pushing some boundaries, sex not for sale . . . sex, destigmatized. Here, in this town, we'll be trailblazing. We already have a waitlist."

I gave Marcia a look—*Find out. I've had enough*—and said, "I should be meeting and greeting and circulating. Thank you for coming, John."

Luckily or not, Vanessa was heading our way with open arms, which earned her a kiss on the lips from our new friend. Did she even know him? Hard to tell, because all she said to Marcia and me was "I see you've met one of our most distinguished guests."

"I don't remember these girls," he said. "But I wish I had reason to."

"We're hoping you'll be back this weekend with your checkbook," said Vanessa.

He was looking surprised. New policy? Lola's Ladies never took personal checks.

I said, "Everything you see here will be for sale."

"We were told Emma is the best in the business," Vanessa said. "And believe me, we asked around."

"Estate of Mind. Her cards are on the bar," said Marcia.

"Estate of Mind," he repeated, each word a tasty morsel. He closed his eyes. "I love that; I love the subtlety."

"Be careful," said Marcia.

John asked why, smiling, as if she meant *Watch out for the wild ride ahead.*

Marcia pointed. "The tall guy by the punch bowl? He's our chief of police? She's dating him."

I waved, and Luke waved back. "So nice to meet you," I said. "Please look around. We hope you'll be back this weekend."

I joined Luke, topping off my glass, though I'd had quite enough. "You won't believe it . . ."

"What?"

"Marcia told that guy we used to work here, as junior Lola's Ladies. I hope he knew she was kidding."

"Did he introduce himself?" Luke asked.

"Just as John Doe, with a wink."

"It's Andy VanMeter," said Luke.

"You know him?"

"I have to. He's our state rep. First Hampshire District. Total asshole."

This was too good to keep to myself. I called to Marcia, "Um . . . when you're free . . . Come say hello to Luke."

47

I'd done my best, publicitywise. I'd pinned the Venus de Milo notices to bulletin boards all over town and sent frequent, tantalizing emails to an ever-expanding mailing list. After many requests, Jeffrey Orwell had written a front-page piece below the fold, titled "The Secrets of Quail Ridge Road." His editor wouldn't let him spell out anything sexual, so it was blander than I would've liked. "Escorts" and "the oldest profession" did make it past the puritanical copy desk, but no mention of money changing hands for favors. The timing might've been good—it ran the Wednesday before the Friday opening—but the sale itself was only mentioned in the carry, on page 8.

Posted hours, as ever, were 10:00 a.m. to 5:00, Saturday, Sunday, and Monday. Beth, Dad, and I arrived at 8:00 a.m. We didn't expect any of the Mankopfs to have straightened up to our satisfaction, nor would they be dressed, let alone out of the house, as the contract had stipulated in what now seemed like another life. The cheese, grapes, and crackers were desiccating on the handsome cutting boards.

But where were the silver cheese knives ($35 apiece), the silver water pitcher ($175), the display of sterling silver, the silverplate trays, the silver ashtrays, the cigarette lighters, cigar cutters, and candy dishes—every single thing I'd spent two days polishing, down to the marrow spoons and pickle forks?

"Where's the rest of the stuff?" I asked Lois, the first one up since we'd rung the doorbell.

She pointed at the leftover refreshments.

"No! The silver!"

"Service for eight in its original box," Beth added.

I sensed something like genuine panic in Lois's reaction. It wasn't the look of someone in collusion with a thief.

"Did someone put the good stuff away?" I asked. "Maybe back in the kitchen?"

"No," said my dad, who'd checked there first.

"I don't know," Lois wailed. "Why would they? I went to bed. I don't know."

"I mean, could a stranger, a guest, have been the last one to leave?"

"Thomas was going to lock up and clean up . . ."

"Is he still here?" I asked.

"Let me check. They're in one of the nests."

As soon as she'd left the room, I whispered, "What if . . . ?" as Beth was repeating, " 'They're?' *They* being Tomáš and Paulina?"

"If someone stole the silver, we dial nine-one-one," said my dad.

"As if he's going to admit it!" said Beth. "Or her!" of course meaning Paulina, the adulterous in-law.

Lois returned with Paulina, in a kimono that was one of the "silky seven" I'd priced individually at $100, despite their polyester content. "What the fuck," she was muttering.

"Is Tomáš here?" I asked.

Spotting Beth, she said, "I wouldn't know."

How diplomatic did I need to be? John-Paul Lewis, the experienced negotiator, mediator, and innocent-until-proven-guilty diplomat, said, "We were just wondering where he put some of the things that were on display last night."

"Like what?"

"Every piece of silver," I said.

And, having done more scouting, my dad added, "The Waterford. The majolica. The Wedgwood."

"Maybe someone bought it?" Paulina said.

"Bought it?" Lois snarled. "All of it? Meaning he sold it?"

"I don't know! Isn't that the idea? Isn't that why everything has price tags?"

"I need to speak to him," I said. "People are already knocking on the door!"

As we three Lewises waited in depressed disbelief, Tomáš appeared, in boxers and undershirt, needing translation. Paulina had clearly filled him in as to why he was being summoned, because he entered the room saying, "What am I accusing of?"

"Nothing yet," I said. "It's just that some things are missing."

Paulina's translation was ten times longer than my two sentences. His answer was one spit-out word.

"He doesn't know what you're talking about," said Paulina.

"Wasn't he the last one here after the gala?"

"I sold nothing," he said in English.

Back and forth. Back and forth. Offense clearly taken. Who had said that? Why should he steal things they'd be needing for *chimica*?

Chimica? Hanukkah? I didn't care. I pivoted back to "Who else was still here at the end of the night?"

"Nikto!"

"No one," Paulina translated. "Nobody."

We didn't answer the constant knocking at the door. My dad and I took turns yelling reminders of the 10:00 a.m. starting time. I was feeling more and more helpless, bordering on the panicked. We'd left the gala, been shooed away, reassured that everything would be shipshape. *Get a good night's rest. Big day tomorrow; a big weekend. We'll throw away the plastic glasses and wrap up the cheese. Go home! Sleep well!*

"We had a cop here all night," said Lois. "What good did he do?"

"If you mean Chief Winooski," I said, "he wasn't here in any official capacity. He was my guest."

"He's her boyfriend," said Beth.

"Call him!" said Lois. And to Tomáš, "Do you not know the way this works? This isn't a free-for-all. This was going to be the sale of the century!"

Paulina didn't bother to translate. She asked, "What else missing? Chemistry is going to need a lot of things when we open. We're going to serve light meals."

All of us Lewises wore the same expression: baffled. I asked, "Chemistry? Light meals where?"

"Here. Once we get liquor license, but my partner won't have trouble getting that."

"Tomáš?" I asked.

"No, my buyer," said Lois. "He was here last night—Andy VanMeter?"

"In what way is he your partner?" I asked Paulina.

"He's owner. I'm hostess, the front of house."

"What's the back of the house?" Beth asked.

"Men and women having a good time, enjoying each other," said Paulina.

"Does that mean that Lola's Ladies is back?" I asked.

Paulina said, "Not like that. Not men buying dates with vimmins."

"As what?" I asked.

"A hotel for people with their minds open."

Beth didn't care. "What are we waiting for? Call Luke!"

Lois was sitting on one of the rented folding chairs, looking utterly dejected. She said, "Thomas has a job when this place reopens. You know who *doesn't* have a job? Who didn't come to bed last night, and isn't here now?"

I did know: Manny Mankopf, who'd left the town of Harrow without benefits or a pension; certainly without a golden parachute. And without selling a single painting.

"I know how he thinks," Lois said. "The silver was a wedding present from his parents and his aunts and uncles. And the rest of it? More wedding gifts. And then our silver anniversary. God. Did we last that long?"

I went to a window that overlooked the driveway. Manny's car was gone.

Beth asked, "Should we call nine-one-one? If Manny drove all night, he could be halfway to Florida."

It was Lois's decision. What he'd taken surely added up to grand larceny in Massachusetts—in any state! The signed contract and the list we'd drawn up could probably turn into a civil suit, but what kind of publicity would that be?

"If taking the silver means he'll never return," Lois said, "he can have it."

"Except we have a contract," I said. "And everything that's missing was on that list."

Loyal Vanessa had been standing by, silent until now. "It all came from Daddy's side of the family. You can't steal what belongs to you." She smiled. "No victim, no crime. And if he's not back, do you want me to give the tours?"

I did not. I called Frank, who should've arrived by now. Though I'd always seen tours as Manny's gimmick, I'd come around. Customers could miss whole floors without a guide. I asked Frank if he could fill in. He knew the house—

"*That* again? Even in the best of times, I wouldn't be good at it. There's so much that's distasteful. I'm feeling exposed enough."

I heard Connie in the background, asking if everything was all right.

"Manny was going to give tours, but he's gone," Frank told her.

"That's only half of it! He cleaned us out!" I said.

"He's gone for good?" Connie asked, sounding hopeful.

"He took off with everything portable, everything fenceable and pawnable, so he's probably not coming back."

Now Connie was on the phone, asking, "When do you need us?"

"I'm not doing tours," I heard Frank say.

"Shush," said Connie. "How hard can it be? 'Here's the master bedroom. Here's where the men waited for their dates. The bells on the wall? Those rang upstairs, a heads-up: 'Joe Shmo is on his way upstairs.' "

"How'd Frank sleep?" I whispered. "He sounds exhausted."

"And cranky . . . but I think the sale is going to do great, and it'll give him a nice shot in the arm."

"The sale is not going to do great," I said. "Most of the stuff I bragged about in every email is gone."

"Did you call Luke?"

"I thought I should do an inventory first. I just want to get through it. People are already here, ringing the doorbell every two seconds. Someone tried to get in through an unlocked window." My voice broke.

"I'm calling Luke," Connie said. And to Frank: "Let's go! Emma needs backup."

I heard a markedly less miserable "On our way!"

48

Frank wasn't the only one who'd lost his mojo.

What had once seemed potentially fulfilling—the selling of bedclothes with a past, the ceiling mirrors, the sanitized sex toys wrapped in tissue paper, secured with a heart sticker and labeled "preloved"—seemed only embarrassing now. Given the previous week, would Frank be able to ring these up with anything like good cheer?

We'd prepared a handout. The first draft was my dad's, and overly apologetic. Proofreader Beth rejected it. "This sale isn't for babies," she scolded, "and this isn't 1950. This is an enlightened college town in Massachusetts, the bluest of states. We are *not* going to be boycotted or shunned." And to me, "Your father's worried about crossing some old line that would get a teacher fired. Please tell him he's his own guy now."

"Dad, you're your own guy now," I said. "And if any lines are crossed, it's me doing the crossing."

We settled on:

Dear Friends,

As the head of Estate of Mind, Inc., I had already agreed most happily to sell the contents of this stately home, the highly rated Quail's Nest bed-and-breakfast. Over the course of my visits, appraisals, and interviews with the owner, it came to light that another kind of commerce had been conducted here, and that was an escort service. Should I, or could I, walk away?

I'd already devoted countless hours to the project. And how does an experienced estate sale professional walk away from an historic house filled with beautiful furniture, valuable artwork, and collectibles?

She doesn't walk away. She takes that leap, and in doing so risks offending her loyal customers. Please know that I made every effort through press releases and emails to prepare our buyers, to attract new ones, possibly to intrigue. . . .

If arriving with children, please confine your browsing to the first and second floors, the cellar, the garden shed, and the garage.

We welcome all, especially our first-time customers. Please add your names to the sign-up sheet. A five-dollar coupon is below.

> *We welcome you and thank you!*
> *Emma Lewis & Associates*

The loyal reunion committee turned out in full force, all six of them, seven if you counted Luke. Up to now we'd pretended to be mere buddies, but given last night's heist, my depressed state, and the imminent lead balloon of a sale, he squeezed my hand when he arrived and kissed me when he left.

Annette caught both and hustled to my side. "What haven't you told us?"

Unable to say anything lighthearted, cute, or untruthful, I said, "He's the chief of police. We wanted to be discreet."

"How long has this been going on?"

I didn't have to answer because a woman was walking toward me with a set of ceramic salt-and-pepper shakers shaped like dice. She asked if $3.50 was the best I could do. "I don't care," I said. "Take them."

Annette reached for the pair and said, "I'm happy to pay three-fifty," prompting my first smile of the day.

"No," said the customer. "I saw them first."

"Oh, all right," said Annette, adding for good measure, "A steal, if you ask me."

I thanked the customer for coming and said I hoped she'd keep shopping.

"Slim pickings," she said. "Not exactly as advertised."

"Everything sold the minute the doors opened," said Annette.

As soon as the woman headed to the checkout table, Annette said, "You're welcome. Tell me now: How long has this been going on, you and Luke?"

I said the partial truth: "Not during the first or second committee meetings." The whole truth was, at least on my part, since the day I came down to breakfast and found Chief Winooski drinking coffee in my kitchen.

Connie did in fact give tours. I tagged along with her first group and heard her hit all the right notes. Starting in the kitchen, she said, "I worked here when my boys were little; I baked muffins and scones and the occasional birthday cake. If you have questions you don't want to ask in the group, I'm here all weekend." Heading up the stairway to heaven, she said, "I have to make this a GP tour, otherwise I might explain what the owner meant by 'heaven.'"

Rep. VanMeter came every day with a wad of cash. He wanted only what he described as "classy." I assigned Beth to him, introducing her as the founder of the company. He bought most of the library accessories—the fake leatherbound books, the standing ashtrays, the tankards, the fireplace tools, the horse paintings and dog paintings. Bed frames, yes, but he'd be buying state-of-the-art mattresses. The ladies' desks, chaises, vanities, every mirror, and the *Downton Abbey*–esque antique bells on the kitchen wall that summoned the ladies ($999), paid only after losing his argument that they came with the house, like sconces and light switches.

Manny hadn't taken any clothes. He could hardly claim Lois's as his rightful property. I changed into a red satin cocktail dress, adding several rhinestone pins to the bodice, then into the next dress (black velvet), and the next one (full-skirted, yellow). Eventually I was back in my own jeans and T-shirt, but still accessorizing with Lois's unwanted costume jewelry, the more the better.

As ever, the bikes, the hammock, the lawn mower, the gas grill, the rakes and garden tools, all went. Lawn chairs, outdoor furniture, except for the embarrassing hot-pink plaster-of-Paris nude statue in the rose garden, not made more demure by any Macmillan-wear, as advised, but decorated with Mardi Gras beads. We'd predicted it would be the sale's white elephant, marked down to nothing by 5:00 p.m. on Labor Day, too heavy to move. Rep. VanMeter didn't want it, even for free. Should we take it to the dump? Exhausted, we left it.

We had the usual headaches: rain on day three, cars both in and blocking neighbors' driveways. The minor thieveries—an egg slicer, potholders, unsellable CDs—we let pass. There were rubberneckers, as expected, snapping selfies along the stairway to heaven, grinning men posing in front of the bird-named dorm rooms. The *Echo*'s Jeff Orwell was present two out of the three days, asking Beth, my dad, and disconsolate Frank questions about his late wife's thieving. Every question was a variation on

"Curious that the people who discovered the stolen art lived in the same house as the thief's widower . . ."

I asked Orwell to leave my family alone. "You already wrote about it. The whole town and beyond knows that millions of dollars of stolen art was recovered." I pointed to Beth and my dad. "And they didn't appreciate your so-called joke about Finders, Keepers feeling like Losers, Weepers. They're heroes."

"Exactly. I'm doing follow-ups."

"Can I speak to you off the record, human being to human being?"

"Okay," he said. "I'll try."

"Frank Crowley has suffered enough. He had no idea that his wife was stealing art. None! It was all hidden, and she was crazy. He's in a state of shock."

"Ask *me* about his state of shock," said a new voice—Connie's.

"You're who?" asked Jeffrey, pencil poised.

"A friend, and a parent whose sons had Mr. Crowley as a baseball coach and teacher. You can quote me as an anonymous source."

"Saying what?"

"Saying that Frank Crowley fainted when he heard about the stolen pictures. You only faint when you hear shocking news, not when you helped with the heists."

I was giving her a worried look; was fainting something that Frank would want the world to know about?

"You were present? You witnessed this?" Jeffrey asked her.

"I was, and I did," she lied.

Had I placed my hand on a Bible? I said, "In my own kitchen. I saw it, too."

"People can fake fainting," said Jeffrey.

"White as a sheet," said Connie. "Can you fake that?"

"I have a sale to run," I said. "If you had your eye on anything, you should buy it now."

"There's almost nothing left," Connie confirmed.

*

Manny left behind a canoe and kayak, his golf cart, the grand-father clocks, and all the furniture that wasn't foldable. Besides every piece of silver, he took Persian runners, lamps, a bocce set, and a croquet set. Had no one noticed he'd attached a U-Haul trailer to his rental car?

Though Beth had been envisioning the sale as the peak of my alleged career, I couldn't rise to the occasion. By Sunday at five, she and my dad suggested I take Monday off. Go swimming. Go to a movie. Find a Labor Day parade. Neither within range of my hearing said what was so obvious: *Emma's not cut out for this.*

Sadly, a 35 percent commission of a fraction of what we should've sold does not add up to a working wage. Did it ever, though? Was I going to live underwritten by parents and rent-free forever?

We followed through glumly on the celebration dinner we had planned before Manny's and Ginger's larcenies. Frank made his excuses; he was emotionally exhausted, please carry on and have a lovely meal. But Connie won the battle. What exactly was he worried about? "Luke would never be joining us if you were a suspect. It's over! Enough!"

We ordered takeout Peking duck for six, an extravagance that belonged to the presale optimism.

We toasted just to having it over. I toasted Connie for being the best substitute tour guide, for jumping in, for keeping every-one's spirits up, and especially for bringing Frank back from the dead.

"Everything could be recovered," said my dad. "Lois could wake up tomorrow and decide to press charges."

"If you mean another Mankopf sale because he's forced to

return all the stuff you can count me out. Good luck to Goldie's Oldies, because I'm not doing this again."

"This sale?" asked Luke. "Or this, big picture?"

"Too soon to know," I said, though it wasn't.

My dad said, his glass raised, "Emma, I know you're disappointed, but this sale is still one for the books. And I don't mean because of Manny's pilfering. I mean, a house of ill repute? The diplomacy and the euphemisms it required . . . I'm not sure Beth and I would've had the nerve to take this on."

"Yes, we would," said Beth, "not to take anything away from Emma."

Luke said, "Especially not that slinky red dress."

"Who bought it?" Beth asked. "Do we know?"

"I did," said Luke.

49

Early Tuesday morning the nude pink statue appeared on our front lawn, delivered by three large men, their labor overseen by Representative Andy VanMeter. He knocked on our back door and explained that he couldn't keep it; he didn't want it on the grounds of his future operation. He'd been about to pitch it, but then thought: It's art, isn't it? We deserved it, and we were closer than the dump. It was a thank-you gift for leaving the place immaculate.

I asked about that future operation he kept alluding to.

"We're calling it 'Chemistry.' "

"We heard that already. Because . . . ?"

"Because it's all about that: chemistry, desire, dating experiences for open-minded people."

"Is this a sex club?" I asked.

"Well, that's the coarse nickname. It's all about sex positivity. Nonmonogamous men and women gathering to explore their sexuality."

Beth asked, "Is this legal?"

"Totally. It's going to be an aparthotel for having fun in a safe setting, for pushing boundaries. No judgment. A *refuge* from judgment." He gave the statue a pat. "This gal had to go. I'm putting a hot tub in the rose garden, and this . . . not exactly a Leonardo da Vinci."

"Paulina will be doing what at Chemistry?" I asked.

"Manager. Screener. Couples have to apply. No weirdos."

"And Tomáš?"

"Handyman, valet, and hall monitor."

"Hall monitor?" Beth asked.

"Consent. It's key. Zero tolerance. No touching until you ask permission!"

Chemistry . . . Might that be *chimica* in Slovak?

Beth was gracious. She said the statue had nice lines. Thank you. But one thing; the way we worked, Finders, Keepers D.B.A. Estate of Mind had to pay him a token amount.

No, no, he wouldn't hear of it!

She explained: They'd learned the hard way. Money had to change hands when something from a sale ended up in our possession. No reflection on him, but she didn't want crazy, greedy Manny Mankopf accusing her of stealing it.

"I'm not going to argue," VanMeter said. "Want to give me ten bucks?"

"One will do it," she said.

I went inside, found my wallet, took out a dollar, went back outside, and gave it to Representative VanMeter.

"This is going straight to Lois," he said. "And I'm going to remember how you do business—very professional. You're no yard-sale hobbyists."

Once he'd driven away, I said, "It's hideous, but I think it was a nice gesture."

"He's running for reelection," said Beth.

Athena dropped by to apologize. She'd been a short-term resident of the house on Greenough, and had no idea, just like Frank, of what it was concealing. What does the district attorney do? Charge dead people? The room was hidden, behind a bookcase. Like in a movie! Who knew there were such things in real life? It was haunting her. Had Stefan helped? Had I heard that fingerprints found in the hidden room matched those on the driver's-side sun visor of Stefan's car?

She'd brought baklava, apologizing that it wasn't homemade, but from the best Greek bakery in Worcester.

Her arrival coincided with our trying to move the pink statue off the front lawn. Athena studied it, touched its forehead, and said, "It's Artemis, the Greek goddess of the hunt."

Was she just mocking our new eyesore?

"Feel . . . a moon. Here. . . . The Roman name for her is Diana. Goddess of the hunt and of the moon."

I too felt a raised crescent.

"Who desecrated her like this?" Athena asked.

"You can bet, Manny," my dad said. Even worse, the statue's fingernails and nipples had been painted red.

"It would look much better unpainted, don't you think?" Athena asked.

"For now, we just want it out of sight," I said. "The neighbors will complain, and Ivy will pee on it every time she goes by."

Athena said she didn't think it was plaster of Paris. A statue this heavy could be marble.

"Should I get a rag and some paint thinner?" asked Beth. "Maybe test a patch?"

"Not paint thinner," said Athena. "Start with water and see if that does anything before trying anything caustic."

Soapy water did nothing, nor did an alcohol pad, nor nail polish remover.

I then said something that would forever be quoted by all concerned, gleefully: "Too bad. It could actually be pretty if it's marble."

*

Since we were the family who'd discovered the college's stolen art, it took only one phone call to Macmillan's grateful curatorial department to schedule a house call.

The department's sculpture expert, Dr. Kobayashi, took measurements and photos, and then examined Diana with a black light under a blanket. She said she'd be sending photos to colleagues at other museums.

"Which ones?" I asked.

"I'll start with the Smithsonian, the Metropolitan Museum of Art, the National Gallery of Art, the Art Institute of Chicago, and the Yale University Art Gallery."

"Because . . . ?"

Rather vaguely, she said, "Its style . . . it's neoclassical," then asked about its provenance.

"Quail Ridge bed-and-breakfast," I said.

"Do you have reason to believe it was stolen and therefore disguised?"

"The B and B was a whorehouse," said Beth, "hence the sexing up of it."

"It might've just been left there from owner to owner as part of the property, like a birdbath," I said.

"Philistines," said Beth.

Snapping more pictures, running her fingers across the forehead's crescent, Dr. Kobayashi viewed her from every angle, then said, "Give me a few weeks."

As a recent, unwilling expert on art thievery, I immediately checked the Art Loss Register and saw no sixty-two-inch Diana or Artemis missing from anyone's collection.

Luke and I hadn't talked in a few days, longer than usual, and this was a good excuse to call him. He might be amused to hear I was the proud owner of the pink lady that no one wanted, a thank-you present from Rep. VanMeter. Also, I hadn't known that Stefan's fingerprints had been found in the hidden room. A moot point, I supposed, prosecutorially, but it would've been nice to know.

I'd been trying to give Luke some time and distance, given the decisions he had to make on Manny, on the dead art thieves, on my housemate dating his mother, and on my hovering parents. And undoubtedly on the glum and occupationally disheartened me.

I texted: Busy 2nite? Doing much better here. ♥

Hours passed. I worried about him in general, out on the streets, crazy people everywhere, drive-by danger of all sorts, even in Harrow. But this was the breaking-up kind of worry. I walked Ivy, scolding myself for so many days of bellyaching. When my phone rang at 5:20, I answered, trying to sound upbeat.

"I was going to call you," he said. "I talked my way into a table at Beardsley's tomorrow night. If you're free."

"Beardsley's," I repeated. "Are you sure?"

"Very," he said.

50

I'd told Luke just to honk when he picked me up to avoid my parents' overly approving hellos and goodbyes, and Frank's ongoing apologies for crimes he hadn't committed. As soon as I got into the car, after a quick hello kiss, I launched into my semi-existential crisis, meant as an apology for my post-sale bad mood: Here I was, living at home like a boomeranging millennial. My parents were in no hurry to leave, maybe sensing my ambivalence about estate sale captaining.

"Seat belt," he said.

I did that. After I checked my lipstick in the visor, I said, "You're looking very handsome tonight," adding an ahem of a fake cough that meant, *And how do I look in the red dress that you bought me?*

"You, too," he said.

I expected, with me in my highest heels, he'd drop me off at the restaurant, but he kept driving, down Market Street, into the municipal parking lot, to the most distant empty space. He turned off the engine, turned to me, and said too solemnly, "I told the restaurant we might be a few minutes late."

Here it was: the inevitable end. How had I misread the signs? He was everyone's favorite Harrow citizen, and its most eligible bachelor. Instantly, my eyes stung. Why had I let my professional failure leach into my personal life? It was all my fault. Would an apology help? I said, "I won't be able to do dinner if you're breaking up with me."

Was he smiling? If that was meant to be reassuring, it wasn't. No contradictions, no rebuttal, no words except, "I need to get something out of the glove compartment."

I was right. The glove compartment was where he kept a box of tissues, and I'd be needing several. I leaned back so he could reach across my lap.

"Close your eyes," he said.

I heard the opening click and the closing one. Then, "Now open."

It was a small maroon box. A ring box, unless I'd been misled by a lifetime of romantic comedy finales. "Is this . . . ?" I managed to ask.

He took it back and opened it. It held a ring. A ring with three not-small round diamonds in a row.

I said, "Luke . . ." I dragged my glance away from the ring. "Is it what I think it is?"

"Yes, it is. And maybe you could say, 'Yes, I'll marry you,' or 'No, I don't want to.' "

I burst into tears. I told him yes, yes, of course yes. I'd been so worried. Like a coward, I'd never told him I loved him, but I did. So much. He knew that, right?

"I knew that," he said.

"The ring. It's so . . . *me*. I mean, I love antique jewelry. *Is* it antique?"

"Mostly."

"Mostly?"

He touched each diamond. "New, old, new."

"Old? From your family?"

"No. Yours."

I knew then. It was built on my mother's engagement ring.

I had to swallow another weepy gulp. I dragged my gaze away

from my left hand. I told him it was the most beautiful ring I'd ever seen. And how was it possible that it fit perfectly? Did Beth help you with that? Like on TV, when the girlfriend slips a string around her roommate's finger when she's sleeping?

"God, I've never heard you babble like this. No. Your dad thought your mother's ring would fit, and because he was choked up, I didn't ask why."

"Her amethyst ring," I said. "He gave it to me on my sixteenth birthday."

Luke gave the ring a wiggle. "Too big? Too tight?"

I told him it was perfect. He was perfect. I touched his warm freckled cheek, alternating fond gazes between his eyes and my left hand.

He said, "I know the car isn't the most romantic or scenic place to propose, but you sounded so worried. Plus I didn't love the idea of taking out a box at the restaurant, in public, with total strangers catching on and posting pictures."

"Pictures!" I said. "We have to document this!"

We both took out our phones. Many selfies, cheek to cheek, a kiss that resulted in an off-kilter shot of the dome light. Shots of my left hand, splayed against my chest, held up midair. And one staged by me, Luke's hand on the glove compartment, obligingly grinning.

"Sending one to my mom," he said, "which means all my brothers will know in thirty seconds."

I said there was no hurry sending photos to my dad and Beth. Those coconspirators had known for weeks.

Once seated at, I swear, the same prize window table as our first date, I asked how the topic of my mother's ring even came up. "I hope it wasn't like 'When are you going to make an honest woman out of my daughter?' "

"Not quite. I told Frank I'd be proposing when I thought he needed something to look forward to. He confided in your dad, who called me and said he'd always hoped that someday, if someone wanted to give you a ring, and if I didn't mind, he'd get Annie's out of the safe-deposit box. It was my mother's idea to add a diamond on either side to make it yours. Then Steve Quinn at Quinn Jewelry made it work. They do all our engraving for the softball trophies."

"Best conspiracy ever," I said.

He asked if I'd seen the inscription.

I hadn't. I slipped it off. There they were, the letters distinct, having been worn for too short a time in too short a life: *Ubi tu es, ego semper ero.*

"Which means . . . ?"

"Your dad knew off the top of his head: 'Where you are, I am always.' "

I didn't want to cry at Beardsley's. I said, "That's going inside *your* wedding ring, if you don't mind me being a copycat." I put it back on. I kissed it. I kissed Luke. If I was making a scene, so be it.

51

We went to my house after dinner to share our news and found Beth and my dad watching TV in the study. I sashayed in and, without a word, delivered my left hand with a flourish.

Hugs and squeals ensued. I said, "You two phonies! You've known for weeks!"

"Weren't we good, though?" asked my dad.

"No! You were terrible. It was written all over your faces whenever I mentioned Luke. Good thing he followed up."

"Is Frank home?" Luke asked.

"At your mother's," said Beth. "God bless that woman."

Luke asked me if I wanted to go over there now.

"Sure."

"You came here first?" my dad asked, his voice choked.

"You're the father of the bride," said Luke. "You get the first handshake, and the first dance."

"Second dance," I said.

Back in the car, he said, "I sent Mom a picture. She knows. Which means Frank knows. Do we still need to go over there?"

"How about tomorrow? We'll bring her flowers. Let's go to your place."

We did. Once inside, I said, "I have my dancing dress on. Could we? To something appropriately just-got-engaged?"

He asked Alexa for John Legend. Not surprisingly, "All of Me" came on.

I said, now barefoot, the two of us interlocked, swaying between coffee table and wall, "It's hard to believe this is our first dance."

"It's not," Luke said. "It's our second."

I lifted my head from his chest. "I don't think so."

"Harvest dance, junior year. For maybe a minute—that dance where you switch partners?"

I said, "Sorry, but . . ."

"You had on another red dress. You smelled nice. And you knew my name."

"Did you ask me for a real dance later?"

"No! I mean . . . I wouldn't have . . . not back then."

I said, "I'm finding this a little sad in the self-esteem department."

His right hand slid down the red satin to pat my behind. "I'm much better now," he said.

I asked Alexa to play a love song from 2010. After just a few notes, Luke said, " 'Just the Way You Are.' Bruno Mars. Entirely possible."

I said, "I like this song. Thank you for cutting in . . . Who do you have for homeroom?"

He caught on after I opened my eyes wide and nodded my encouragement.

"Oh, right. Miss Finnegan for homeroom. We think she's a hundred. She puts Kleenex up her sleeve."

We switched to swaying in place, teenage style, my wrists on his shoulders. "Do you play any sports?" I asked.

"I can't. I have band practice every day."

"That's nice. What instrument?"

"Drums. All of them: bass, timpani, snare, xylophone, tambourine, triangle, glockenspiel."

"That's so cool. What's your name again?"

"Luke."

"Luke. I like that. I think I have a crush on you. Want to get married in fifteen years?"

"You mean it? That'd be awesome. Wait'll I tell the guys. But fifteen freakin' years? Can't we get married sooner?"

"How's December?" I asked.

52

Frank, of course, had already heard the marvelous news. Connie, he said, was tickled. Now all four of her boys would be settled.

He had Ivy's leash in hand. I asked, "Can you give me a few minutes to change?"

Five minutes later we set out with Ivy in the rain under one big black umbrella. I asked how he was doing.

"I can go for longer periods without thinking, Ye gods! How did I not know!"

"Which is when I bet Connie says, 'Snap out of it. You didn't do anything wrong!'"

"Two things on the topic of Connie," he said. "I'm going to move in with her." He managed a smile. "And you'll be happy to know she's given me two weeks to stop whining, then I have to see a therapist. Maybe it's about time."

"Good. I think it's taking up every cell in your brain."

"I know," he said, "and probably yours, too."

I covered his hand with mine on the umbrella's handle and said, "She's very lucky. You're the best housemate. I'm so glad to have been your landlady."

He said, his voice shaky, "Thank you. Me, too. It changed my life."

For fear of my voice going shaky too, I didn't ask him to elaborate. Instead I asked when he'd be moving in with Connie.

"Soon . . . well, as you can imagine, there's the sorting of George's things with the sons. New wallpaper, new bedspread, new bed. Not that I minded. But she wants me to feel as if it's *our* space."

"So nice," I said. "And I know at least one son who's all in."

He nodded, smiling. We drifted into small talk—the forecast, Ivy's appointment with a groomer. And news, still to be held as confidential: Alex's wife was pregnant with what would be Connie's third grandchild.

"Which reminds me," I said. "Marcia Kirshner's pregnant! The opposite of confidential!"

There was a pause that I knew to be a delicate one, which translated to *Who's the father?*

"It's Gideon's baby. They're reconciled, house arrest, ankle monitor, and all. Plus she'll be visibly pregnant at his trial, sitting a row behind the defense table."

"What a gal," he said.

Ivy had been stopping every few yards to shake herself vigorously like a dog in a cartoon. She'd done her business. We turned around.

Beth was at the kitchen table, at her laptop. "I want to host an engagement dinner," she said. "I don't mean an engagement *party*. That'll happen. Just a dinner with us six . . . I'm thinking cold poached salmon with a green sauce."

"When?"

"Tomorrow night, if everyone can make it."

Frank said, "I was supposed to have dinner at Connie's tomorrow night."

"Is that date set in stone?" Beth asked, "because I can call her."

Frank was toweling off Ivy, who was licking his face, postponing an answer. Then there was the making of a new pot of coffee, after opening a new vacuum-packed bag of beans. Finally, he sat down. "I'm going to propose," he said softly.

I burst into tears, surprising myself and alarming Ivy. "No, I'm fine. I'm thrilled. You've been through so much. And she's been great."

Frank said, "She doesn't let me wallow." Then, with a shy smile, "She adores me. Would you believe it?"

"I *so* believe it. I saw it! From day one. Actually . . . from *night* one. And I don't mean just the pie . . ."

Beth opened the cellar door and yelled, "John-Paul! Get up here!"

Frank said, "I haven't asked her yet."

I said, "We'll postpone the salmon. First things first."

When my dad appeared, Beth said, "Frank's going to propose to Connie tomorrow."

"More wonderful news!" said my dad.

The ring-happy me asked, "What about a ring?"

"I have one," Frank said.

"Not Ginger's, I hope!" said Beth.

He winced at that question, and for the first time I sensed that he had lived quite long enough with the Lewises. "No," he said. "Ginger didn't need an engagement ring. She liked the big square one that Stefan had given her."

"Red flag number five hundred," I said.

"I'm giving Connie one that was my mother's."

I took another teary inhale over that.

"How soon?" asked Beth.

"If you mean when we're getting married, I don't want to step on Emma's toes, wedding-wise, and I know Connie will feel the same way."

My wedding, Beth's favorite topic. "Not before the Greenough sale," she said, eliciting a groan from both me and Frank.

"Could we please not make a big deal out of the sale?" I said. "I don't want emails that say 'the house where Harrow's only lightning fatality lived and where stolen art was hidden.' I'm sure the girls don't want that either."

"I think it's sufficient to say 'huge quantities of furniture, cheap,' " said Frank.

Beth didn't answer. I knew she had ideas: Ginger, posthumously, was notorious; 44 Greenough had been referred to—sarcastically, by Jeffrey Orwell under his five-column headline—as "the secret museum annex."

"We know," said my dad, patting my hand. "We know . . ."

"Know what?" I asked.

"What the Mankopf sale took out of you."

"We're happy to do it all," Beth said. "We're thinking the weekend before Thanksgiving."

No longer Columbus Day weekend, but six weeks later? "But you'll be going home between now and then, right?" I asked.

They looked surprised. No, they'd be here the whole time, with so much to do.

My dad said, "Hon, we're now thinking that the condo might have been just an investment property that we'll rent out through Airbnb."

"But you love it there! The hiking, the ocean, the buying lobsters direct from the lobstermen!"

"The Mankopf sale gave us a booster shot," he said.

"The Mankopf sale was a disaster!"

"It was not a disaster," said Beth. "Maybe it wasn't the windfall we thought it would be. But it got the old juices flowing."

Frank asked helpfully, "What about starting up a Finders, Keepers on the Cape?"

"The condo in Buzzards Bay is eleven hundred square feet," said my dad. "We miss having space. We miss the house. We miss you. We even miss Harrow where our soon-to-be son-in-law is our chief of police!"

"We thought we were ready for retirement," Beth said.

"Or was it a way to give me a job and a place to live?" I asked.

"Honey, we never regretted—" my dad began, but I held up my hand. "I think you have *several* regrets: giving up the business, retiring, moving. But you're coming back. It's your house. And you're getting your bedroom back, as soon as I empty out the bureau drawers and change the sheets."

I put my right index finger to my lips to stave off an expected foldout couch argument, but there was no protest.

"And how about taking Finders, Keepers back, too? I mean not just in title but in practice?"

When Frank laughed, I asked why.

"Have you *not* noticed it's already back?"

53

We were afraid to indulge in what-ifs. What if our pink statue *was* valuable? So valuable that we'd be selfish to keep it? What if we couldn't insure it? Would we be morally obligated to donate it to the Macmillan College Museum of Art?

We waited weeks to hear back about who or what she was. Something like progress came in a follow-up visit from Dr. Kobayashi. She'd brought with her a professor who'd done his thesis on nineteenth-century American sculpture. He hadn't come to render an opinion; he'd come for the thrill of seeing our Diana.

He recoiled at the pink and the red but caressed the moon on her forehead. "Why?" he moaned. "Who?"

Dr. Kobayashi said, "I warned you."

"Now what?" I asked.

She asked if we'd trust them to hire a moving company that handled fragile artwork and would carefully transport her to the best art restorer they knew. Not far away, New Haven?

Yes, we said, of course.

"We'd cover that expense . . . should the statue come home to Macmillan."

I didn't like that "come home to," and Beth must not have either. "Thank you," she said, "but we're covering whatever it costs. And we'll need you to sign something that says you took her; otherwise we can't just put her on some moving truck."

"Understood," said Dr. Kobayashi.

Beth went inside. She took a while, probably conferring with my dad, then returned with a handwritten piece of notebook paper. She showed it to me. It said, "The statue known as 'Diana' or 'Artemis' is the property of Emma Ann Lewis, DBA Estate of Mind, of 110 Montpelier Ave., Harrow, Massachusetts. We the undersigned will return it to owner Lewis, safe and sound."

"Me?" I whispered. "Mine? Are you sure?"

"Very," she said.

I handed the contract to Dr. Kobayashi, and while she read it, I explained that we'd suffered a big reversal when someone stole all of the high-value items from the last estate sale.

"The same idiot who painted this priceless statue!" said Beth.

"Awful on all counts," said Dr. Kobayashi.

"You can tell us your hunch," I said. "We won't hold you to it."

No, she couldn't . . . she shouldn't. But her colleague had either lost patience with her discretion or just couldn't contain himself.

"We think it's a Hiram Powers," he said, and clasped his hands in prayer.

Hiram Powers, July 29, 1805–June 27, 1873. Born in Vermont. Famous, very. His sculptures were at every one of those museums that Dr. Kobayashi had consulted, and countless more.

It took ages, or so it seemed, to get Diana back. Uncrated and unwrapped, she was so beautiful, so classic, the marble so smooth and milky white, that I wanted to apologize for ever having thought *plaster of Paris.*

"We believe this was done before his 1843 *Greek Slave* made him internationally famous, after his bust of Andrew Jackson," Dr. Kobayashi said.

I had a flash of retroactive disgust over how Diana had been denigrated, painted garish pink and put out to pasture. Poor Hiram Powers! He'd turn over in his grave—at the Cimitero Protestante di Porta a'Pinti in Florence, Italy, my obsessive research had shown.

The Macmillan College Museum of Art tried again. They promised the sculpture would have its own alcove. The Lewis family would be credited with its discovery; we'd be reimbursed for its (very expensive) round trip to New Haven and its restoration.

But again, because we were the family who'd returned paintings and pocket-size sculptures worth millions to her very museum, we squeezed a number out of Dr. Kobayashi. "Off the record . . . I shouldn't say; ethically, museum curators don't . . . but at least six figures at auction."

We had a family powwow to discuss our moral obligation to Art. On one hand, I wanted scholars of American art and lovers of sculpture and students of Greek mythology to see the goddess Diana/Artemis, to write papers titled "Hiram Powers, Genius of Marble."

On the other hand, I was broke.

Speaking from that narrow, selfish lane, I made the argument for us cashing in: Sure, rich families donated important art to museums and colleges, but we weren't rich. If the high bidder at an auction, let's say, paid six figures to win it, they would surely cherish it. They'd invite their friends to catered dinner parties to show her off.

"I agree. Let's flip it," said my dad.

We'd start at the top, with Christie's and Sotheby's; if need be, we'd work our way down the auction ladder until someone wanted and appreciated our recovered goddess. Dr. Kobayashi strongly recommended we find out how it ended up in the rose garden. Provenance? Was there an original owner?

"Ask Manny," Frank prompted.

Did I have to? I hadn't talked to him since he took off with most of the valuable loot, and I didn't want to start now. I said, "My asking about the statue will only make him suspicious."

"You're not going to mention its restoration," my dad said. "Start by saying you're not pressing charges for his running away with the sharp end of the manse's contents. . . . Tell him you were just curious about the statue. Did it come with the house? Did he buy it? If so, from whom? Just curious. Tell him you might put it in another sale."

"Maybe I can ask Lois," I weaseled.

"She'll wonder why you want to know. Manny will wonder too, but he's not coming back here, probably ever, and certainly not to retrieve a statue he had so little regard for."

If this was the next step on the path to putting Diana up for auction, I had to comply. I dialed Manny's number, and to my surprise he answered. "Emma Lewis here," I said.

"Well, well, well." The nerve of him still sounding smarmy after what he did to us.

I said, "I'm not calling about . . . what you think I'm calling about. We know Lois isn't pressing charges."

"Smart woman," he said.

I forced myself to continue. "The pink statue in the rose garden. I'm curious where you got it."

"Why?"

I expected that, and I was ready. "It didn't sell. Maybe its original owner would like it back."

"I won it in a poker game. Joey some-Italian-last-name said he had a naked statue, that it could be worth something, and I said,

'A naked woman? Let me see her.' So he took me out to the garage. I said, 'Fine. I can put her in the yard. She just fit in the back seat of the cruiser.' "

"Do you think he'd want it back?"

"No. His wife didn't want a naked woman in the lobby of their restaurant. In Agawam, Italian, nothing special. So he put it in his garage. Besides, he's dead."

I was recording the call. "Okay, just making sure you didn't need it or want it."

"What would I do with it? It's all yours, doll."

Both giants of the auction world invite submissions. We followed the steps on their websites:

Tell us about your item

Add dimensions, history, and any documentation

Upload photos

Take front and back images of your item

Review and submit

Our specialists will review your submission

I did all of that. I was confident we wouldn't have to talk our way in, because I'd sent three photos of this, now ungummed, visible, and undeniable:

HIRAM POWERS

Sculp.

54

It sold, with Luke and me in attendance at Sotheby's, which had been the most gaga in response, and had sent a specialist from their Americana Department to Harrow to see Diana in person, in our living room, behind a baby gate to keep Ivy out.

The auctioneer introduced the lot by calling it a beautiful lost Hiram Powers. We were numb and nervous, but feeling better and better when the first bid went up. He took his time, scanned the room, smiled, pointed, teased to induce higher numbers from the competing bidders. "Fair warning," then hammer down at $220,000, the best return on $1 that Estate of Mind/Finders, Keepers had ever dreamed of.

Luke and I celebrated at an Italian restaurant on Lexington Avenue, in honor of Hiram's many decades in Florence. I confided to the waiter as he poured our first glass—from the bottle of Chianti Classico we splurged on—that we'd just sold something at auction, at Sotheby's, no less.

"Congratulazioni," he said.

"A sculpture that no one else wanted!"

"Until tonight," said Luke.

We toasted the unknown buyer, the charming auctioneer, Dr. Kobayashi, Athena, each other, and, with a twinge of guilt, and soon a little drunk, Representative Andy VanMeter.

*

Our reincarnated Diana's whereabouts were unknown for only a
month. I'd left a thank-you note at Sotheby's for the anonymous
buyer, the way birth mothers leave their wishes in an adoption
agency's file. Most generous on all counts, the benefactor wrote that
Diana had been donated to the Metropolitan Museum of Art, New
York. She'd be standing for all of eternity next to a sister, a bust of
Proserpina, goddess of the underworld and springtime, likewise
lovingly fashioned by Hiram Powers.

55

Even though I called Ginger's sale my swan song, of course I helped. Beth and Dad needed all hands on deck, minus Frank, who didn't want to cross that threshold ever again. Beth had advertised the sale as overstocked. "You can furnish a whole house from the contents of a single room. All offers considered. Own a piece of Harrow headline history."

We took turns leading the curious behind the bookcase. Beth had curated it into a gallery of Ginger's framed posters, mirrors, lamps, worthless art, and tchotchkes. Against my wishes, and never reported to Frank, she crisscrossed the secret door to the crime scene with police tape, begged from a disinclined Luke.

People bought the good, the bad, the ugly. Luke, his brother Peter, and Peter's husband helped buyers lug the heavy purchases, their eyes rolling over what other humans wanted to own. I helped half-heartedly. I surely didn't greet customers wearing anything from Ginger's closet, never before curated and filled with designer labels. Returned from the evidence room, not just one, but two minks, a brown one and a blond one, both with oversized, customized inside pockets. I thought it was tasteless to display them on rented dress forms with signs that told their outlaw history, but I was no longer in charge. They sold in a two-lot silent auction to the same bargain-hunter at a disappointing $501 apiece. But all told, the sale brought in $17,526, a record for Finders, Keepers.

My refusal to take one cent was meant to be an unmistakable
"I'm out."

Frank and Connie were married as soon as a Saturday was available at St. Sebastian's and the Harrow Inn. Of course my dad was
best man, returning a thirty-three-year-old favor. All of Connie's
sons and one son-in-law were groomsmen. Michael, the oldest,
walked her down the aisle.

Connie looked beautiful. Her suit was a gold brocade that
matched her hair. I was a bridesmaid, along with her two
daughters-in-law, none of us in matching dresses due to the time
crunch. I re-rented my flouncy peach chiffon gala dress, fond
tears running down my face throughout.

The priest knew Frank and Connie. He began his homily, "I
marry a lot of couples, but may I say—with apologies to those of
you present for whom I performed the sacrament of marriage—
this might be, for me, the most personally rewarding, uniting two
loving, wholehearted, and resilient people who found each other
in these parlous times."

I recovered enough to join Luke in a toast at the reception,
a small gathering almost entirely of ex-teachers and Connie's
relatives. We told our own met-cute story—Luke showing up to
arrest me—well, maybe just to investigate, and, just like a guy,
didn't want to pass on Frank's regards to his mom. Was that
such a big deal, a mere hello? "Well," I continued, "he managed
that much, because a sympathy card followed, conveniently with
Connie's phone number and email, which I had to translate for
Frank as 'Call me! Come over for coffee and an apricot muffin!'"

We'd rehearsed. Luke put his arm around me. "She's leaving
out the best part, which is where her hounding led." He picked
up my left hand, which I was happy to rotate in a queenly wave.

In unison, his brothers hooted *Luke Luke Luke!*

Luke said, "Don't change the subject." He lifted his glass. "To Mom and Frank . . . especially to Frank. I speak for my brothers, my sisters-in-law, my brother-in-law . . . all of you please stand up." They did, spread across the room. Luke continued, "Frank! We owe you! Huge thanks for taking over! It's a big job, but worth it!"

The bride called from the head table, "Bums! The lot of you!" beaming like the proudest mom on earth.

56

People! We have a lot to discuss tonight," said reunion co-chair Chris at our next meeting. Then, with a nod to his grinning wife, he raised his voice and said, "I move that Emma Lewis and Luke Winooski tie the knot at the reunion!"

"Second!" cried everyone except Luke and me.

"Have our *wedding* at the reunion?" I asked.

"It would be the ultimate drawing card," enthused Melissa. "Two classmates getting married at the reunion? Are you kidding me? Who wouldn't come to that?"

I refrained from calling it the worst idea I ever heard. Instead I said it was a very nice idea, but what about parents, relatives, and nonclassmate guests?

"Plus," Luke added, "it would mean that people are buying tickets to our wedding. I'm not comfortable with that."

"And I suppose you'd want bridesmaids and groomsmen who aren't fellow alums . . . ," said Brooke.

"Let's move on," said Annette, followed by a stage-whispered, "I don't know why it had to be such a big secret."

A day later, as we were washing and drying dishes in his tiny kitchen, laughing over that crazy motion, Luke said, "But here's what I've been thinking, venue-wise . . ."

I expected a review of the contenders—the Harrow Inn, or Beardsley's for sentimental reasons, or the chapel at Macmillan . . . but what he said was "I've been thinking about the gym. I don't mean at the reunion, but during Christmas break when school's off."

I wasn't a snob, but I wasn't a pregnant teenager, either. The high school gym for our wedding? I said, overly generously and insincerely, "I get why you're thinking of it, and it's so sweet—"

"What if there were lots of flowers? Even trees? With chairs—nice ones. Tablecloths. Candles? Music?" And with a smile, "Valet parking? It could be arranged."

"We'd have to explain it. It would have to be a footnote on the invitation—Luke and Emma danced together here for thirty seconds, fifteen years ago."

He continued anyway. "People have weddings in barns and bowling alleys and all kinds of weird places. It's the getting-married part that makes it work."

I said, "I'm sorry. I just can't see it."

The whole valley, it seemed, regardless of religious affiliation, needed a venue, a caterer, a band, an event planner, a photographer, and a tux the weekend after Christmas. It was a no from Beardsleys and everywhere else, in a tone that seemed to be asking, *December 27? What were you thinking?*

After a no from the caterer in Hartford that Marcia had used for her wedding, and one in Amherst that Rep. VanMeter would be using for his orgy's canapés, we decided on an elevated taco buffet from Buena Comida. It would have every garnish, multiple salsas, guacamole and cremas, a festival of proteins, two kinds of cheese and two kinds of tortillas. My goal: *alta cucina*, I explained, nothing that would remind guests of *la cafetería de la escuela secundaria*.

*

I had to admit, there was something municipally spirited about getting married at Harrow High School. We were alums. My dad had taught there, Frank had taught there, my mother had met them both there. Valedictorian Marcia Kirshner would stand up for me, and every Winooski groomsman had earned varsity letters as Harrow Hawkeyes.

Who to officiate? Connie lobbied for the priest who'd married her and Frank, but I wasn't Catholic, and the high school wasn't a church. We settled on the Superior Court judge whose wife had taught with my dad and Frank—not math, but even more fittingly for a gym wedding, phys ed.

What dress? It was long understood that if any of the siblings—Unity, Pamela, Celeste, or John-Paul—had a daughter, and that daughter was getting married, no matter when, or to whom, she'd wear her grandmother's lace and satin dress, preserved in a cedar closet since Valentine's Day, 1950. Long-sleeved, heart-neck-lined, deemed perfect for a winter wedding, then and now. My grandmother had been taller than I and a little stout. No problem, the aunts insisted. All had dressmakers, one more brilliant and talented than the next, who could do the job, and did—something old and something borrowed rolled into one. The something new: my thin gold wedding band.

At six p.m. on December 27 I was waiting for my cue, poised on my dad's arm between the girls' locker room and the botanical wonderland that had transformed the gym. I heard the opening notes of Mendelssohn's wedding march, tinny but true, seemingly a solo.

I looked around. It was Luke at the glockenspiel, making this music, mallets hitting keys softly, him looking up to smile, as much as the task allowed. My father had to remind the dumbstruck bride that the point of the march was to march.

I'd never seen Luke play, and I'd never heard anything so beautiful.

57

Marcia, now late in her second trimester, had invited me to lunch at the faculty dining room, which for some reason was famous for its Manhattan clam chowder.

"What's next?" she asked airily, as if she didn't have an agenda.

"I know this much: I'm out of the family business."

"Good! I saw it all over your face at the Mankopf fiasco. You were in shock. Do you remember me taking the handouts away from you? You couldn't even smile at the arriving customers and rubberneckers. You looked as if you were handing out programs at a funeral."

"Or maybe as if someone had just robbed me blind."

A short discussion followed, the one we knew by heart: the morally corrupt, bent cop Manny Mankopf. Not in jail. Fencing silver. Painting and drawing unsellable art.

Returning to the topic of jobless me, she asked, "You're not going to sit home, are you?"

Home. I smiled. Luke and I were renting what had once been a gamekeeper's cottage on the grounds of one of Harrow's only estates. In search of trustworthy neighbors, its owners had rejected applicant after applicant, no doubt violating fair housing laws. And who was more trustworthy and stable than the newly-wed chief of police, his cruiser always parked on the property? We shook hands. Deposits were waived.

But here in the college faculty dining hall, with its white stucco walls and white tablecloths, Marcia was saying, "You're not letting the auction money keep you from getting back to work, are you? Because a windfall isn't a job."

I said I knew that. We were being careful.

"I have an idea, a job idea," said Marcia, "which you may not love at first."

"Here? At Macmillan?"

"No. But hear me out, okay?"

"That bad?" I asked.

She blotted her mouth before saying, "An internship with the *Echo*. No, wait. It usually goes to Macmillan students, but not always. Do you want to hear why this is a brilliant idea?"

Knowing she wouldn't need my consent, I waited.

"You have at least one degree in journalism, right? Or creative writing or something like that? And some random courses?"

"True . . ."

"Students of mine have done it. You tag along with a staff reporter, but soon enough—since they're short-handed and don't want to pay a lot—they hire you. If you're thinking, why would they want a thirty-three-year-old intern, I can tell you why: You're mature. You have a car. They'd be getting an adult brain, and adult judgment. Not to mention, you're sleeping with the chief of police."

"You're not doing a great job selling this. Does it even pay?"

"Gas and mileage. But that's just until you're promoted. And you will be."

"Is this a Jeff Orwell tip?"

"No! We haven't spoken since I'm back with The Husband. And he's gone on to greener pastures, some daily in New Jersey with a fifteen-minute commute to and from Manhattan."

Of course she'd printed out the application. I was folding it to take home, to discuss with Luke, and no doubt throw it away. She took it back. "No, let's fill it out now."

I obeyed. My experience: not terrible. I'd written for the *HHS Banner* and had a few bylines in the *Daily Collegian*. I'd done all the press releases for Estate of Mind. Relevant courses, fiction and nonfiction. And I'd been reading the *Echo* my entire life.

Marcia said, "Put my name down as a reference. Oh, wait . . . use Gideon's last name. Arthur knows me as Marcia Siegel."

"Arthur?" I asked.

"The editor in chief." She took a gulp of her milk to wash down a large neonatal vitamin. "We go to the same temple. And Purim's coming up."

58

The *Echo* did take me on. Among us three interns, no one else wanted to do obituaries.

I volunteered for two reasons: It looks good to take a beat no one else wants, and, mostly, because of my experience reaching out to the bereaved. I vowed to make these phone calls journalistic and empathetic. No longer would I use an address to assess what size house in which neighborhood I might help empty.

In less than a semester's block of time, I've achieved my goal, which is to put more meat on the bones of the obits, to make them miniature biographies, to put the best spin on dead persons' accomplishments, whether they had any or not.

Months of writing about other people's lifespans have made me think about the arc of time, about how the present can cheer up the past. Frank met Connie after a lifetime of romantic disappointments. Dad and I suffered the heartbreak of losing my mom, and then Beth appeared with a chocolate cake. My selling alcohol without a license brought Chief Winooski to my door.

I write about old loves who met at fiftieth reunions and married at seventy. About a ninety-five-year-old who'd been diagnosed with cancer fifty years earlier then died of something else; about the son who dropped out of college against his parents' wishes, causing a long rupture, who went on to win a Tony for lighting direction, his parents in the audience. Posthumously, such good news become my ledes.

Luke reads the paper at breakfast. Headlines first, then the obituaries. He's a good critic; often he knows the person who's died; sometimes he's arrested the deceased, and might say about my overly positive summary, "Wow. What a stellar human being. Who knew?"

I don't mind the teasing; it's our back-and-forth. He moves on to the sports page, a fellow intern's turf, then off to the shower, reappearing shaved, uniformed, and crisp. Unfailingly, for my amusement, he adjusts his cap with a leading-man swagger and a wink.

Before we leave, I ask about dinner. Should we defrost his mother's chicken cacciatore or Brunswick stew or turkey tetrazzini? Or should we eat out—a more frequent luxury made possible by Hiram Powers and his goddess of the moon, a framed photo of her at the Met, on the mantel.

We drive the two miles into town together. When he drops me off at the paper, we kiss goodbye across the mountain of police gadgetry. Every morning without fail, since I composed my first obit, he's called after me, "Knock 'em dead!"

And every morning, still, I laugh.

Great thanks to:

Jonathan Greenberg, who inspired the Artemis/Diana discovery. When I was three-quarters of the way through the book, he happened to tell me about a whitewashed sculpture found at a Liverpool school while he was working on a museum project. It turned out to be *La Carità Educatrice* by Lorenzo Bartolini (1777–1850).

Stacy Schiff, prize-winning friend and sentence polisher. She was the official editor of my first two books, and for the next fifteen, my advisor, first reader, and safety net.

Millicent Bennett, my dear, wise editor, champion, and ideal everything.

Assistant editor Liz Velez, who answers all my questions, big and small, quickly, graciously, and even enthusiastically.

James E. Mulligan, former chief of police in Georgetown, Massachusetts, and police commissioner in Rockport and Rowley, Massachusetts, once again my indispensable cop on the narrative beat. Everything that Luke Winooski says and does as Harrow's chief of police was approved and often refined by my friend since fourth grade.

Amy Roost, who reached out when I asked Facebook friends to suggest names for Emma's company. Her experience running estate sales and her long, witty emails were a huge help, and many of her insights inspired Emma's point of view.

Barrie Blake who shared entertaining anecdotes and trade secrets about the biz.

Robin E. Black suggested the name "Finders, Keepers" for the family business. My indispensable neighbor, Dirk Dyson, supplied "Estate of Mind" when Emma thought she needed rebranding.

This book is dedicated to my agent, Suzanne Gluck. I could never, ever be in better hands.

About the Author

ELINOR LIPMAN is the award-winning author of seventeen books of fiction and nonfiction, including *The Inn at Lake Devine*, *Isabel's Bed*, *I Can't Complain: (All Too) Personal Essays*, *On Turpentine Lane*, *Rachel to the Rescue*, and *Ms. Demeanor*, which was a finalist for the 2023 Thurber Prize for American Humor. Her first novel, *Then She Found Me*, was adapted into a film directed by and starring Helen Hunt, with Bette Midler, Colin Firth, and Matthew Broderick. Lipman, the 2011–12 Elizabeth Drew Professor of Creative Writing at Smith College, divides her time between Manhattan and the Hudson Valley.